The Other Side of Through

ALL THINGS WORK TOGETHER...

Cynthia Middlebrooks Harris

T.O.S.O.T. Ministries, LLC
(The Other Side of Through)

i

Scripture taken from the King James Version of the Bible.

Published by: T.O.S.O.T. The Other Side of Through Ministries, LLC and can be ordered by contacting:

T.O.S.O.T. Ministries, LLC
P.O. Box 565
Waynesville, MO 65583
http://www.tosotministries.org
Email: tosotministries@gmail.com

Imagery provided by: Cover model Stephanie Harris and such images are being used for illustrative purposes only.

ISBN: - 13: 978 - 1480094703
ISBN: - 10: 1480094706

Library of Congress Control Number: 2012919439

T.O.SO.T. Ministries, LLC rev. date: November 1, 2012

Acknowledgments

First and foremost to my Lord and Savior Jesus Christ; for taking a gift of imagination used for worldly pleasures and redirecting it to be used as a ministry tool. Without him I would be nothing, and with Him I can be anything.

To my husband Minister Kim Harris, who has endured my countless days and nights of solitude. His sacrifice has been as endless as the love and support he has given to me and the ministry.

To my son Dominique; whom God has carried to the other side of through by changing in him what could have been a disastrous life and made it one of many accomplishments.

To my daughter Stephanie, who has been a magnificent camera person and make-up artist. She has sacrificed much mother-daughter time for the sake of the project.

To Jasmine Walthall, a wonderful friend who out of the love she has for the craft and her spirit of excellence, found many of my grammar and spelling errors.

To Shawndelin Hall, and Minister Sir Avington, who by far are the books biggest fans. I have had countless discussions with them concerning the authenticity of the story line in relation to scripture and believability.

To Minister Tannisha Smith; best friend and personal motivator. Everyone needs that one person who will constantly remind you of the gift you possess; how important you are to the body of Christ; to correct you when you're wrong; to encourage you when you're down; and make you laugh at yourself! Tan, there are too many situations to mention what you have meant and mean to my life. They themselves would be a novel.

To Lynetta Powell, who in pursuit of her dream as a gospel music artist inspired the title of the book. During her album debut she sang a song titled *"Reasons."* The song is a direct challenge to go through with grace and to maneuver through with haste because God is waiting on the other side. The song contains a line that says, *"So here I stand today, on the other side of through."* The song *"Reasons"* is not only the inspiration behind this work and countless other books now in the birthing phase; but it is also the theme song of the ministry.

Also at the same time Lynetta was debuting her album, a long time Evangelist friend of mine, Susan Marshal of Still Useable Ministries requested that I write a screen-play for her annual women's conference. The theme of the conference would be "Lord My Soul Thirst for Thee." Susan is a true mid-wife mandated by God and helped to birth in me the ministry of authorship. She is one that just won't let you settle for less than what God has for you.

The characters' lives mirror the lives of countless Christians today. Any comparison of your life to any of the characters is purely coincidental. Other than the public knowledge of obvious states, cities and colleges, being a native of Georgia, most of the locations are fictitious. The characters, places and situations were developed fresh from the throne room of God and placed into my spirit. I have no knowledge that some of the restaurants, churches, street names, or any other locations mentioned in the play or this book even exist. If they indeed do exist, it is the work of the Holy Spirit's knowledge or just purely coincidental.

It is my desire that the story of these characters lives will minister to countless women and men and open discussions in book clubs and groups on sensitive subjects on a global market. Though fictional, it is my desire that what God has inspired me to write will minister on a non-fiction level. On the following pages, I believe, is what He wants the readers to know will be waiting for them on..."The Other Side of Through."

~Chapter One~

"Oh God...no! Brandon, don't do this to me! No, baby please...look at me! Baby...no...stay with me! Hang in there sweetheart, the ambulance is on the way! No! God please don't! In the name of Jesus, death I command you to release your hold...you have no authority here! I love you too baby, now stay with me...look at me sweetheart, look at me! God...no...please, God please! Yes you can baby...just breathe slowly, you're going to make it, you have too, you're going to be a father! Yes you are Brandon, now breathe! Brandon...baby please don't leave me! God you said these signs shall follow them that believe! God I'm laying hands on my husband, please meet me half way! Don't let him die God! I need him! I can't do this without him. We're a team, God please help me! Brandon look at me...look at me, keep your eyes open. Yes sweetheart, I said you're going to be a father, now fight Brandon fight! Bernard? What about Bernard! What do you mean Brandon? What does he have to do with...no baby not Bernard...you're going to be a father! Brandon please sweetheart you have to fight. Now fight baby fight...please! I need you sweetheart...don't do this to me... Noooo! Breathe Brandon, breathe!..."

Talinda sat motionless in a fog of disbelief as the ambulance attendants tried feverously to revive her husband's lifeless body.

They had arrived five minutes too late. This was the man of her dreams. It had to be a nightmare. There is no way this was happening. Talinda and Brandon had been happily married for seven years. She was going to tell him she was expecting their second child tonight after they returned home from the church's quarterly youth rally. She already had the sparkling cider chilling to celebrate. But instead, she declared to him in desperation as he lay in her arms dying. It was a futile effort to inspire him to fight for life. He would have been so excited, considering they had been so afraid to try again for another baby and in fact, weren't even trying now. Their first child, a beautiful baby girl they named Lydia had been still born five years earlier. Since that night, Talinda had been barren. They had resolved to allow God to decide when and if she would conceive again. They used no form of birth control, and just waited on God for the right time. Her mind drifted back to their first encounter.......

She was twenty-two at the time, fresh out of college and very much frustrated with the male population at her local church in Newport News, Virginia. Her father was the pastor and she was one of the lay-ministers. She recalls countless days sitting in church wondering when her knight in shining armor would come a sweep her off of her feet. All while fighting the opposition that most of the men there seemed determined to be the one to take the virginity of the pastor's prized possession.

"God," she would say, "I know you are preparing me and him, wherever and whoever he is, for this awesome marriage. But could you speed it up a little, my hormones are starting to get out of control." She could feel the desperation settling in. For as long as she could remember, she had always wanted to be a wife. She was somewhat relieved college was over and she had indeed graduated. She had no real desire for a career outside her home other than ministry with her husband. She only went to college to please her father and therefore pursued and earned a degree in Old Testament Theology. She was a true pastor's wife to be. Well, at least that's where her heart was.

She often complained to God and her father saying, "I'm so tired of being alone. I want to be a wife, to work side by side with my husband in the ministry."

"In His timing baby girl," her father would always say, "In His timing."

It seemed as though her life had become an uninspired hum drum of routines and programs. She sat in church Sunday in and

Sunday out pretending that she was complete and content at, "*whatsoever state she was in.*" But the truth to the matter was she was anything but content. Although she knew that in God she was complete, she longed for the completeness in being one with her soul mate. Because of the prophecy she had received about her future husband, she envisioned that she would have this ultra-romantic first encounter with him.

She recalled the day she received the prophecy. She stood ready to assist with those that would answer the invitation to the altar call Prophetess Hayes extended at the conclusion of the message. As she followed her with oil and drapes for those slain in the spirit, she was oblivious that she would soon the object of prayer that Sunday morning. Without warning, Prophetess Hayes turned toward her and began to speak into her life. She started out by saying to Talinda that God was preparing her husband for her at this very hour. She began to share what the Lord was telling her about her future husband.

Then, sensing that every single man in the room was way past tuned in to her words, she turned the microphone off. Asking the ushers to please take a few steps back, she leaned in even closer to Talinda. Called her parents over, and was now speaking barely above a whisper. She told Talinda that she would know her husband's voice when she heard it, because God would begin visiting her in her dreams concerning him. She said that Talinda would even recognize his smell and his heartbeat would move in perfect unison with hers. She smiled as she told her that he, just like her, would be a virgin. That he had been keeping himself just for his wife. That he had been brought up in a strong Christian house with parents that had strong values. She told Talinda that the first night that they met they would share a kiss of betrothal. She was told that within the next year she would meet and marry this man. Prophetess Hayes then told them that they were not to disclose the words of this prophecy with anyone, just to pray, prepare and wait on the manifestation.

She recalled that Prophetess Hayes was so specific in her description and details concerning her husband. She was told that he would love children and they would work in the youth ministry together. Then, she stopped and just looked at Talinda, as if contemplating whether or not to say what the Lord had just shared with her. She could hear God say, "No. Do not reveal that," and continued on in what God would allow her to proclaim. She looked at Talinda's mother with an, "I know your secret", look. She then turned back to Talinda telling her that she would develop a strong relationship with her mother. Which she remembers brought her mother to tears. She told Talinda that she would call her son BJ, but was unsure what her husband's actual first name would was. She shared with her that the nature of her delivery would be very special to a lot of people. She paused and smiled, but once again did not reveal what God had just shared with her.

She told her that the courtship before marriage would be very short, but to trust God. She then turned to Talinda's father and said, "Tonight, God will visit you concerning Talinda and her husband. You have been grooming her as a pastor's daughter, but He is about to shift gears and send your training of her in a different direction." The last thing she said to her was, "Get ready Talinda, your wait is almost over."

Talinda remembers falling to her knees at those words and weeping. Through her tears she praised God. She thanked God over and over and began to sing a song of worship. She ministered to God in dance as she sang the song.

She remembered that a new level of song and dance was birthed in her that night. She would often go to a garden she discovered and minister to God in song and dance. She would take her streamers and flags to worship God as she sang. Most of the time, there would be no music. When there was music, there would be no words. God would minister to her what to sing and she spent countless hours serenading her Lord. She would dance all her cares away and let God minister divine revelation about her life.

Because of the prophecy, she would often sit and daydream about how the first encounter with her husband would be. She imagined it would be the most romantic fairy tale adventure ever told. She just knew that bells would be ringing and it would be one of those glowing divine moments that would make every woman in the room go, "Awwwee" through teary eyes.

But it wasn't like that at all. In fact she was so caught up in her blissful imagination of her dream encounter and marriage, that she didn't even notice this tall handsome stranger enter into church accompanied by her ex-high school sweetheart.

Sunday school had closed out and worship service had begun. She had been totally oblivious to her surroundings. She was shaken back to reality by a new, but divinely familiar voice. She looked up and was instantly frozen in time. Her mind raced back and forth recalling the prophecies concerning her husband-to-be. She had heard this voice in her spirit and dreams for the last eight months and couldn't believe she was hearing it audibly...or was she? But there he was, standing and making his declaration as a first time visitor. Professing how he loved the Lord and was glad to be there. He was visiting one of his college buddies Tommy Davis, on his way back home from a business trip.

Tommy Davis was Talinda's ex-high school sweetheart, who almost was, and everyone expected would be, but...that's...another story. She and Tommy were still very good friends. They severed their relationship just after high school and ended up hundreds of miles apart in college. Tommy was off to Athens, Georgia and she journeyed to Oklahoma to Ramah. Tommy was pushing to take their love over the top intimacy wise and Talinda wasn't about to ruin eighteen years of virtue. She remembers telling her father that she and Tommy just had too many differences of opinion, as not to ruin his reputation in the church. Lately, the agape love of God had not been the driving force in their relationship for quite some time. Something had changed in him during their senior year and it seemed as though she had to get reacquainted with him spiritually on daily basis. She was relieved that during college he regained his focus and was back on fire for the Lord. She would learn later, that it was due to a strong influence by her future husband.

But this voice...this voice that so gingerly captured her while she was sitting there lost in her thoughts, was so divinely accurate. It was the voice of prophecy coming to pass. It was the voice...of her future. "Wow! How did I miss him walking through the door?" she thought. Her eyes were fixated on him and she had to keep telling herself to breathe. Everything inside of her told her that this gentleman was the one who would walk into the prophecy of her life. His voice confirmed so many things inside of her about her prophesied husband. She squirmed in her seat as she forced herself to look away from him before their eyes could meet.

All of a sudden, she was asking for a tissue to wipe her dampening palms. She was feeling something on the inside that she couldn't control. Although, he had not even looked in her direction, she felt as though his eyes were fixed on her.

He was breathtakingly handsome with a caramel smooth complexion, tall and buff in all the right places. He was very clean shaven, and had deep to-die-for dimples. He had a million dollar smile that just sent warm tingles all through her, and "Oh my God," he loves the Lord! "It has to be him God...it just had to...but what if it wasn't...mmmm, he's got my temperature rising either way...stop it girl! You're in church lusting over a man you don't even know and may never meet! I do hope Daddy invites him to the visitor's brunch after church. I just have to get close enough to him to measure him against all the prophecy and word of knowledge I have received about my husband. My heart is already saying that this is him. He's the only visitor and I can have him all to myself," she remembers giggling out loud looking around to see if anyone noticed as she pondered her thoughts. She was absolutely about to explode on the inside, "Oh God this is him...I just know it is. I would know that voice anywhere. And those dimples, I have seen those dimples and that smile for the last eight months in my dreams."

She wanted to stand, clear her throat loudly, or walk in his direction as though passing by to some unknown destination. She just had to do something to get him to notice her. She was both terrified and desperate to get his eyes on her. But knew that she had no idea what she would do once she held his gaze. But terrified or not, she just had to think of something. If it had been the following Sunday, he would have seen her because of the church annual park outreach program. The dance ministry team always ministered during the park events. That was it! All of a sudden she thought of an announcement she needed to make about the park outreach program. She got the attention of the worship leader to get a moment during announcements. Surely if he was her husband he would see her and be blown away. She was sure that the prophecy spoken in his life would come to reality for him as well. She had been told that the one being prepared for her, was well aware that he was indeed, being prepared for her. She was told, that the Holy Spirit would confirm the encounter in both of them.

She made sure she didn't look in his direction while making the announcement; partly, because she didn't know how she would react if their eyes met. She was sure she would just lose all composure. Everything in her inner most being told her that day, that prophecy was being fulfilled in her life.

She sat in church the whole service doodling the name Brandon Travis on her note pad, while maintaining her efforts not to look in his direction. There again, because she just didn't know what she would do if their eyes met. She just could not shake the overwhelming presence of the Holy Spirit. Although

6

they were sitting in a crowded sanctuary full of people, she felt as though they were the only two in the room. Then it hit her...Brandon Travis! The prophecy...Prophetess Hayes said her son would be called BJ, after his father! "Oh God...Oh God...Oh God!" She heard the words as they escaped from her lips. She had hoped she hadn't said them loud enough for anyone to hear that wasn't sitting in her immediate vicinity. To her relief, only those around her had heard it and she covered it up by making a comment about the word of God as though she were into the message being delivered by her father.

In actuality most of the sermon had gone unheard by her that day. To her disappointment and dismay, he left without so much as a first, much less second glance at her, or so she thought. But the truth of the matter was, he had stared at her for most of the service looking away occasionally to avoid getting caught.

On top of her initial disappointment, her father as he gave the benediction didn't invite him to the visitor's brunch. He hadn't even mentioned the visitors brunch. And when she looked up, much to her dismay and disappointment, he and Tommy had exited the church. Well...at least that's what she thought.

"How could he?!" Her mind raced. "I was so sure!" Her hormones were seriously beginning to get out of control, and her emotions not only had a loud voice they were screaming at her. "God, I was so sure I heard and felt you." In total frustration, she exited the church at the last "Amen." She skipped the visitor's brunch to go for a ride.

Had she missed God? Out of her yearning for her husband, had she force-fit this man into the prophecy? She felt confusion and despair overtaking her. She needed some alone time with God to get it together. She thought out loud as she pulled away from the church parking lot, "Talinda you have got to get yourself together girl, you're getting desperate. Don't force it Talinda...you're going to have to do what your father said and just wait on God's timing." She paused as tears she could not control streamed down her face, "I was so sure I felt you God...his voice...the presence of the Holy Spirit...I just don't know any more God...I just don't know...it must be him God...but..."

She spent the afternoon in her secret garden praising, worshipping and dancing before God. Oh, how He was the lover and restorer of her soul! Feeling much better, she decided to go home and apologize to her father for not attending the visitor's brunch. Ministers were required to be in attendance. Even though her father had not mentioned it, it was a given to all ministers that it was a part of the first Sunday service every month.

As she pulled into the driveway, she noticed an unfamiliar car with Georgia license plates. She figured her father must be counseling someone, or a minister friend of his was over for a visit. She thought nothing of it. She went in, kissed her father and apologized for not remaining at church after service for the brunch. "Sorry I missed the brunch daddy. I needed some God time, so I went to my garden." It couldn't be! Out the corner of her eye she thought she saw...no, it couldn't be! "Oh my God it is!" she thought. Her heart started to race so fast, she thought she would have to run and catch it, to put it back inside of her chest.

About that time her father said, "You didn't miss the brunch baby girl, we didn't have one today. By the way princess, I would like for you to meet Minister Brandon Travis. He was a visitor with us at church today. He was recently offered the youth pastor position at the church he attends located just outside Atlanta, Georgia. He wanted some counseling concerning the position. Tommy suggested he talk to me, so we didn't have the brunch today. We talked briefly in my office right after church and from there I invited him over for dinner. I wanted to pour into his life all I could, considering he leaves tomorrow returning home."

"I think I'm going to pass out," she thought. "Oh my God he is drop dead gorgeous. Those beautiful hazel eyes, are they contacts? They must be contacts."

She put on her, "I've been brought up in church all my life and know how to conduct myself", posture. Extended her hand and said, "Nice to meet you." When he touched her hand, all the emotions of the day came rushing back over her and she thought she would lose her balance. Everything froze in time, and the air went out of the room.

She was resuscitated by a very sexy voice greeting her, "It's very nice to meet you."

She fought off an audible sigh, as she thought, "Oh my God his voice...it's mesmerizing." They stared into each other's eyes for what had seemed like an eternity. She was sure the fireworks she felt could be seen in the natural and the supernatural. She was absolutely starting to melt inside. The silence was broken by her father, who being very uncomfortable with the moment, realized he could be getting ready to lose his baby girl. There was something very prophetic about that young man, and he went into shepherd mode. He wanted to both protect his daughter and help propel her into her prophecy. As long as the man of God being prepared for her had not manifested, he could stand strong in what God had promised. But now that he potentially stood here in front of him, the thought of losing his baby girl became a strong reality. He began to watch the scene more careful eyes, the words of the prophetess ran through his mind. He began to seriously ponder, if Brandon was indeed the one.

Clearing his throat, he said, "So Brandon is there anything else I can help you with? Like I mentioned earlier, the opportunity you have been offered, will be a life changing experience."

Brandon, not taking his eyes off of Talinda responded, "Sir, I couldn't agree with you more." Then it hit him, what he is doing. Realizing this was the pastor's daughter and he was indeed in the pastors house, he let go of her hand, looked at the pastor and said, "I mean yes sir, I'm really looking forward to it, I mean...the opportunity that is, sir."

"I think I know exactly what you mean son," her father responded, clearing his throat again and eyeing him with much curiosity.

"Oh, daddy," Talinda sighed, feeling very embarrassed and flushed. Talinda, desperately wanting to cool the temperature down in the room, asked Brandon, "So have you always liked working with children?"

"Well," Brandon responds, "It's been a passion of mine since my early teens; I mostly worked with troubled youth while I was earning my degree in Sociology at the University of Georgia located in my home town of Athens. After graduating, I started working with children of broken homes and victims of diverse circumstances, situations and tragedies..."

"This is crazy," she thought! It wasn't getting any cooler; the sound of his voice just escalated her body temperature all the more. Her hormone monitor was telling her she was way above and exceeding safe zones. The more he talked, the more Talinda heated up. She was captivated, but so was Brandon. She was not keeping her cool. Oh, she looked together on the outside, but inside she was a melting mess and just knew that he could sense it. But this was of course, not the case at all. Little did she know, he was just as out of control emotionally inside, as she was.

"Oh my God!" she just realized he was the perfect height. His cologne...the cologne she had smelt for the last eight months was filling the air. She had always dreamed of laying her head in her husband's chest, at just the point of his heart, in the perfect position for his strong arms to comfort her in time of need. To listen to the soothing effect of his heartbeat, and for him to caress her in times of intimacy. She thought, "This is too much, I can't take it! I have to get some air!" "Ah, excuse me," she exclaimed, "I need to get some things from my car I'll need later. Be right back."

"May I help you with anything, I mean, is there a lot that you have to get?" Brandon asked.

"Oh, you may help me all right," she thought. "Talinda, get your thoughts together girl, you're losing it." She took a deep breath and answered, "No thanks, its just my bible and notes for women's meeting this week. I'll need them later in my study time." Well, it wasn't actually a lie, she did leave her bible and note pad in the car, so she thought. And they did have women's bible meeting that week. She breathed a sigh of relief as she stepped outside the house. She decided to take a few minutes to gain her composure before going back in, after she had retrieved her bible out of the car. But to her surprise, neither her bible nor note pad was in the car.

"Oh that's just great!" she exclaimed in frustration and bewilderment. "That's just perfect! It's already in the house. Now, how do I go back in without my bible?"

Back inside, Brandon turned to Talinda's father. Unsure how to proceed, he knew an apology is always appropriate. He looked him in the eyes and said, "Pastor Thompson, please accept my apology sir. I know how my actions just now with your daughter must have appeared to you. To be honest, I'm just a bit overwhelmed myself. But I assure you sir, that my motives and intentions are very respectful towards her."

"I see," Talinda's father responded. He was somewhat perplexed, and eyed Brandon yet again with curiosity.

Brandon continued, "You see sir, about a year ago..."
"Excuse me," her father interrupted. "Did you say a year ago?"

"Yes sir, why?" Brandon replied very nervously.

"Nothing, continue," her father answered as he motioned with his hands in a "come on and give me the rest of the story" gesture.

10

Brandon continued, somewhat hesitant because of her father's demeanor. "About a year ago God showed me my wife in a dream, vision, or something. He has been preparing me all year to meet her. He told me he was well pleased with me for keeping my purity and waiting on my wife. That he would reward me with a wife that had kept her purity as well. He even told me when and where I would meet her and that she would be a pastor's daughter. But now she was being prepared to be a pastor's wife...more specifically, my wife. I was so excited to come on this business trip for the shelter where I volunteer, because I knew I would finally get to meet my wife. The woman God had been preparing for me and preparing me for. It's been an awesome year in the Lord for me. My prayer life has grown to a level that I could not have even been told I could ever reach. I was feeling very discouraged that this was my last day here with Tommy and I had not yet met my wife. But when your daughter Talinda stood up in church, I almost yelled out Hallelujah! It was her, the breathtaking and lovely creation of God that He showed me in a vision. I remember thinking...she is real...I wasn't dreaming, it was you God! But honestly sir, I was seeking your professional counsel on the youth pastor position. I know this must seem a bit much sir and a little overwhelming, I'm overwhelmed myself...," he was interrupted by Talinda's father who had tears in his eyes.

"Not at all son, about a year ago, a prophetess came to our church and spoke into Talinda's life concerning her husband. She said that night; God would awaken me in the wee hours of the morning concerning instruction about Talinda. God told me He was preparing her husband, and to enjoy her because she wouldn't be my little girl much longer. He also said that it was time to stop teaching her how to be a pastor's daughter and to begin teaching her how to be a pastor's wife. The prophetess said that her husband would be a powerful man of God that had been keeping himself pure. She also said that we would know when he came into our life, because he would fulfill prophecy. We were told that there would be no mistaking who he was. But until you and Talinda stood face to face just now, it didn't hit me what was so familiar about you that I couldn't quite put my finger on."

Talinda's father looked up towards heaven and began to praise God, "Oh my God, you're so awesome!" Brandon threw his hands up and began to praise and magnify the Lord! Her father watched as Brandon praised God so freely and with genuine passion. He wept and thanked God for answering his prayer in supplying his daughter with a godly husband.

Brandon gathered himself together and turned to Talinda's father, "Sir I have no idea what to do. Please help me. What do I say, what don't I say, all of a sudden I'm very nervous."

"You'll be fine son, she is just as nervous as you are," her father replied.

"Really?" Brandon exclaimed.

"Yes son she is. She went out to the car to get her bible right? Well Brandon, its right here on the table. She brought it in with her like she always does after church every Sunday. She just felt overwhelmed with the moment."

An angelic voice from upstairs called down, "Is everything all right down there, Pastor?"

"Everything is fine dear, and I don't think you have to be formal with this guest, sweetheart." Talinda's mother Valetta came to the top of the stairs. She had missed that day, ill due to food poisoning at a dinner engagement the night before. She had been upstairs lying down and had not yet met the house guest.

"What do you mean by that dear?" She responded and as she descended down the stairs. She was taken aback by the gentlemen in her living room. For some reason she felt as though she knew him already, or that she should know him.

Brandon spoke first as he extended his hand. "How do you do Mrs. Thompson, my name is Brandon Travis?"

"Minister Brandon Travis," Talinda's father beamed, as he placed his hand on Brandon shoulder and gave him a slight squeeze of approval.

"Not feeling my best, but it's nice to meet you." She turns to her husband and asks, "What is this all about honey?"

"I'll explain it all in a minute," he turned to Brandon and said, "Why don't you go outside and talk with Talinda. She's probably not going to come back into the house." He replied with a slight chuckle, "She hasn't figured out yet how to enter without the bible she went to the car to get." As he exits, Talinda's father turned to her mother and began to explain the details of the last fifteen minutes.

Brandon finds Talinda sitting in a lawn chair, half facing him. He gathered himself, took a deep breath and walked toward her. She caught a glimpse of him out the corner of her eye but pretended she didn't notice. "Oh God here he comes, stay calm Talinda stay calm," she thought.

"Excuse me Miss, I thought I would come and check on you."

"Wait a minute! That wasn't Brandon's voice...!"

≈

...The paramedic slightly touched her on her shoulder to gain her attention, "Excuse me Miss, are you hurt? Is any of this blood on you yours?"

Talinda, thrust back in her tragic reality responded in a voice that was barely a whisper, "No."

"Ma'am would you like to be transported to the hospital to get checked out just as a precaution?" Talinda just sat there. "Or...is there someone from the crowd here that could escort you home? Miss...Miss, are you going to be all right?" Talinda continued to sit. The paramedic walked away to get his partner for assistance. The senior paramedic came over.

"Excuse me ma'am but we need to get you checked out, are you injured?"

Once again, she answered with barely an audible whisper, "No."

"I'm very sorry ma'am, but we need to transport your husband's body to the hospital, and..."

"Please wait," Talinda interrupted, "I would like to ride with my husband. I need to be near him."

The paramedic responded, "That would be fine ma'am."

She felt sick and light headed and asked the paramedic, "Please just give me a minute."

"Are you okay ma'am, you don't look well. Please have a seat and allow me to check your vitals before we leave." He replied assisting her to sit down on the back bumper area of the ambulance.

A police officer walks over to where Talinda and the paramedic are. "Excuse me ma'am, I know this is very difficult for you, but I need to ask you a few questions. Can you tell me what happened here tonight?" The paramedic continued to check her vital signs as she talked to the police officer. Suddenly, he stopped and looked at her. Their eyes meet and she realizes he has heard the fetal heartbeat. His eyes are filled with compassion for her and without an audible word being said, he spoke volumes to her spirit. She nods her head in affirmation to his unspoken question. She then turned her attention back to the police officer. She took a moment to redirect her thoughts before answering. She recalled being in a meeting with another dance team member, when a very hysterical teenager ran into

13

the office yelling and screaming and gesturing. Unable to get the words out of her mouth about her fallen leader, she had grabbed Talinda's hand leading her to the front of the church.

"I was told everything was going great, the youth were enjoying themselves and out of nowhere...Oh God I don't believe this is happening!" She turns to the paramedic, "Are you sure...I mean are you positive...you could have made a mistake?"

The paramedic responded, "I'm sorry ma'am he was already deceased when we arrived, we couldn't revive him, I'm very..."

"Are you sure because God wouldn't do this to me, this is my husband, we're going to have a baby. I was going to tell him tonight. I'm going to wake up...I have to wake up...this is not happening for real...somebody please wake me up...Brandon, oh Brandon...why Lord why...I don't understand...I waited so long for him...we've been believing you for another baby Lord...oh God please help me!" Talinda buried her head into her very shaky hands.

The police officer touched her on the shoulder, "Ma'am, I'm very sorry about all of this, but please try to tell me what you were told happened here tonight. Who stabbed your husband? We need to find the people responsible for this." As Talinda sat there, everything began to go in slow motion. She couldn't seem to make out the words that were being spoken to her. She was thinking of Brandon again, and everything went black.

≈

"Ahhmm hello...I mean, your dad sent me out here to check on you," Brandon said as he approached her.

"He did...really?" replied a surprised Talinda.

"You've been out here for quite a while," replied Brandon.

"I guess so," Talinda responded in a low daddy's little girl voice.

"Did you find what you needed?" Brandon asked her.

"No, I didn't. I must have left my bible at the church," Talinda replied somewhat bewildered hoping her bible hadn't been noticed on the table.

"Actually...it's on the table in the house," Brandon replied in a loving and comforting voice. Talinda just sat there unsure what to say next. Brandon broke the silence, "It's okay, I think we were both feeling the same way in there."

"I don't think so," Talinda thought but responded, "Really?" quite puzzled but relieved at the same time.

"Listen Talinda," Brandon said as he pulled a lawn chair up and sat directly in front of her. He grabbed her by the hands and looked into her eyes.

She thought she would faint. "His touch...oh my, his touch," she thought. He was looking deep into her soul. It was all she could do not to scream. She sat silent for fear of what would come out her mouth, if she had opened it.

Brandon, not looking for or expecting a response continued, "I know what I'm about to say is going to sound like the biggest come on line in America. But believe me, it's all true." A very nervous Talinda continued to sit in silence, shaking on the inside hoping it couldn't be felt on the outside. He was still holding her hands, and the more he talked...well, need we go there again?

Brandon took a deep breath and continued, "I would like to share with you, what I told your father inside a few minutes ago. And no doubt, what he is now sharing with your mother."

Talinda sat and listened to Brandon as he shared with her the conversation between him and her father. She sat both in disbelief and uncontrollable excitement at the same time. "Oh God it is him...it's my husband," she thought. After he finished there was an awkward pause.

"Well, aren't you going to say something?" Brandon replied with a half chuckle and demeanor as though his devious plan had been found out. Talinda stood and took a few steps away from him, she needed to turn away to hide her tears of joy.

"I knew you would think this was a come on. I'm sure every single man in the church has probably already told you he is supposed to be your husband." Talinda continued to stand with her back toward him, no longer able to fight off the physical appearance of her tears.

"If he only knew," she thought. Brandon sensed her tears and approached her. He turned her around and wiped her tears with his fingers. "He's touching my face God, I'm going to lose it, I am going to lose it any minute now," Talinda thought. She dropped her head and broke his touch removing his hand from her face.

"I'm sorry Talinda. I'm not trying to upset you. It's just that...I am so excited! I mean...for the last year I've been wondering if you were real or some self-imposed fantasy of mine. I was so eager to meet my future wife, and when my trip here was almost over I thought I had missed God, that I had imagined it...that I had imagined you. Then, when I saw you making the announcement at church today, my heart raced and my soul magnified the Lord because you were real!"

He placed his right hand under her chin and wiped a tear with the other. He lifted her head to look into his eyes and said very softly, romantically, but firmly all at the same time, "You are my wife, Talinda Thompson. God said it, and for me, that settles it!"

His words penetrated deep into Talinda's soul, she was speechless. She had absolutely no idea what to say or do. She had never been at this place before. She always thought she would know what to do, what to say, to the man of her dreams. But here he was, and she was speechless as if frozen in time. Brandon continued to wipe her tears, "Talinda, you are so beautiful, just like God said you would be. I am so blessed." All she could do was weep, she kept trying to form words with her mouth but nothing would come out. Brandon, finally understanding, pulled her into his arms and just held her.

"Oh God, I can't take anymore," Talinda thought. There she was, in the arms of a man she had just met. She felt a warm peace like she belonged there, like she belonged to him, probably because...she did. She seemed to fit perfectly in his arms. She was laying her head at the perfect height of his chest with those strong arms comforting her, enjoying the sweet aroma of his cologne and the rhythm of his heart beat soothing her. It was just as she had envisioned and dreamed about so many times. The fullness of the prophecy hit her like a ton of bricks. The prophetess told her that his voice would speak to her inner most being in a knowing way and that she would feel his heartbeat. Unable to control the nervousness that was about to overtake her, she pulled away and turned to run but Brandon caught her by the hand.

He shook his head left to right as he exclaimed, "Talinda, I'm sorry, I shouldn't have...I've over stepped my bounds. Please accept my apology."

"No, Brandon, that's not it at all. You haven't done anything wrong, it's me. I'm scared. This was prophesied to me and then God showed it to me in a vision. Now it has manifested and I'm scared. I don't know what to do," she replied looking down as though embarrassed.

Brandon pulled her back into his arms and softly said, "Don't do anything, just let me hold you. I've been in love with a woman for the last year that I wasn't even sure existed...so

16

Talinda, please...just let me hold you. Let me enjoy this moment, with you and God."

~Chapter Two~

"Doctor, I think she's coming around," the nurse said while taking Talinda's blood pressure.

Talinda could hear voices as she was coming to. She groggily asked, "What happened...where am I?" In a panic, Talinda realized where she was and what has happened. She sat straight up and grabbed her stomach screaming terror, "My baby!"

The comforting tone of female voice responded, "Your baby is fine ma'am, but you gave the paramedics and us quite a scare."

"Brandon...where's Brandon?" Talinda asked in an uncertain tone.

Nurse Veronica Gregory very nervously responds, "Ah ma'am, your husband is..."

"I know...I know...where is he? I want to see him." The OB/GYN doctor appointed to her when she was brought into the ER, stepped in to the conversation at that moment and replied, "Mrs. Travis I don't think that's a very good idea right now, you're dehydrated and under duress. We would like to keep you through the night to continue monitoring you and the baby."

She remembered thinking that Dr. Trevor Johnson seemed extremely young to be an OB/GYN doctor. She learned later that he was actually in his internship under one of the more seasoned doctors there in the ward. She responded to his refusal, "Isn't he here at the hospital...I mean, shouldn't he be here...somewhere? I remember the paramedics were about to transfer him here...I mean, I just need to see him please."

"Okay ma'am, I'll check the status to make sure it's a presentable sight for you. But if you start feeling overwhelmed,

18

I'm going to get you out of there." Dr. Johnson left the room to check Brandon's condition in the morgue. She had been covered in blood when she arrived in the ambulance, he could only imagine the condition of her husband's body.

The nurse turned her attention back to Talinda and asked, "Okay ma'am, let's get you presentable for when you are cleared to go down stairs. I'll get you a robe to go over your hospital gown."

Talinda sighs, shaking her head as she replied, "I just can't believe this is happening. I keep thinking that I'm going to wake up any minute and this would all have been a nightmare. But I am awake aren't I, and it's not a nightmare is it?"

Veronica responded in a very compassionate and sympathetic tone, "I'm afraid it's not ma'am...I'm afraid it's not. But hey, you know what?" She said in a tone attempting to brighten the moment. "Your pastor and his wife have been praying for you constantly and waiting for you to come around. Shall I get them while we wait on the doctor to return?"

"You know...I think it is a nightmare, only I'm just not asleep." She seemed to be momentarily having a conversation with herself. Then she responded to Nurse Gregory's suggestion about her visitor's, "I don't know...I mean...I'm not sure I can handle seeing anyone. I know that sounds a bit strange coming from a Christian. I mean...not wanting to see her pastor in a time of crisis. I'm not sure how I feel right now. I don't want to speak out of my hurt and devastation if that makes any sense. I just don't think I can take the, "Minister Travis, I'm so sorry", story right now. I just don't know if I want to see anyone from Grace Tabernacle." Talinda looked down and buried her face in her hands. Out loud she said, "Oh God Talinda this is so selfish...what are you talking about, they care about and you don't want to see them?"

The nurse interrupted, "No, it's not selfish at all Mrs. Travis, and I understand how you feel. I think it's wise to want to guard what you may say, in your time of hurt. More Christians should be concerned with what they might say that is hurtful to others at a time like this. Most Christians would use the crisis as an excuse to say hurtful things they always wanted to say, because the crisis makes it easier to go back later and apologize for being ugly toward someone." Her tone suggested to Talinda that there was some pain behind her voice and personal testimony to what she had said.

A very surprised Talinda responded, "Thank you."

"For what?" Nurse Gregory asked.

"For not judging me," Talinda replied.

"Mrs. Travis, unfortunately I have seen a lot of tragedy in my profession as an ER nurse, which is mainly the reason I work in OB/GYN now. People don't always respond controllably to devastating news. I have respect for you for admitting you need time to get your emotions under control, so that you don't say or do something that is out of character for you." Tears welled up in Talinda's eyes, Nurse Gregory really did understand. Talinda wasn't sure she would respond well right now. She didn't want to sound accusing to anyone, because she desperately wanted to blame someone, anyone for what she was feeling. And being pregnant wasn't helping the situation. She had to admit she was both hurt and angry.

"I'll go and let them know we are recommending no visitors tonight. I'll inform them, because of your condition, we are keeping you overnight for observation to monitor you and the baby's vital signs. I'll tell them you are resting at the moment and you won't be available for visitors until in the morning."

"Thank you," replied Talinda. She was instantly grateful for Nurse Gregory. "They will probably be a little surprised, and excited. They don't know about the baby, we've been trying for so long after losing the first one five years ago. I only just told Brandon tonight."

"I'll take care of it," the nurse replied as she walked out the door. Talinda, feeling tired from all the events of the day, decided to lie back down while she waited for the doctor and nurse to return. She started to think again of that day she met Brandon, before she drifted off into a much needed and God given, peaceful rest......

≈

Brandon wasn't the only one enjoying that moment with God. Talinda couldn't control her tears, she no longer wanted to. God had given her the man of her dreams. He was real and everything she thought he would be; handsome, strong, and on fire for the Lord. She would spend the rest of her life with this man, she just knew it.

Just as they were about to release their embrace, he lifted her chin with his hand so she would make eye contact with him and just stared at her. She nervously started to ask him why he was staring at her and was there something wrong; when he kissed her with such passion she almost lost her balance. Everything
20

inside of her went to mush and it was a wonder that she stayed on her feet, then again, maybe he was holding her up. Either way, she no longer cared. She would never be the same. She felt like there was warm peach fuzz growing inside of her. She was warm, tickly and on fire inside all at the same time. It was an indescribable feeling. The kiss seemed to last forever, but was broken up by her father as he yelled out, "Is everything all right out there?"

"Yes daddy," Talinda responded barely above a whisper, without taking her eyes off Brandon and gently glided her fingers vertically down the side of his face, "everything is just fine, in fact, it's perfect."

Brandon smiled at her response that only he could hear, as he slightly turned his head in the direction of her fingers, kissing them ever so gently as they moved along his jaw line. When he looked into her eyes time just seemed to stand still, and she felt like she was inside of the rainbow.

Brandon answered in a louder, more audible tone for her while still engaging her, "Yes sir, everything is fine." He rubbed both his hands through her hair on either side of her head just above her ears and down the sides of her face. He slightly caressed her cheeks as he repeated the response in a whisper that only Talinda could hear, "Yes sir, everything is fine indeed." She was absolutely weak in the knees and wondered if she would be able to walk back to the house without stumbling around like she was intoxicated. She could have easily just stayed right there in that moment all night. She didn't want it to end, and was silently screaming at him with her eyes to kiss her again.

As suddenly as the thought entered her mind, Brandon smiled and chuckled softly as he pulled her back into his arms and kissed her again. But this time, the kiss seemed to speak to her. He kissed her gently but caressingly as if he said, "I love you so much, Mrs. Talinda Travis."

It was at that moment, that she remembered what the prophetess had said about their first kiss. That it would be one of betrothal and consummation. She knew she would never forget that night. They released their embrace and turned to walk back towards the house. Talinda asked him as they were walking, "Okay, so what do we do now?"

Brandon stopped and looked at her with a serious face, "I guess we could go to the courthouse in the morning to get our license and your father can marry us by noon tomorrow. You can pack and head back to Atlanta, Georgia with me by night fall. Of course I'll have to take some more time off work, because I have to take my bride on a honeymoon. How does a cruise to the Bahamas sound? Or maybe we could fly to Spain..."

Talinda had such a stunned look on her face that Brandon decided to let her off the hook. "Just kidding," he laughed as he put his hand on the side of her face and stroked her ever so lightly and played in her hair. "We wait on God and follow His instruction. He prepared us to be together, so I'm sure he has designed the entire relationship. In the meantime, we'll spend as much time together as we can. I want to know everything and every part of the woman God has betrothed me to. May we start with dinner tonight and spend some time together tomorrow, if you're not busy that is?"

It was now Talinda's turn to tease and she responded jokingly, "Mmmmm...let me see. I'll have to check my schedule and get back with you." They both laughed and as they continued to walk Talinda asked, "Hey wait a minute, I thought you were leaving out going home tomorrow?"

Brandon smiled as he reached out for her hand, "I was, but I'm sure I can delay a little longer. Pastor Tills wanted to ordain me Wednesday night at bible study and I was scheduled to start the following Sunday. But I'm sure pastor will understand and I'm not due back to my real job for another week. I took two weeks off, because I wasn't sure how long the youth conference would last. I got some good ideas for both the shelter and the youth ministry at church as well. I also knew that I would meet my bride this week and thought I would need the extra week to spend a little time with her, before leaving her. I'm sure pastor won't have any problem with my delay. He has been praying over me and ministering to me all year. He is my spiritual father and a strong part of my Christian life. He'll be just as excited to meet you, as my real parents will."

Talinda couldn't believe this was happening, a few hours ago, she was hanging out in frustration ally. Now, she was talking to the most incredible man, other than Jesus Christ and her daddy that she had ever met.

"This is too much!" Talinda thought.

"What's too much?" Brandon replied.

"Oh...wow, did I say that out loud, I didn't mean to. It's just, I'm in awe of God and how your life can completely change in a matter of hours. I should be confused and reserved, but everything in me tells me this is God. That this is a divine appointment."

They both smiled, still holding hands as they continued in their conversation walking back toward the house.

~Chapter Three~

The next morning, Talinda felt quite rested considering the circumstances. She realized that Dr. Johnson had no intentions of allowing her to view Brandon's body the night before. Nurse Gregory's job was to occupy her until she had fallen asleep. It was almost noon, boy she must have really been exhausted. Either that or the restful magic of Nurse Gregory had intervened to ensure she would sleep for at least ten hours. The latter was probably more accurate.

She also had a surprise visitor waiting for her, her father. Her pastor had called him the night before after finding out about the baby. Her father was in the waiting room and Brandon's parents were on their way as well. The pastor had not yet shared the news of the baby with Brandon's parents. He had thought maybe Talinda would want to be the one to share the news. He did, however, informed her father who was curious as to why she was admitted in the hospital. He reassured him she was not hurt in the incident the night before at the church youth rally.

Nurse Gregory was in a shift change and checked in to get Talinda ready for discharge before leaving for the day. "Well good morning, I trust you slept well last night," she asked Talinda.

Talinda responded, "I'm sure you had something to do with that."

"Wasn't me, no meds were prescribed for you. It was divine intervention," replied Nurse Gregory. "Hey, you have a visitor this morning. He wanted to wait here in the room but I convinced him it was against hospital policy with all the new privacy act regulations. I wanted to be sure you were up to it."

"Thank you Nurse...," Talinda started to reply.

"Call me Veronica," Nurse Gregory said cutting her off before she could finish her sentence.

Talinda sighed, "Okay, Veronica, I'll talk to my pastor today. But first, I would like to see Brandon."

"I knew you were going to say that," Veronica responded. "But the visitor is not your pastor. The gentleman says he is your father."

"Daddy!" Talinda jumped up out of the bed. Nurse Gregory barely had time to react.

"Whoa! Wait a minute Mrs. Travis. I'll go to the waiting room to get him," Veronica replied as she turned to leave the room. About a minute later, Talinda's father walked into the room. Veronica didn't return with him, giving them a private moment. It was a small miracle that he was able to get on a last minute flight out of D.C. to Atlanta, after her pastor called and shared the news about Brandon and the baby. Pastor Tills had picked him up from the airport and offered to no avail to take him to his house to freshen up. Of course, he wanted to get to the hospital to see Talinda, although Pastor Tills had informed him she could have no visitors tonight. By then, it was in the wee hours of the morning and visiting hours were way past over. Pastor Tills had only that morning informed Brandon's parents, after finally finding their contact information in the church records of the ministry staff.

"Oh daddy," Talinda yelled as she ran into her father's arms. She felt five years old again running to her father for comfort after taking a fall outside playing ball with neighbors.

"Princess, I'm so sorry," her father responded as he embraced her. "Your mother will be here tomorrow after she reassigns some of her patients to other care providers."

"I don't understand daddy...why...why would God give us a baby and take Brandon?" Talinda exclaimed with her head still buried in her father's chest.

"Only He knows princess, only He knows. We just have to trust him." Her father replied.

"We were so happy daddy," Talinda managed to reply through her tears. "I mean really happy...I just don't know what to do."

Her father sighed. He was unsure what words he could possibly say to her to bring any real comfort. He felt helpless as a father. This was something that he simply could not fix for his baby girl. He kissed her forehead and said, "God will comfort you sweetheart, the Comforter will come. It's a promise from

God. It may not seem like it now, but you will feel the comfort of the Lord."

"I know daddy, I know. It's just so hard, and I'm so...so...oh daddy." Talinda exclaimed, once again burying her head in her father's chest.

"I know princess...I know," her father replied squeezing her even tighter in his arms for comfort. Nurse Gregory and Dr. Johnson entered the room.

Dr. Johnson picked up her chart. After giving it a once over he said, "Good morning Mrs. Travis, if you're up to it, I need to give you a final check and you will be ready to go."

Wiping her tears, Talinda responded, "Thank you so much Dr. Johnson for last night. I wasn't in any shape emotionally to view Brandon's body."

"I was just doing my job Mrs. Travis," he responded as he checked her vitals. "Everything is okay for you to go down stairs this morning, if you would still like to spend some time with Mr. Travis before leaving the hospital."

An emotionally grateful Talinda replied, "Thank you for not saying the dead body or the morgue or anything harsh like that, I appreciate it very much."

He only smiled, "Well Mrs. Travis, it appears we are done here. I will go to the nurse's station and have them discharge you, so you can go downstairs. When you are done there, you will be ready to go. I know you have business that needs to be tended to. By the way, I know this is probably not the best time to mention it, but the police would like to continue their statement with you and asked me to have you wait for them downstairs if you are up to it."

"That will be fine," Talinda responded, "I have to get all this over with. I have to begin to deal with it, thanks again."

"Ah, Mrs. Travis, there is one other thing," Dr. Johnson added.

"Yes," Talinda curiously replied.

He continued, "I would like for you to allow Nurse Gregory to check on you at home several times over the next few weeks to check yours and the babies' vitals. Emotional trauma could put a lot of stress on the fetus in the first trimester of pregnancy."

"I would like that very much," Talinda replied. She had the feeling this was the beginning of a close friendship with Veronica.

"Great, I'll make the arrangements, and again I am very sorry for your loss," he interjected again as he prepared to leave the room.

"Thank you, you have been great. You and Nurse...I mean Veronica have just been so wonderful. God had you right where I needed you." Talinda's father also expressed his gratitude before Dr. Johnson left the room.

As they reached the hospital morgue, her father turned to ask her, "Are you sure you want to go in there alone?"

"Daddy I have to do this. I need to do this...and I need to do it alone. I'll be fine. I just want to spend some final moments with my husband before I have to be the strong grieving widow." Talinda responded trying to sound as reassuring as possible.

"Okay princess, if you need me I'll be right here, just call for me," Victor said as he took a seat outside the entrance of the morgue.

"Okay daddy," Talinda replied. She breathed heavy and walked into the morgue. She spotted the medical examiner and got his attention. To her surprise he was waiting on her. Dr. Johnson had prepared everything for her.

"Yes ma'am, I have been waiting for you. I have Mr. Travis here in a private room for your visit with him." Dr. Stewart gestured for her father to enter the morgue. "Your father may wait just outside the room for you in case you need him. Take as much time as you need to."

Talinda was overwhelmed, she responded with tears in her eyes, "Thank you so very much Doctor...,"

"Stewart and you are welcome ma'am," he responded.

"Everyone has been so wonderful," Talinda thought as she took a deep breath. She looked at her dad for reassurance and entered the room. To her surprise and relief, the scene was very presentable. Brandon lay there, in a hospital bed slightly inclined, as though he were a patient asleep. The medical examiner had gone the extra mile to make the visit less painful as possible. Talinda stopped a moment to thank God for his love and kindness, in hand picking her and Brandon's caregivers.

Talinda walked over and touched Brandon's hand first, half expecting him to be cold and lifeless. To her surprise and amazement, he was almost as warm as usual. She stroked his cheek as tears ran down her face.

"Oh Brandon, I miss you so much already. I love you and don't you ever forget that. I know as much as you love me, given the choice, you wouldn't come back to this world. Take care of Lydia, I know she was there waiting for you, and I'll take care of the little one you left here. Sweetheart, I don't understand why, but I know God must have a plan. I have to confess, I'm struggling right now in trusting that plan. But I'm sure in time...God will...will mend my broken...my broken heart."

She was barely able to speak through the tears and heaviness she felt from the grief she could feel entering the room. She couldn't fight off the overwhelming feeling that rushed over her as she realized she would never rest her head in her husband's chest and feel his strong arms around her again. She wanted to just put her head in his chest now, but she just couldn't bring herself to do it. She was afraid of the emptiness that would be there. There would be no caressing of his strong arms, no gentleness of his voice, and no rhythm of his heartbeat to comfort her. She wanted to look under the cover to see the wounds, but once again she couldn't. She didn't want her memory of Brandon to be one of death, but of life. The life through God, that Brandon had placed inside of her. A life, she thought as she stroked her stomach, that would keep the memory of Brandon alive for her. She wanted to remember the life they shared, and the love they exchanged.

"Oh God," she said aloud. "If I could just feel his arms around me, hear him say I love you and be soothed by his heartbeat and his loving touch one more time." It's funny the things you think of at a time like this. Just at that moment she reminded herself not to wash all of his clothes when she returned home. So she would have something to sleep in every night that smelled like Brandon. She smiled as she chuckled and said aloud, "The things you think of...uhmmnn."

So she sat there, for what seemed like hours, crying and talking to him. Not wanting to leave or to say goodbye. This was her moment, her alone time. She knew the next few days would be very crowded and she would have to be something she never thought she would have to be, a strong grieving widow. She was so grateful for Dr. Johnson, Nurse Gregory and the medical examiner for making this time less painful as possible, softening the hurt of losing her beloved. Most people viewed their loved ones on a slab in a room where there may or may not be other bodies, and the bodies are cool and lifeless to the touch. But here Brandon lay, in a hospital bed, tucked under covers as though he were asleep awaiting the doctor to come in. At slightly above room temperature and seemingly full of life.

Talinda was grateful to God for favor and begin to cry yet again because she could now feel the Comforter come into the room, and chase away grief and despair. She looked across the

28

room and saw a vision. It was of her just after delivery. She was holding a baby boy, Brandon Travis Jr. She looked back down at her husband and said, "I'm going to make it through this Brandon...I will with God's peace, get to the other side of through."

She leaned over and kissed him on the cheek and said, "Goodbye sweetheart, I promise I'll take good care of Brandon, Jr. Tell Lydia mommy loves her and one day, we will all be together." She turned to leave wiping the tears from her eyes as Brandon's parents entered the room.

Meanwhile, seven years earlier at approximately the same time that Talinda and Brandon were joining together in holy matrimony, another wedding was simultaneously taking place. Nevette Naythia Graham was about to marry the man of her dreams.

She stood looking in the mirror as her aunt put the finishing touches to her makeup and secured her veil. This was a bittersweet moment for Nevette. She wished her mother was alive to see this moment. A moment she had groomed Nevette for her entire life, teaching her to be a chaste woman of elegance and grace. She had lost her to cancer five years earlier. She was very grateful for Lindsay, her matron of honor, her aunt and Justices' mother Shaundra, who all stepped in and prepared her for this day. Tears began to flow from her eyes. Until this moment, she hadn't realized just how much she indeed, looked like her mother. She forced a smile through her tears as she remembered that her mother always called her a "Nubian princess destined for greatness."

"Oh, Naythia, what is it baby?" Justices' mother asks.

Her aunt, understanding what was happening said to Nevette, "Sweetie you're gonna make me cry and mess up all my hard work on our faces...I miss her too, baby girl." That being said, they were all close to tears now fanning themselves with their hands trying to keep their mascara from running.

Nevette responded through her tears, "It's just that...I'm so happy and she's not here to share it with me. To see the fruit of her labor...to see that I was listening to everything she taught me. That I remained virtuous and pure...that I did it."

She looked up toward heaven and declared, "I did it, mom. Thank you for all those times you said no...wait...not yet...and be

29

patient. He's perfect mom, I waited on God and he sent me a perfect man."

Shaundra, Justice's mom, looked on and smiled at Nevette's comment. "Thank you Jesus for the man of God he has become," she thought.

Lindsay in tears as well interjected, "Yes! He is at the altar waiting for you, and you've got all of us a mess. If we don't pull ourselves together, we're going to have black streaks all over our dresses from our mascara. Not to mention, they are going to think you jilted poor Justice at the altar." They all burst into laughter. Leave it to Lindsay to lighten any mood and get you back on track.

Heading to the door Lindsay said, "I'll grab an usher to tell them we had a minor setback in the preparation stage and should be out shortly."

"That's why you are my matron of honor," Nevette replied. She paused, remembering a déjàvue moment. "Hey Lindsay, this is too familiar," Nevette declared.

"What's that Nevette," Lindsay replied as though attempting to guess what Nevette could be referring to.

"Remember," Nevette answered. "You had to get me together and stall with Justice on our very first date."

"Churchy girls," Lindsay chuckled. "Some things never change."

They burst into laughter as Justice's mom asks, "Churchy Girls?"

Nevette and Lindsay both reply in unison as they look at each other smiling, "We'll tell you later." Fifteen minutes later she was altar ready once again and the ceremony was beginning.

She was a beautiful bride, the picture of purity and loveliness. Finally, here she was, walking down the aisle with her father to meet her groom. Her father, being the pastor of the church, was torn between walking her down the aisle to give her away and performing the ceremony. He had always teased that he could do both. Walk her down the aisle and then switch to take the role to marry her. But conceded to allow the associate pastor to marry his baby and take his role as the father of the bride only.

Everyone looked so lovely. Her colors were gold, black, and white. Her matron of honor and brides maids were beautiful, and Nevette was stunning in her dress.

She was holding back the tears of joy she felt inside. She chuckled as she saw her groom and her two older brothers as they smiled and whispered to one another, as they stood at the altar and watched her advance down the aisle toward them.

She remembered the first day her family met Justice. He was so nervous to meet them. They were coming up from Columbus, Georgia for a visit...and...well, things didn't get off to a good start.

She remembered that Justice had spilled something on his shirt, and it was just coming out of the dryer, which was positioned in the hall closet right outside her bedroom door. Her dad Theodore and brothers Teddy Jr. and Jason had come through the front door just as Justice was walking down the hall. He was pulling his shirt over his head and buckling his pants up after tucking his shirt in. It was a very awkward moment to say the least.

She remembered her older brother Teddy Jr. said, "Oh heck no, what is going on here? Nay Nay you better still be a virgin!" The look on Justices' face was just priceless.

She had added fuel to the fire when she walked over to Justice slightly pulling on his shirt as though she were attempting to pull it back out of his pants. She responded with a very sarcastic, "What do you think?"

Justice grabbed her hand and said, "Naythia what are trying to..." as Teddy lounged for him.

He dodged and held his hands up as if under arrest and said, "Whoa, whoa, whoa man she's a virgin, Naythia talk to them baby." She could no longer keep a straight face. She laughed as she shared with her family what was going on. They all got a good laugh out of Teddy and Justice's interaction.

Teddy, finally laughed and said, "Man you should have seen your face. Boy you were getting out of the way fast."

Justice responded in humorous relief, "I was trying to figure out how I was either going to get out the door or fight all three of you off..."

"Now look at them," she thought out loud as she walked down the aisle, "There is nothing they would not do for one another." It was as though Justice had been there all their lives. They really are brothers because they are brothers in the Lord. She loved listening to them discuss God's word and praise Him when they got together. It got to a point when they would come to visit Justice and forget she was even there. She remembered being just a tad bit envious of their relationship at times. Being the only girl and the baby of the family, she had always been the center of attention where her brothers were concerned. She looked up at her father and notice tears rolling down his cheeks.

She stopped walking and turned toward him. She leaned up to kiss her daddy and said, "God is well pleased with you daddy, you did well. You and mom brought me up with value and instilled greatness in all of us...I know daddy...I miss her too."

Those words were bittersweet to her father, bringing both pride and pain. Pride because of his daughter maintaining her purity and at her level of maturity in God. He was pleased at the conformation of the Holy Spirit being evident in her life. Pain because he did not have his loving wife there to share the moment or the rest of his life with.

She looked up as they began yet again to journey down the isle of matrimony and there Justice stood, handsome as ever with tears in his eyes waiting to receive his bride. That man's smile always melted her and sent tingles all through her body. Justice was the picture of romance and always made her feel like she was the most important thing in his life, next to God that is.

The wedding was beautiful, just like the fairy tale. There were unity candles and praise dancers, singers, poems, a salt ceremony, a solo serenade from her any moment-to-be husband and of course, they shared personal vows. Everything was perfect, just like she had imagined it would be. It seems like it took forever for the associate pastor to say, "I now pronounce you husband and wife, you may now kiss your bride."

After they released from the kiss, Justice whispered in her ear, "Let's just skip the reception and go straight to the honeymoon."

She laughed and responded, "Is that what you and Teddy were discussing back and forth as I was walking down the aisle?"

"What else?" Justice laughed.

The photographer was a barrel of laughs and they had some very different poses. He was everything opposite of traditional. Nevette was cherishing every moment. They took a picture where she and Justice stood face to face. The fire that burned in her for this man was getting uncontrollable and scary all at the same time. In this particular pose, he had one hand on her waist and the other gingerly cupping the side her face. She tilted her head resting it in his hand. The room grew quiet and everyone was captivated by their love.

Justice did not say a word. He just let his love speak for him as tears filled his eyes and they stared at each other as the room stood still. The love in his eyes for her spoke volumes to her spirit and the Holy Spirit whispered in her ear... *"his love is so unfeigned for you that he is just as willing to die for you as the Son was."* These words almost took her breathe away and made her start to cry. Just as the tears started to fall, the photographer snapped the picture encasing this moment forever...her and the love of her life, filled with tears of love for each other, as the lover of their souls looked down on them with joy. As far as she was concerned, there was no one in the room but her and her husband, as they shared a sweet kiss. It was at this kiss not the one at the altar that he relished his love on her.

It was a kiss of consummation that spoke to her spirit and as they released their embrace she whispered, "He loves me," and Justice answered, "Yes he does." There wasn't a dry eye in the wedding party. It was a good thing this was the final picture and they were about to advance into the fellowship hall for the reception. The mistress of ceremony introduced Mr. and Mrs. Derrick Justice Goodfellow II, as they entered the room.

≈

"Brandon!" His mother screamed, as she dropped to her knees. "Oh God, my baby, my baby, my baby! Lindy what happened...where...why...what? Oh my God, oh my God! This isn't real...please God, tell me this isn't real. All the way down here I kept telling myself this wasn't real. My baby can't be dead! God please no...Brandon!" She turns to Brandon's father who had kneeled down beside her. "Do something Roger, please...this is my baby...my only baby...Roger please...no...God no...why God why...I don't understand. Lindy, are you sure?" She exclaimed as she grabbed Talinda's arm. Talinda had knelt down beside her and was in tears again. "Did you check Lindy...are you absolutely sure? Talinda managed to nod, for no words would come out of her mouth. "No...there must be some mistake," she exclaimed as she stood and rushed over to Brandon's body, "Brandon! Brandon! He's warm Lindy! There must be some mistake!"

Brandon's mother was beginning to breathe very fast. Talinda turned to her father-in-law with tears streaming down her face. In a very shaky voice she said, "This isn't good dad. She needs to get some air."

"Honey, come on let me take you out," Roger said as he tried to pull Brandon's mother away. "Sweetheart, come on...let me take you out...please Helen...come on, let's go out so you can catch your breath."

"No, Roger...but he's warm...he's warm Roger...Brandon...oh God my baby...this is not happening...Roger please...do something...," she panted managing to speak in between her fast breathing. Seeing that his wife was about to pass out, Brandon's father gathered her up in his arms and took her out of the room and Talinda followed.

Talinda's father called for the medical examiner when he saw Roger carrying Helen out of the room.

Dr. Stewart rushed over to where the Travis' were. "Okay let's get her on the gurney and get her out of here. She'll be fine, this isn't uncommon. This can be just a bit overwhelming. We'll get her some oxygen just to be on the safe side." He called for an attendant to take care of Brandon's mother and turned his attention to Talinda, "Are you okay Mrs. Travis? Maybe we should get you all out of here for now, I will leave Mr. Travis in this room for a while longer until after his mother is feeling up to the visit. But not too much longer, I will need to cool the body down soon for preservation purposes."

"I'm fine thank you, are you sure she will be fine?" Talinda asked Dr. Stewart?

"Yes I'm sure," he reassured her. Talinda walked outside the morgue to join her father and the Travis'. Helen was coming around and breathing better already.

"Honey don't talk, just lie down, breathe and try to relax," Brandon's father said to his wife as he gently nudged her back into position on the gurney. Unable to speak with the oxygen mask on her face, she complied and relaxed. Everything seemed to be getting under control when the police officer walked up. He needed to speak to Talinda about the events of last night.

"Good morning Mrs. Travis, my name is Officer Jeffries. I spoke with you briefly last night," he stated as he approached them.

"Yes, I remember," responded Talinda. "I'm sorry about..."

"No need to apologize ma'am," he interrupted. "Everything was understandable. Are you feeling up to some questions today?"

"Yes," Talinda responded.

"Okay," replied Officer Jeffries, "Why don't we step over here for a minute."

"Do you need me, princess?" Talinda's father asked.

34

"I'm fine daddy, but I would like you to come just the same," she responded.

"Okay sweetheart," her father replied.

"Now, Mrs. Travis, this is what I have so far. You were in the back office, when one of the youth ran in hysterical and said you needed to get out front. She said that everything was going well, and then something happened."

"Correct," replied Talinda. "Jessica ran in and said that the Knights had come to seek revenge on Raymond, who had given his life to God and renounced the gang. They repeatedly stabbed Brandon as he was trying to regain control of the situation."

"They have been on the blotter a lot the past few months," Officer Jeffries said interrupting her. "Excuse me ma'am, please continue."

"Brandon and I had so been so excited for him when he gave his life to the Lord. Brandon was such a proud father that day at church. Raymond has become like a son to us both. It's not very many Hispanic kids that get help and get off the streets. Sad to say, sometimes minorities are prejudged and written off by society. He's practically lived with us for the last seven or eight months. Brandon had been working very closely with Raymond and mentoring him through the difficult times of shedding his gang life, for the life Christ has for him. He said they had had a few brushes with the Knights recently but there was nothing to worry about. I remember thinking I didn't believe him, he just didn't want me to worry," Talinda paused to wipe her tears and get her thoughts together.

"That's fine Mrs. Travis, take your time. I'm in no hurry here," replied a reassuring Officer Jeffries.

"Thank you, some things you can never prepare for. You just never know how you will respond until you're in the middle of it," Talinda sighed.

"I understand Mrs. Travis. Unfortunately, I've had to interview this line of questioning too many times before. Just continue when you are ready," replied Officer Jeffries.

"You see, Brandon and I are the youth pastors. We organize these jamborees for the children every three months on the third Friday of the third month. We have music groups over, youth speakers from various ministries, and lots of fun, games, and food. I guess the Knights decided this was the perfect place and opportunity to send a message to Raymond and anyone else who might be thinking of getting out of the gang."

"This scene, Mrs. Travis, is all too familiar when it comes to the Knights. However, the church is usually not involved. It's good to know there are those who haven't given up on these kids," Officer Jeffries sighs. "Kids turning into killing machines, when will it end Lord, when will it end?" he said in a defeated voice as he held up his hands in despair and looked up toward heaven.

Talinda not surprised by his response said, "Unfortunately Officer Jeffries, until I can talk to Jessica and the other youth, that's all I know at this point. But if I may get your card or something, and as soon as I know more I will contact you. I know this is somewhat an unusual request, but I would like for you to please not do anything until after we have my husband's memorial service. I don't want the children affected by the negative publicity. They are hurting and I don't want them being interrogated just yet. I feel that God is doing something with this and I'm just going to trust him. I know you have to do your job, and I respect that. But I think God is going to use this death to turn a lot of young people around, including the gang leader."

"Well, that is a usual request, but one that I understand. I'll try to sit on some paperwork and leads through the weekend. But I'm not sure how long I will be able to justify it. Here's my card, please call as soon as you know anything else. I probably have enough to pick the Knights leader up for questioning with what I have already. But I will hold off by telling my superiors that I'm having a hard time securing anyone to interview as a potential witness."

"Thank you, Officer Jeffries for your patience and understanding. Again, I am sorry about last night. I just lost it. Everything was just too much I guess," Talinda replied.

"Don't mention it, and again no need to apologize. We'll be in touch and please feel free to call if I can answer any questions for you. Stay in the faith Mrs. Travis," Officer Jeffries responded as he shook her hand and walked away.

Talinda and her father headed back down the hallway to check on Brandon's parents. His mother was sitting up in a chair and no longer had the oxygen mask on. She saw Talinda and began to cry again.

"Mom, we'll all get through this together," Talinda said as she knelt and grabbed her hands.

"Please stand up dear, I'll be fine. I was sitting here thinking of Brandon as a baby and some of the cute things he used to do

36

that made me laugh," she said as she tried to muster a smile.

"Yeah, well you gave us quite a scare," Talinda replied. She couldn't help but to laugh as she remembered that these were almost the exact words that Nurse Gregory used the night before. She said them as Talinda was coming to, after being transported to the ER by ambulance.

"Yes, I don't know what came over me," Helen replied. I'm usually very calm in a crisis. But when I saw my baby...I don't know what happened to me. It's like I was someone else. I wanted to be someone else, anyone else, so this nightmare wouldn't be happening to me. I just can't believe he's gone...it doesn't seem real. Everything seems so artificial, if that makes any sense."

"It makes perfect sense," Talinda replied in agreement.

Helen grabbed Talinda by the hand looked at Brandon's father and said, "I think I'm ready to see my baby now, I need to say goodbye to him."

"Honey are you sure you're up to this?" Roger replied watching for her response.

"Yes dear, I'm fine now, I had my moment but I can do this. I'm ready," she replied.

Talinda stepped back so Helen could get up out her chair. "I'll give you some time alone with Brandon, I've had my special moment to say good bye. But I do have something I would like to share with the both of you before you go back in the morgue. In light of the situation, hopefully it will comfort you."

Brandon's parents looked at her with both curiosity and concern as Roger said, "What is it Lindy? Is there something else we should now about what happened to Brandon?"

Helen replied, "If so, please wait until after I come out to share this with us."

"No," Talinda responded. "It's nothing like that. It's just...you see...wow, I think I am finally able to be a little excited about this." As she grabbed her stomach she said, "thank you Lord!"

Brandon's parents both together reply, "What is it Lindy?"

Then it hits Helen. She looks at Talinda and yells out, "Oh my God Roger, she's pregnant!" Talinda couldn't hold back the tears of joy and comfort that came over her. "That's it isn't it Lindy, you and Brandon are expecting another baby. What else could it be? At this point, nothing else about what happened to Brandon could change anything!"

Brandon's father interrupted, "Lindy is it true, are you pregnant?"

Talinda nods her head in an affirmation. She was so overcome with emotion that she spoke barely able to whisper, "I told Brandon last night as he lay in my arms at the church just after everything happened. I wanted to give him something to fight for, but his wounds were too much, he had lost too much blood. I had just found out that afternoon and hadn't had a chance to talk to him. I had wanted to tell him at home that evening after the church festivities."

"Oh Lindy," exclaimed Brandon's mother as she looked up toward heaven then buried her head in her hands. "Oh God, thank you."

Talinda remembered the vision God gave her as she was spending some final moments with Brandon. She grabbed Helen's hand and said to her, "Mom...there's more, earlier when I was with Brandon before you and dad came in, God showed me a vision. It was me holding a baby just shortly after delivery and it was a boy, Brandon Jr. I felt such a peace pass over me and I knew at that moment, though this would be a trying time I would get through it. That God would be there to comfort me all the way. He will be there for the both of you as well."

"My, my, my, a boy!" Brandon's mother beamed. "I'm ready. I need to see Brandon. I need a moment alone please. You don't mind do you Roger?"

"Of course not dear, if you're sure you're going to be alright," Roger replied, watching her for any hint that she wouldn't be able to handle it alone.

"I'll be fine honey, be right back," Brandon's mother said as walked back through the double doors leading to the morgue. Dr. Stewart was there with other staff members. He sees her and dismisses himself from the group and walks over to meet her.

"Well, Mrs. Travis, I see you're doing much better. You certainly look better," he said as he approached her.

Helen smiled and nodded her head. "Yes, thank you. It was a rough time. I was caught me off guard. You never really know how you'll react to situations like these, until you're in them. I would like to see Brandon now, do you still have him in the room or has he been moved?"

"No ma'am, he's still here. I figured you would be back. You may enter whenever you like. Rest assure we'll stand ready just outside. Should the need arise again, just call," Dr. Stewart replied.

"Thank you doctor, you've been great." Helen took a deep breath and said a short prayer for strength before entering the

38

room. She walked over to Brandon and pulled up a chair. Although she knew he is gone. She couldn't resist the urge to check for a pulse. Knowing there would be none. He felt so normal, she thought and smiled realizing she hadn't had much experience with dead bodies enough to know how they are supposed to feel. She was very grateful for the extra care to make him appear less waxy, if that made any sense. She picked up his hand and caressed it as she began to talk to him.

"Brandon, I am so grateful for the life we have shared together sweetheart. So thankful that just yesterday morning I was talking to you on the phone. That I was able to tell you that I love you and that I was so proud of your ministry and the strong man of God you had become. Baby boy, I'm so thankful that I don't have any regrets at all, about anything concerning our relationship. Thankful that there was nothing that needed to be said or done. That there is nothing that feels unfinished between us. And now, God has entrusted me to care for your son, just as I cared for you."

She paused for a moment, as the tears began to flow once more. "Brandon, I promise I will help Talinda to take good care of him. I'll try not to be to overbearing and selfish concerning him and give time to the other grandparents. But I have to admit, it won't be easy," she chuckled trying to make light of the situation. "I'm sure it will be like watching you grow up all over again. I couldn't be more blessed at this moment, other than you being here with us to share the experience. I'm sure it will be bittersweet for all of us the day he is born. But I know you'll be there in spirit saying, *"Push Lindy, come on baby you can do it."* She paused again, feeling overwhelmed. "Oh, Brandon it's not supposed to be this way. No parent wants to bury their child." She could feel her breathing began to feel sporadic again and took deep breaths to calm down.

"No, I said I could handle it and I can...no I can't! Oh Brandon, baby, I'm going to miss you so much. I'm so angry sweetheart, I'm just so angry! Baby, I'm so angry and I want to know "why"? Oh God Brandon, mommy is just so sad baby. Sad...heartbroken...confused...and just plain...overwhelmed! You know it's funny, just now it's like I could hear you say, *"its okay to be in despair mom, just don't stay there. God is your refuge."* That's just like you to minister to the end and beyond. You are such an awesome son. I will always love you. I have to confess, I'm a little envious. You're standing with the almighty God and everything in your life has come full circle. And now everything

39

makes perfect sense. Your mind is as infinite as time, and you are no longer constrained by or subject to the laws of nature. Enjoy your Savior sweetheart...I know you will. You enjoyed him while you were here on your earthly journey, how much more are you enjoying him in his full manifested presence. This fulfills your favorite scripture Brandon. *To absent from the body is to be present with the Lord.* Take care my love, and we'll do our part here. It won't be easy at first I'm sure, but with God we'll get through. Your dad and I will take good care of Lindy and the baby. Goodbye son, say hello to grandma, grandpa and Lydia for me, okay?"

Just then Brandon's father entered the room. "I came to check on you, are you okay sweetheart?" He stated as he approached her.

"Yes, I'm fine dear," she replied as she paused to pat Brandon's hand once more. Fighting back tears she said, "Just saying goodbye to my baby boy." She leaned into her husband arms losing the battle, in tears yet again.

"We'll make it through baby, we'll make it through." Roger said as he looked down at Brandon for the first time. He had been so concerned with Helen that he hadn't come to the reality of his son lying there. Tears roll down his checks as he thinks of all the wonderful times he shared with him. All the things he taught Brandon and all the things Brandon had taught him as well. He at that moment, realized there would be no more times of teaching and learning with his son. His mission with Brandon had come to an end. Feeling a bit overwhelmed, he dropped to his knees and began to pray through his tears with his wife kneeling down beside him.

Lord,

I'm struggling right now. I miss my son. God, I love him so much. I know I have to trust what You have decided for his life and ours. I don't always understand Your way, but God help me to trust You. You loaned him to us for thirty-one years. Such a short time and entrusted us to rear him in the admonition of the Lord. We did exactly as You instructed us to do. Lord I'm being just a bit selfish right now because I miss my son...his smile would engulf a room. He had a way of bringing the best out in everyone he met.

No father wants to bury his son, it just doesn't seem right Lord...it's not natural. Jesus I'm hurting right now...so very badly. I know you will comfort me but Lord right now I'm angry...and just a bit scared. All I've ever wanted to do was to be a good husband and father. I hope I pleased you Lord...please help me to deal with this with a good Christian heart. God help me to forgive...and to love Lord. Send Your Comforter God. We stand in need of Your guidance today.

In Jesus name,

Amen

As Roger and Helen stood he leaned over and kissed Brandon on the cheek and said, "Goodbye son, I love you." They turn and walk out of the room. Talinda and her father who are just outside the door. As much as Talinda was hurting, her heart was breaking for Brandon's parents. She too, was an only child and could imagine how devastated her parents would be if the situation were reversed. The Travis' were such a close family and she enjoyed the times they all shared together. She remembers thinking that Roger was just like her dad, a great example for her. She had grown to love them as she did her own parents. From the beginning, she was made to feel a special part of the Travis family. She was actually closer to Helen than she was her own mother. She had been such a daddy's girl, and at times could feel the resentment her mom displayed about her relationship with Helen. But that was all about to change. Talinda was about to realize just how strong her mother had been in her life. She had at times taken her for granted, not understanding she couldn't always be her friend. A role Helen Travis had freely played in her life.

Helen, seemingly rising to the occasion, said as she is wiped tears away, "Lindy, I guess we need to get ready to make some arrangements. Just let us know what you want for Brandon and we will help with whatever you need."

"Thanks mom," Talinda responded. "I will check with pastor to see if there is anything in particular he wants to do. He was like a son to pastor. I don't want to leave him out of the process. My mother won't be here until tomorrow and flowers and colors are her specialty. So, for now, I guess we need to find out when the hospital will release his body. And find a funeral home." Talinda paused for a moment and then continued. "This is too much to think about...I mean...I don't know who...mom, I think maybe we should take Brandon home to Athens. What do you think? Can you please contact a funeral director there to come and get Brandon? When mom gets here tomorrow, we can begin making all the arrangements."

"Of course, Talinda," Helen responded with tears of relief in her eyes. "Thank you for allowing us to take him home." Talinda only nods. She could feel she was on the verge of giving in to grief again.

Her father, knowing his little girl well said, "Why don't we get out of here and try to go get something to eat. You have to feed my grandson."

"Thanks daddy," Talinda said as she leaned into her father's bosom for comfort.

"That's right," Roger replied. "We want that boy to be big, strong and healthy."

Talinda looked at each of them and whispered through tears, "I don't know what I would do without each of you in my life."

As they walk toward the elevator to go back upstairs and exit the hospital, Dr. Stewart approaches them just before they exit the morgue. "Here, Mrs. Travis, you will need to sign a release form to allow the funeral home to receive your husband. Just give this form to whoever you decide to use for your services. They'll know to bring it when they come. The number for the hospital mortuary and all the information they will need is on the form."

Talinda was very grateful but emotionally exhausted as well. She responded, "I can't thank all of you here enough. You have all been so wonderful to me and Brandon. You have made this time of difficulty much easier than it could have been."

As Dr. Stewart shook her hand he said, "You're welcome. May God bless you and keep you Mrs. Travis. Our prayers are with you."

They enter the elevator and head back to the OB/GYN ward to make sure they were released. Dr. Johnson met with them at the nurse's station and set up times for Nurse Veronica Gregory to check in on her over the next few weeks. She had already left for the day. He gave Talinda a check list of things to watch for, including Veronica's work cell phone number as well as his.

"Please don't hesitate to call anytime you feel you need to Mrs. Travis. All the numbers you need are listed on the bottom

42

of this check out form. If you have any of these symptoms what so ever, call immediately. Be sure to follow the instructions to the letter," instructed Dr. Johnson.

"Oh, don't worry doctor," Helen responds as she takes the paper. "We'll make sure of that."

"You all take care and again, I'm sorry for your loss," Dr. Johnson replied. He shook all their hands and walked away.

As they prepared to leave, Talinda said to her father, "Daddy, please remind me to send thank you gifts to the hospital staff and comments to patient care administrators' office after I get settled."

"Okay princess. I think that's a great idea," her father replied. "Now, where are we going to eat?"

Talinda held her stomach and said, "I'm not really..." but was cut off before she could finish her sentence by Brandon's mother.

"Oh, no you don't young lady. You will eat, just a little something at least. See, right here on the paper," she states sternly as she shows Talinda the form. "Continue with normal diet. While stressful times often make you lose your appetite, an expecting mother has to consider the baby's nourishment."

"Okay, I need to take this paper from you. How did you get it anyway?" Talinda chuckled shaking her head as she replied to Brandon's mother.

"Never mind that, you're going to eat," demanded Helen.

"Okay, mother," Talinda replied in a sarcastic be playful tone. She was actually very relieved someone would be there to help her stay focused. She knew she would have allowed grief to take over her without proper supervision. This was such a delicate time for her.

~Chapter Four~

The reception was just as wonderful as the wedding itself. Nevette was on cloud nine the entire evening. Although, in the back of her mind, she was preoccupied with what would happen later that night. A phrase kept reoccurring in her thoughts, sending cold chills through her body... "The wedding night is coming, the wedding night is coming."

She just couldn't shake that phrase. She was so looking forward to it and terrified of it at the same time. She could feel the intensity heating up. Justice was sitting next to her with his arm around her. His fingers were slightly toying with her at her waistline. She was overwhelmed with the emotions of the atmosphere.

Justice, sensing that his touch was creating a whirlwind of thoughts in her mind, looked into her eyes and said, "Don't worry sweetheart...I got you." She was so amazed at how he could read her thoughts. He was so in tuned to what she was feeling. He always knew all the right things to say, at the right moments.

Her brothers bombarded their way in to break up their private moment and snatched Justice away for some male macho bonding time, to counsel him before she, "ruined him for life", they said. She chuckled at that the thought of the ball and chain theory and thought, "Justice...never!"

"God, this man is so for me," she whispered as she looked at him across the room engaged in laughter with her brothers. There was so much love in her heart for him. She was so happy, that it almost seemed unreal and impossible. She pondered in her mind, words she remembered hearing her mother say to the young women in the church on several occasions. "When you

44

wait ladies on the one that GOD has for you, he will be everything you dreamed he would be. You won't have to compromise anything. Not your integrity, not your body, not your desires. Wait on what God has prepared for you and everything, not some things, but everything will flow and fit perfectly together. You will truly be a match made in heaven."

She was so deep in thought, that she didn't see Justice standing right in front of her. She smiled when he cupped her face and said, "Hey beautiful, they want us to be seated at the table, because it's time for the toasts and cake cutting ceremony." As he assists her to their seats, Teddy and Lindsay were moving toward them at the head table.

After Teddy gave her the "ladies first" gesture. Lindsay, the matron of honor stood and began her toast. She cleared her throat and began to speak.

> "First of all, I would just like to say to Nevette. It is such an honor, not only to be your matron of honor, but to be your friend and sister in Christ. It was a godsend that we were roommates the first two years of college. You stepped up in a time in my life last year, when I was so angry with God. You showed grace and you didn't judge me. Even in all my anger and hurt, watching you always made me afraid to get too far away from God. I always envied your relationship with God, because you were so sure of yourself and your foundation was so strong. I remember when you told me Derrick said he would sit in the back of the campus chapel watching you teach bible study. Well, I already knew that, because I was also sitting in the back of the campus chapel trying to be unnoticed.
> I never told you this, but when Derrick got hurt at that game, I could tell by the fall he was going to need therapy. So I went to the chief therapists and told on you."

There was a look of bewilderment on Nevette's face through the tears that were falling from her eyes at Lindsay's previous words. Justice was holding her hand as they both listened. Lindsay continued,

"I knew the one thing you were not confident in, was close encounters with male patients..." At Lindsay's words, Justice smiled as he looked at Nevette, remembering the awkwardness of his first therapy session with her. *"...And so, I told him that you were extremely uncomfortable with male patients and needed to break that fear. So why doesn't he give YOU the football player that was coming in."* Everyone in the room started to laugh as she continued, *"He agreed. But the main reason I did it, was because one day while I was sitting in back of the chapel at bible study, I caught a glimpse of Derrick watching you."* She paused to fight back tears, *"I didn't really know him personally. But the love that man had in his heart for you as he watched you just filled the room.*

I knew that once you two got together, the love he had for you would take over. It was because of the shielding of God that you never saw him sitting in the back of that chapel. Because love that strong and powerful stands out, even in a room full of people."

Justice was still holding her hands and tears welled up in his eyes as he smiled at Lindsay's comment and looked deep into Nevette's eyes. And again, no words needed to be said.

Lindsay continued, *"God had a perfect plan for your meeting, one that you wouldn't be able to escape from."* She laughed, and regained her composure. *"I have not seen a man more faithful, sincere or honest than Derrick..."* she stopped and laughed then continued saying in a low imitating a male voice tone, *"...but you can call me Justice...Goodfellow."* With that being said, Justice couldn't help but to laugh as he remembered the moment she was referring to. *"But seriously, Derrick you are an awesome man of God, who understands God's love."* Justice nods his head in positive affirmation as if saying "thank you".

Lindsay returned the nod as if saying "you're welcome" and continued. *"Nevette, you are a picture of purity. Not many women keep themselves after leaving home and the direct influence of their parents. But I watched you and how you carried yourself. You stood firm on your convictions..."*

She paused once again to no avail to hold back tears. She failed at, because looking at Nevette made it an impossible task. And so, she continued through her tears,

"...and I was ministered to by your life. It blessed me tremendously. I wanted so much to be like you and be your friend. I was so glad when we were selected to be roommates the first two years of college.

We had so much fun together. I was so excited for you in your relationship with Justice. I not only enjoyed, but cherished the moments that I got to share with you. The girl talk sessions that went way into the wee hours of the morning. Heck, some went into the next morning. You were such an inspiration to me. God is well pleased with you Nevette. I'm going to miss seeing you on a regular basis.

I know we won't have as much time together, because marriage itself is a ministry and you'll need to spend time developing it. Although we're all moving to Atlanta, we won't see each other as much as we did in Athens. I am so happy for you and would like to thank both of you, for allowing me to be a special part of your big day." She paused, cleared her throat, wiped her tears and picked up her glass. She motioned for everyone to follow suit as she proposed the toast, *"So, to Mr. and Mrs. Derrick Justice Goodfellow II. I pray that your love will continue to bless all that you encounter. I pray that God will richly bless you and that your love will manifest into the pitter patter of little Goodfellow feet. Love you both, and may God bless you!"*

Everyone raised their glasses. Some were in tears, some laughter, but all shared in the love as they drank to the toast of the matron of honor.

Teddy stood as the room was settling back down from Lindsay's toast. He started out by saying:

"Wow...maybe I should have killed chivalry and went first..." a comment that totally cracked the room up into laughter. *"I just want to say to Justice...I know that name doesn't roll as sexy off my lips as it does Nay Nay's, but I'm going to call you Justice any way,"* more laugher followed. *"But seriously, Derrick or Justice,"* he said as he smiled at his little sister. *"I never thought the day would come, when I would say that someone. That anyone would be good enough for my baby sister. Derrick you asked me to be your best man. But I stand here today saying, you sir, are the best man."* Nevette was crying again and Justice pulled her into his arms as Teddy continued. *"Derrick, you are the man of God that all fathers and big brothers pray for their daughters and little sisters to meet and marry.*

Although, our first initial meeting was a little bit rocky. I instantly didn't like you because it looked like you were coming out of my sister's bedroom putting your shirt on and zipping your pants up." The room both laughed and looked surprised. Justice dropped his head with a chuckle remembering the situation Teddy was referring to. Teddy continued, *"I remember lounging at you saying something like, oh unh unh, it better not be. Nay Nay you better still be a virgin. You were yelling for Nay Nay to...get me, get me, talk to me...as you were dodging me, because I was chasing you around the room."* The room was in total laughter as he continued, *"It still took a while for you to come close to me after Nay Nay said something had happened...that you had spilled something,"* Justice, Nevette and Teddy all laughed as they said at the same time, *"on your (my and his) shirt,"* he continued by himself, *"And she had washed it for him, so we wouldn't tease him about needing a bib to eat."*

Justice smiled and shook his head in amusement as Teddy continued. *"She knew her big brothers well. We always gave her boyfriends a very hard time. Men had to pass the test, if they're going to survive in the Graham house. But Derrick, you proved yourself to be an honorable man of God. Like Lindsay said, the love you have for my sister overwhelms a room and is obvious in the way you talk to her and treat her.*

I remembered when you made a vow to my father..."

He started to tear up. Justice swallowed hard holding back tears himself, which of course started Nevette again. Teddy had to take a moment before he continued,

"...you made a vow to my father, with me and my brother Jason both standing there. We were going to leave you two alone and you said to us no...stay. I want you all to hear this. I want to be accountable to all three of you. And you said this, as you looked each of us in the eye with unwavering honesty.

You said to my father...to all of us, that you would never defile, dishonor or devalue his daughter...our sister. You said that we could trust you with her, because you loved her. That you would protect her from harm and give your life to save her, should the need arise. I could see the genuine love you had in your eyes and I believed you...I believed you. At that moment, I had no doubt you were sent into her life. I was so grateful to God for you...I was grateful."

He paused as Justice shook his head in affirmation with tears in his eyes remembering the vow. Nevette was just as moved. She held on to Justice with her head on his shoulder and partially in his chest. She shed silent tears at the words spoken by her brother. The room was silent, outside the sounds of sniffling and attempts to stifle tears.

He gathered himself and continued, *"Derrick, you, I, and Jason have grown so close over the last year. We got to the point where we started wondering...was Nay Nay good enough for you!"*

The room once again burst into laughter. But Teddy knew he made the statement, only to lighten his own mood to get through his next comment to his sister. One that would include thoughts of his mother.

He paused to collect himself and continued, *"Nay Nay."* At saying her name he started to fight the tears. Nevette braced herself in Justices' arms. She knew what was coming and that she would be in tears yet again at her big brothers words. Teddy continued through teary eyes and a shaky voice,

"Bear with me everyone...I'm going to get through this...Nay Nay, you have always been my baby sister...the princess of the house. We spoiled you rotten. But now, you are a beautiful woman. I was mesmerized at the sight of you walking down that aisle today. I thought as I fought back the tears...mom," he swallowed hard to try to contain himself before he continued. *"...mom,"* he paused again to look up toward heaven to gather strength to continue, *"...mom, would be so proud...so proud of the woman you have become. Because...you have become her.*

You have always carried yourself with respect and integrity. I was always proud of you. Dad and mom taught us well and you made very good decisions in your life. So, when you wanted us to come and meet Derrick, we all three knew we were about to lose our princess. You had never wanted us to come meet any of your boyfriends before. You always tried to no avail to hide them from us. But there was love in your voice when we talked to you on the phone. I knew something was different and I told Dad. I said...Nay Nay is in love Dad, so get ready."

Her father sat there in tears. It was another bittersweet moment for him. Teddy continued, *"And as I raise my glass to the both of you, Mr. and Mrs. Derrick Justice Goodfellow II. I would say to the both of you, always leave communication open. Continue to love and cherish each other. I pray now for success in your marriage and your ministry together. Nay Nay, you're not our little princess anymore. Today...you became his queen."*

Everyone raised their glasses, most of them in the room still in tears and drank to the toast. Nevette was still nestled in Justices' arms. She was unable to speak or drink to the toast. She just enjoyed the moment through bitter sweet tears, as she watched her father look on in pride because of the men and woman of God his children had become.

Teddy moved and stood behind Nevette and Justice and hugged them both. They exchanged "I love you's". Lindsay joined them in the private moment they shared.

They were interrupted by the voice of the mistress of ceremony, announcing that it was time to cut the cake. Justice and Nevette headed to the table to slice the cake together. They decided ahead of time that they would not smash cake in each other faces, because they wanted the moment to be remembered as a sacred communion between them and God and not entertainment. So, as they fed each other, it was as though there was no one else in the room but them. The guests all stood and watched silently as they said to each other, *"Take...eat...this is part of me going into you, a bond that cannot be broken. We will share our lives together in Christ, I love you."* You could hear the ooo's and ahhh's in the room as they sealed it with a kiss.

Now that everyone was seated with dessert, her cousin's dance ministry team ministered in sound and drama. Everyone seemed to be enjoying themselves. It was now time for the bride and groom to share their first dance as man and wife. Justice sings to her as they dance and everyone looked on with teary eyes and smiles. Afterwards the dance floor was open for everyone to join them. And of course, you don't have a black wedding until everybody on the dance floor is doing the electric slide.

Later on after both the garter and bridal bouquet had been thrown by the bride and groom, Teddy teased Nevette, whispering in her ear as the reception was coming to a close, "Okay girl get out of here, this is what you've been waiting for."

With tears in her eyes, she turned toward him and whispered in his ear as she hugged him, "Teddy I'm terrified." They release their embrace and Teddy is about to reassure her, but she continued speaking before he can interject. She continued in an intimidated voice, "I've never done this before and he is very experienced. I mean, I've waited for this moment for what seems like an eternity. I even challenged him on several occasions knowing he wouldn't give in, that he wouldn't break our vow, and the one he made to God, you, daddy and Jason. I pretended so many times to be ready, to say I don't care. I don't want to wait anymore, knowing all along I was terrified. He even threw me into a cold shower once to get away from me," she said through laughter and a trembling voice. "But now this is different, there is nothing standing between me and him anymore."

"Very experienced huh?" Teddy says in a teasing tone.

She playfully but seriously tapped Teddy on the shoulder as she said, "Come on Teddy don't...I'm being serious, don't tease me. I'm really nervous about this. What if I'm not all he anticipated I would be? What if he is disappointed? Teddy I..."

He grabbed her by the hands as he cuts her off, "Nay Nay stop! Will you listen to yourself? It's your wedding night and you're a virgin. He is not going to expect anything from you. Sweetheart, I think he knows you're inexperienced. Believe me when I say. He is going to enjoy the journey of showing you love."

She shook her head and looked down with a sigh. "Teddy are you sure...I mean...what if..."

Teddy cut her off as he said, "No more what ifs or I don't knows...I'm sure you'll be fine Nay Nay. Derrick is going to take very good care of you. Now quit stalling and get out of here, your husband is waiting on you."

"Thanks for being such a good big brother, I love you," she said as she hugged him.

"Love you too little princess, I mean Queen Nevette Naythia Goodfellow," he said with a humorous and sarcastic bow, "Now go!"

She rounded the corner of the banquet hall to see her father and husband in a very emotional conversation. So she decided to give them a minute.

"Derrick," her father said. "I'm very proud of you for not devaluing my daughter. As Teddy said earlier, you held true to

52

your vow to me and her brothers. I wanted to lay my hands on you, pray for you and speak into your life before you left."

"Shall I go get Naythia?" he asked

"No son this is just for you." Justice closed his eyes and lifted his hands ready to receive. Nevette stood still and began to pray for them both. Nevette's father began to pray as he laid his hands on Justice.

"Father,

I come before You in the name of Jesus Christ. Lord I ask You to bless Derrick and Nevette. Father You said that it was not good for man to be alone. You created her for him, now teach him how to care for her. Send your Holy Spirit to over shadow him and fill him. Give him wisdom in guiding his home and caring for his wife. Prosper him where so ever he goes Lord. Order his steps Lord God, and strengthen him in You. Bless the fruit of his hands and the fruit of his loins. Father God, I decree that great things will come out of him..."

Justice began to shake, cry and magnify,"...*The Holy Ghost is a gift Father. Breathe on him God and ignite him from on high Father. Yes God...thank You for Your Spirit God.*

Yes that's it Derrick! Praise God! You're right there son, just receive it Derrick. Yes son, let the tears flow son, let them flow...just magnify the Lord. There you go son, you got it...you're filled. You're baptized in the Holy Spirit, thank you God!" Justice was speaking in tongues and magnifying the Lord. Teddy, Jason, Justices' mom, dad and sister all rushed over and revival broke out. He spoke in tongues as the Spirit gave him utterance and they all magnified the Lord with him.

Out of nowhere he yelled, "Where is my wife?"

"Here I am Justice," Nevette responded through tears of joy.

"Naythia...now baby! Now I can be your husband. Now I have the power to be your husband. I wasn't sure before. I knew I was in love with you, but I wasn't sure spiritually I could lead you...but now I know...I know!" Justice exclaimed.

"Yes sweetheart," she responded as they embraced.

As the presence of the Holy Spirit lifted, Nevette and Justice were saying goodbye to everyone. It was now well after ten and the reception was originally scheduled to be over by eight.

"I love you daddy," Nevette said as she hugged her dad. He squeezed her so tight she thought he would break her.

"My little princess is becoming a queen," he declared as he let go of her. Justice and her brothers were hugging and engaged in their goodbyes.

Nevette chuckled as she looked around her father's shoulder at them. They were acting as though they would never see one another again. She laughed inside as she thought, "You wouldn't have guessed we'll only be gone for three weeks, the way they were carrying on."

Justice's mom walked over to them, hugged Nevette and said, "I'm so proud of you. God is well pleased. You are a blessing from God for Derrick, and you will be a good wife."

"Oh, thank you mom. I am so blessed...Justice is," She paused losing the battle to fight back tears, "...is everything I ever dreamed of for a husband. His love is so powerful." Shaundra wiped her tears and they both hug again as Justice, his dad and sister came over to the side of the limousine where they were.

They were on their way to the Hyatt Regency hotel for the night. Justice had an action packed, romantic, exotic three week honeymoon planned for them. They would spend the night in Atlanta and fly to Miami for the next three days. There, they would enjoy the sites before boarding a two day cruise liner bound for the Bahamas. They would stay in the Bahamas for five days, and then fly back to Miami. Spend the night there, and fly out the next day to Paris, France for the remainder of the three week romantic honeymoon of the century.

As they pulled into the Regency parking lot, Justice could sense her nervousness. He grabbed her by the hand and turned her toward him. He placed his hand under her chin lifting her bowed head as he said, "Baby look at me...it's going to be okay...alright. I'm going to take very good care of you."

She looked up at him as she mustered a smile and said with a nervous shaky voice, "And they two...sh...shall become one flesh."

He smiled as he stroked her cheek and replied in that sweet sexy romantic voice of his that always sent her over the edge, "Two become one." He paused then said again as he leaned in to kiss her, "Two...become one."

54

They exit the limousine and head up to the room, after checking in. He opened the door, sweeps her up in his arms and carried her over the threshold. She is overwhelmed by all the care Justice has taken in preparing the room. Everything was so elegant and grand. The floor was completely covered with red rose pedals, with a path of yellow rose pedals leading to the Jacuzzi tub, located just at the foot of the bed. There was a very intricate aroma in the room that she couldn't quite place, but it was very soothing. The bed was elevated and had three steps leading up to it, giving room for the tub to inset in the ground just at the foot of the bed. It was a hot tub style square shaped Jacuzzi, that you stepped down into from the bed and had floating candles and more rose pedals in it. Overall, the bed and tub seemed to be elevated in throne room style. He had wine chilled, non-alcoholic of course, and chocolate covered strawberries in a tray on the side of the tub. There was also a wide silver goblet of fresh cherries at the bedside. The covers were pulled back with a beautiful white lace negligee laying ever so delicately on the pillow and a note that said, "For my Queen."

He had thought of everything. "When did he have time to do all of this?" she wondered.

She stood there nervous and barely breathing as he began to unzip her dress and undo the clasps of her bra, kissing her ever so lightly and sensual on her neck and shoulders. Nevette is so nervous that she didn't realize she was actually shaking. Her mind was in a whirlwind of thoughts. But the most prominent one was, "Oh my God, it's about to happen. Lord please be with me...help me to be good...and enough for him. I want to be all he has anticipated." Sensing her intimidation, he stopped and turned her around to face him. He held her in his arms and said, "Naythia, listen sweetheart...it's okay...I got you baby...I am going to be so good to you...it's going to be okay. This is going to be the most memorable night of your life." He kissed her and then teasingly said, "I mean, outside the day you accepted Jesus as your Lord and Savior...I don't think I can compete with him." Leave it to Justice to make her laugh and completely relax her. He turned serious again and said, "Sweetheart, we're going to take this very slow...I'm a very patient man and I love you...I'm going to take you inside love and show you how sweet it is."

His words both calmed her and excited her all at the same time. He finished undressing her, taking time to give her gentle sweet kisses on her neck and shoulder as he did. She started to relax under his touch and got a little more confident, as she also started to undress him. He escorted her to the tub and held her hand as she stepped in and followed her. They enjoy sparkling cider and feeding each other chocolate covered strawberries, while having some gentle and non-threatening caressing moments. They listened to the intimate but sacred love songs that played in the background. She enjoyed the wholeness of the atmosphere and began to relax. Then without warning, Justice got up out of the tub. She watched him as he walked over to get a towel and she thought, "Oh my God, my husband is sooo fine. Thank you Lord. Mmmmm...can I handle all of that? Ooh God, please help me."

He came back over and assisted her out of the tub. He dried her off with more gentle loving kisses. He led her over to the bed and laid her down. She looked up at him with innocent school girl eyes and asked him if he wanted her to put on the negligee. He responded, "No, not just yet baby. Let me give you a relaxing oil massage first."

She absolutely melted under his touch. It was sensual, intensive and sent her to another place. As his hands moved gently across her body, she wondered if every woman was this blessed in her marriage. She wondered if their husbands took the time to please and romance them. His touch was gentle, warm and intimidating all at the same time.

Justice picked up the negligee and said, "Here sweetheart, I was going to dress you myself, but I think I want to be surprised at how you look in it. So, why don't you go in the dressing room to put it on and then come back to bed."

"Okay," she said as she leaned over and kissed him with such passion, he almost didn't let go of her. "Down boy...down," she teased and walked away with the teddy in her hand, trying to look sexy and experienced so she wouldn't trip over anything. She was walking away from him unclothed, and though she was his wife she was still a little...shall we say shy about being undressed in front of him. Up to this night, no man had ever seen her unclothed before. Discounting her infancy, of course. He watched her walk away and poured more sparkling cider for the bedside and placed the goblet of cherries in the middle of the bed.

She emerged from the bathroom in the beautiful lace negligee, handpicked by her husband. Just as she reached the edge of the bed, there was a knock at the door.

Justice looked toward the door, then back at her and smiled, "Oh, I almost forgot, I have a surprise for you baby girl." She climbed over him and onto the bed as she gave him an inquisitive look. He threw on a robe and answered the door. She crouched there on her knees resting on her feet crossed behind her, and nervously twirled her fingers around each other with her hands in her lap. She anxiously waited to see what her husband had ordered for her.

She noticed Justices' tone changed slightly as he said, "What is this, this is not what I purchased for my wife to be delivered tonight? This isn't even close. There is a very expensive...I mean some things are missing from this tray, and where is the wardrobe cabinet?" He didn't want to give away the gift or show his frustration, so he stepped outside the door pulling it closed, to speak with the bellhop.

She anxiously awaited his return. Finally Justice came back in and said, "Sweetheart I have to go downstairs to get this straight. If it wasn't so important, I wouldn't bother with it. But it sets the stage for the rest of our honeymoon, so I have to get it right. Besides, there's quite a pretty penny invested into it, so I have to find everything."

He paused and looked at her, "You are so beautiful...I'm so sorry this night is turning out to be not so perfect, but baby I...,"

"Shhhh," she said she kissed him and pulled him down on top of her. She looked deep into his eyes and said, "This night has been perfect so far sweetheart. You go get the room service order straight. I'll be here when you get back."

She kissed him again and stroked his face as he pulled away. He said, "Oh, I'll be right back baby...mmmm...I will definitely, be right back." He threw on his pants and shirt and left to go straighten out the order.

She lay there looking up at the ceiling fan waiting for her newly wed husband to return from downstairs. She began to snack on a few of the cherries in the silver goblet in the middle of the bed. She was wondering just what in the world was he going to do with them. While she awaited his return, she took advantage of the time and began to pray and gather her nerves concerning the consummation of her marriage. She had been so ready a few moments ago, but now the intensity of the massage was fading and she could feel the nervousness returning.

She looked down at the beautiful negligee. It was so elegant. "He's such a gentleman," she said out loud. This was the night she had been waiting for all her life. Tonight she would become a woman, his woman...his wife! She would give herself totally to her husband. She had waited. It wasn't always easy, but she had indeed waited. She had been faithful to her vow to God, and pledge to her family. She felt an overwhelming rush of the Holy Spirit, which confirmed that God was pleased with her.

"Wow, how did I get here, to this place called joy?" she said with a smile. "I'm married to an awesome man of God and I am about to give myself to him...literally. Oh God!" She was once again in a panic, "I have absolutely no idea what to do!" Her hormones and emotions were all over the place. She could feel her heartbeat elevating. She realized that was why the Holy Spirit was present. To keep her calm until her husband retuned. So she relaxed in the Lord and thought about their first date, first kiss and the encounter that first brought them together......

≈

After getting a bite to eat they pull up in front of the church. Talinda wanted to touch basis with Pastor Tills and apologize for appearing so distant with him and his wife. She wanted to know what if anything he wanted in particular for Brandon's memorial service, before she made any solid plans. So far, the only sure thing was, he would be buried in his home town of Athens, GA.

She hadn't taken into consideration that this was indeed a crime scene and when they arrived, police tape would still be in place. The crime scene investigators had not yet released the scene for cleanup. She could only imagine that Brandon's dried blood would be everywhere and her mind was thrown back into the horror of the night before.

"Please daddy, drive around the back. I don't want to walk through Brandon's blood," she said to her dad.

"Sure baby girl," her father replied barely above a whisper. "I'm sure they probably have the front taped off due to the investigation anyway." Brandon's parents sat in silence. They could only imagine the horror of the night before and how difficult and terrifying it must have been for Talinda and everybody involved. Helen's eyes again filled up with tears and she realized her life would be full of emotional ups and downs for many days to come. Roger instinctively grabbed her hand, and she leaned over into his chest as they continued to sit in silence. There were just no words to describe or fit the situation at hand.

Talinda's father parked the car around back. She turned to Brandon's parents and informed them that they can remain in the car if they would like to. Because she couldn't be sure what they would see inside. She didn't remember much about location of where she had found Brandon, or anything from the night before. It seemed like a blur for some reason, even though it had all taken place less than twenty-four hours ago.

She turned to her father and said, "Daddy would you come in with me please?"

"I already planned on it sweetheart," her father replied. "I wouldn't dream of letting you go by yourself."

Roger and Helen looked at one another as Roger responded to Talinda's option to stay in the car. "If you don't mind Talinda, we would like to accompany you both into the church. We just feel like we are all supposed to stay together on this. There is strength in numbers."

"Thank you," replied a very relieved Talinda as they all stepped out of the car.

They did not have to travel far into the church because pastor's office was close to the back. All doors leading to the front of the church were closed and taped off, to Talinda's and her party's relief.

Pastor was sitting at his chair behind his desk. He appeared to have a lot on his to do list. He was just sitting there as though time had no meaning, because at this particular moment, it didn't. There was a faraway look of disbelief and devastation in his eyes. Talinda, seeing the emotional state of her pastor, was now very remorseful about her selfishness toward him and his wife the night before, when they were waiting to visit her. Brandon was like a son to them. She had not taken into consideration their position or their feelings for her and Brandon. She was too caught up in her own grief.

There was an awkward pause when he looked up to see Talinda and her family standing almost in front him. He had not heard them enter the room. He had not, for the last twenty four hours, heard much of anything for that matter. Time seemed to be a non-constant for him at this moment.

Talinda broke the silence, "Pastor, I'm so sorry about last night at the hospital. I was being extremely selfish in my actions. To be honest, I wasn't sure how I would react so I chose to just be alone in my grief. I owe you and First Lady Tills a huge apology..."

Pastor Tills cut her off in the middle of the sentence, "Daughter, there is no need to apologize. Beatrice and I sat out in the waiting room trying desperately to decide what would be appropriate to say to you. Questioning and blaming ourselves for even starting the program in the first place. Debating on whether or not I missed God in my choice of Brandon for youth pastor. I was thinking on how events of the last few hours might be different, if I had made different choices..."

Now it was Talinda who interrupted as she rushed over now in tears to embrace her pastor. There was such a rush of the Holy Spirit the moment she touched him that she realized she indeed had made a mistake in not seeing him and his wife the night before. She could have used what she felt at this moment with her pastor. There was such comfort and peace in the room and in his arms.

"Pastor," she said, finally able to muster up a sound to come forth. "I was so angry, not at any one in particular, but just angry, confused and hurt all at the same time. Please Pastor, do not allow the enemy to bring confusion to you. With or without your decision, Brandon would still be in the morgue. His love for troubled youth was not your decision; it was a mandate from God. If it had not been here, then it would have been someplace else. Brandon has run his race and has finished his course. Nothing you could have said or done would have changed the events of the day. In time we will understand fully what happened yesterday and will grow in God because of it. Until then, we just have to trust God and enjoy the many memories He has given us with Brandon. They will carry us through this troubled time that we all must share together."

At these words Pastor Tills was broken. He fell to his knees and began to sob uncontrollably. Talinda's father came over and began to pray for him. Roger and Helen joined them in prayer and thanksgiving to God. Suddenly, there was a break through and a spirit of praise broke out in the office. They danced, sang and gave God so much glory that the Shekinah cloud appeared before them. They all found themselves flat on their faces in God's presence. They were in awe of the presence and the pressure of the Holy Spirit in the room.

Then the unthinkable happened. God spoke with an audible voice......

"BE OF GOOD CHEER MY CHILDREN. HE HAS SACRIFICED MUCH TO SAVE MANY. HE HAS LAID DOWN HIS LIFE FOR A FRIEND. LIVE, LOVE AND FORGIVE THAT HIS WORK MAY BE COMPLETE."

Then as quickly as it came, the moment was over. They all lay there in silence for what seemed like hours, but was most likely only about ten to fifteen minutes. No one wanted to move or speak, at an attempt to extract everything out of the encounter as possible.

Pastor Tills finally stood and said, "Before I say what I thought I heard, let us pray and thank God for his divine presence at this divine appointment today." They all stood hand in hand and prayed, thanking God for his direction for their lives.

"Wow," Brandon's father said, to break the seriousness of the moment. "That kind of takes the fun out of grieving for a love one doesn't it? I mean if that makes sense at all. Of course this is not a fun event."

"Or," Talinda's father interjected. "More like changes the meaning of it. Roger, we understood what you meant. Sometimes, we glory in our infirmities and sort of wear our grief like a God earned trophy."

"Exactly," Roger replied, in relief that he had been understood. He certainly didn't want to make light of his son's death in any way.

Talinda looked Brandon's parents in the eyes and said, "I have a divine calm about me. I don't quite understand it, but I feel absolutely no anger, confusion or hurt what so ever about anything, or anybody. I know whatever it is God wants to complete by Brandon's actions, I am willing to allow. We are going to be tested in the area of love and forgiveness, and I don't know about you, but I plan on passing the test the first time." She paused and looked up to heaven, "God use me. I am available to you. Lead me in your divine direction, and I will answer the call."

Helen looks on knowing exactly what God was saying through Talinda. She knew in her heart that it was of God. She also knew it would take God for her to fulfill the task. So she stood there, in the moment, wondering what she would do when she came face to face with the situation. With the person who so viscously took her son, her only son, from her in a single act of vengeance. She instantaneously learned the truth of the scripture; *"he knows your thoughts,"* for God spoke directly to her spirit and said:

"OH MY PRESCIOUS DAUGHTER, I AM NOT ASKING OF YOU ANYTHING I HAVE NOT

ALREADY FULFILLED. VISCOUSLY YOUR SON WAS TAKEN, VISCOUSLY MY SON WAS GIVEN. YOU WILL FORGIVE. YOU MUST FORGIVE, THAT HIS WORK MAY BE COMPLETE."

Helen cried out with a loud voice, "Yes Lord, I will forgive. I will forgive...thank you Lord...you are God and God alone!"

There was such a spirit of praise and worship in the room, that it was impossible to contain your tongue from magnifying the Lord. His presence and healing power was overwhelming and awesome in the room.

"Oh what a service this will be," cried Pastor Tills who began to write down a few ideas about Brandon's home going service. He turned to Talinda and said, "You must dance in all white." He then addressed everyone and said, "As a matter of fact, no one is to wear black at all. Only colors of purity, redemption, royalty and glory!

"Wow," Talinda responded. "Silver, gold, purple and white, my mother will have a field day with this!"

Pastor Tills instructed Talinda, "Only use the dancers who share in the vision God has given us. So if that means you have to solo, then solo it is."

"Yes sir," Talinda said in total obedience to God and her pastor's command.

Helen interrupted, "Are you sure it's okay, I mean in your condition and all."

Pastor Tills responded apologetically, "I'm so sorry Minister Travis. In all the excitement, I completely forgot about your condition."

Talinda replied with a chuckle, "My condition, pastor I'm pregnant not handicapped. Mom, I plan on dancing all the way to the delivery room. I'm fine and the baby will be fine as well."

Roger shook his head in a disbelief manner said, "If someone would have told me a two and a half hours ago, I would be rejoicing after viewing my son's body in the morgue. I probably would have told them to get delivered off the drugs they were obviously taking and come down to the real world. But I learned today, that heaven is the real world and that's where Brandon is. If I want to see him again, I must follow everything in this." He paused to pick up a bible, "B-I-B-L-E, Basic Instructions Before Leaving Earth. So forgiveness God?" He said as he looked up toward heaven, "I CAN do all things through Christ which strengtheneth me!" They rejoiced all the more in God.

They all sat down and began to make the plans for Brandon's memorial service. About an hour later, as they stood to leave, Talinda turned toward Pastor Tills. "Okay pastor; let me see if I'm with you so far. You want praise and worship by a mixed praise team of adults and youth. Communion, a dance, a youth presentation of some kind involving a candle lighting service and you will do an altar call at the end of service. Oh, and we only have about three days to get this all accomplished. Have I missed anything?" Talinda asked.

"No that's sounds about right," Pastor Tills replied. "And we will have to give the rest of the service to the Holy Spirit, who is welcome to change any and everything on the program."

"Amen to that," Talinda's father replied.

Helen turned to Talinda and said, "Lindy we better get going we have a lot of work to do."

"Okay," she replied. Let me grab a church roster. I have a lot of members to contact tonight. We will have to get together starting tomorrow night, after we get back from Athens, if we plan on being ready by Wednesday."

"Wait a minute Lindy," her father replied. "Tomorrow is Sunday. Will the funeral home even be open for business?"

"Well, if I recall correctly, they are usually open seven days a week. Quite a few people in Athens have home goings on Sunday," Helen answered.

Talinda interjected, "Daddy, I know tomorrow is the Lord's Day, but we only have a few days to get things settled." She turned toward Pastor Tills, "Sir, if it's alright, we will attend church in Athens with the Travis'. We'll be back here Monday afternoon, to start decorating the church and the getting the youth ready. Daddy, would you please stay here with Pastor Tills tonight and bring mom up tomorrow morning. That way, we won't have so much back and forth travel time?"

"Sure sweetheart," her father replied. "See you tomorrow princess. Try to get some sleep tonight."

"I will daddy," Talinda responded.

"We'll take good care of her Victor," Roger replied.

"I know you will Roger," Victor paused and then continued. "Well, I better get a hotel. I came straight from the airport to the hospital."

"Now we'll hear none of that," interjected Pastor Tills. "You will stay with Beatrice and me."

Victor protested, "Now Pastor Tills that's not necces...,"

Pastor Tills lifted his hand toward Victor in full protest, "Now I won't hear of it, you're staying with us and that's final."

Everyone gives Victor a, "you're outnumbered look", and he gives in to Pastor Tills. "Thanks Pastor Tills, I appreciate your hospitality."

"You're welcome," Pastor Tills replied. "And please, call me Denson. We are all equal in the Lord."

"Alright Denson." He then turned to Talinda and said, "Okay baby girl, see you tomorrow in Athens after I pick your mom up from the airport.

They all exchange hugs and bid their goodbyes for the day.

~Chapter Five~

Talinda arose the next morning feeling surprisingly quite well rested and normal. They decided not to attend church that morning. They desperately attempted to convince themselves that their reason was so they could get a good start on Brandon's arrangements. But they knew all too well, the main reason was, they just weren't ready to be the center of attention at church just yet. The news about Brandon had travelled quickly throughout the church community, after the Travis' had shared the news with their pastor before heading to Atlanta the day before.

She sat in bed remembering how sick she was during her first pregnancy with Lydia. Her thoughts trailed off to how compassionate Brandon had been. He had catered to her every need and was so excited about the baby......

"Here sweetheart, I brought you some crackers and ginger ale just like you like in the morning," Brandon said as he kissed her on the forehead.

"Thank you baby, you are too good to me," Talinda replied. It had been the longest seven and a half months of her life. She thought that the morning sickness would have stopped long before, but she had literally been sick every day for the whole seven and a half months. It had simply never let up and she was feeling particularly sick and uneasy that morning. If she would consume the crackers and ale before rising, she would sometimes win the battle of losing her dinner from the night before. But something was very different about her sickness that day. The nausea was accompanied by sharp pains along the bottom half of her stomach, deep in her uterus. She had spent the whole night off and on in pain and felt extremely heavy, with a lot of pressure in her pelvic area. As she tried to rise for her morning visit to the restroom, she was hit with an almost unbearable pain and she cried out in agony as a gush of pinkish fluid rushed out of her body.

"Honey what is it, what's wrong?" Brandon asked as he reentered to room responding to her cry.

"I think my water just broke, but...I don't know, something is wrong, something is very wrong. I need to go the hospital, I need to get dressed," Talinda responded in tears already.

"Okay, sweetheart I got you," Brandon said as he gathered her up in his arms to head for the door. As he picked her up he noticed there was blood in the bed where she laid. Now, realizing the urgency to get her to the hospital, he rejected the idea of her changing out of her night gown.

"Oh my God, Lindy, we don't have time to change baby. We need to get you to the hospital now," a panicked Brandon declared.

Talinda did not need to ask nor did she care about what terrified Brandon, because she was feeling the contractions coming closer together. Between shallow breathes said, "Okay." It was as though life was draining from her.

Brandon drove frantically while calling the hospital to alert the doctor and praying to God all at the same time, as Talinda sat in pain beside him breathing erratically.

An OB/GYN nurse met them at the ER entrance when they arrived and whisked Talinda away while Brandon parked the car. When he arrived inside, they had already taken her to labor and delivery.

"What's happening," a frantic Brandon screamed. "My wife...our baby...what is it?"

"Mr. Travis, we need you to scrub and get into the delivery room. Your wife is about to deliver, we don't have much time," exclaimed Talinda's OB/GYN doctor.

"I don't understand, it's not time is it...I mean we're a long way from nine months," Brandon yelled out in desperation.

"Ready or not sir, she is coming Mr. Travis. We can't stop the process it's too far gone. Your wife is fully dilated. She was probably unknowingly in labor all night. Now get ready, your wife is going to need you," responded Dr. Yolanda Harrell.

The neo-natal unit had been put on alert for a preemie. Dr. Harrell had little hope she would survive the delivery. Her vitals had already dropped to dangerously low levels. If she couldn't

66

push baby Travis out relatively soon, they would be forced to do an emergency C-section. Something, that Dr. Harrell was reluctant to do, because she had little hope that baby Travis would survive. She had little or no vitals already.

Brandon entered the delivery room where Talinda was. Took her by the hand and began to pray for the Lord to intervene in their lives.

"Okay, Mrs. Travis, when the next pain hits you, I want you to bear down and push," Dr. Harrell instructed.

"Oh God, Brandon help me...it hurts so bad...I can't do this!" Talinda exclaimed. She was extremely tired from enduring the pain and lack of sleep during the night.

"Yes you can baby. You have to, now push sweetheart push," Brandon instructed as he supported her back. Talinda let out a yell as she pushed with all her might.

Dr. Harrell in reply to Talinda pushing said, "Okay Mrs. Travis, that's good. Now next time...,"

She was interrupted by a very frantic Talinda who yelled out, after she noticed that the monitor was silent, "I don't hear her heartbeat anymore, my baby! Dr. Harrell...Brandon, what's happening to my baby?"

"Mrs. Travis, I need you to concentrate on your pushing. We have to get her out in a next minute or so, now please, with the next contraction push.

Talinda in a real panic screamed out, "But I'm not feeling any contractions, I'm not feeling anything! Oh God no, please no! I'm so sorry Brandon...I didn't know!"

"I love you baby...it's not your fault...it's going to be okay. Now come on and focus baby...okay...you can do this!" Brandon replied.

"Mrs. Travis," interrupted Dr. Harrell. "You have to concentrate. Now when I count three, you need to push with everything you have, okay? One...Two...Three, now push!"

Talinda pushed, yelled and cried all at the same time, now feeling what the outcome of the delivery would be. Dr. Harrell yelled for Talinda to stop pushing.

"Okay, Mrs. Travis, stop pushing I have her. The cord is wrapped around her neck and I need to cut it," responded Dr. Harrell. They soon had baby Travis on the table working feverously on her. They were massaging her, and working to get any sign of life out of her at all. Talinda and Brandon anxiously awaited a sign, any sign, of life from their baby girl.

Finally, after fifteen minutes, Dr. Harrell called the time of death. Little baby Travis had been still born, never taking a breath of her own outside her mother's womb.

Talinda seemed to be detached from the situation, as Brandon tried to no avail to get her to respond to him, "Lindy, sweetheart talk to me. Talinda, baby say something, are you alright? Come on Lindy, talk to me sweetheart." She just laid there, staring at the ceiling as Dr. Harrell delivered the after birth and stitched up her tear from forcing Lydia out. There had been no time for an episiotomy.

"Lydia," Talinda whispered. "Her name is Lydia."

Brandon responded to her, very grateful that she had finally spoken and appeared to come back to the reality of the situation. "Yes sweetheart," he said as tears ran down his cheeks. "Her name is Lydia. We're going to be okay Lindy. We're going to make it through this."

"I'm so sorry Mr. and Mrs. Travis. But as we run the tests on both you and Lydia over the next few days, we are hopeful we will find out what happened. In doing so will, secure successful pregnancies in the future. I will return to check on you in a short while," declared a very compassionate Dr. Harrell. She then turned and left the room. She had grown particularly close to the Travis' and was feeling very emotional and inadequate at that particular moment.

The nurse had Lydia cleaned and wrapped in a delivery blanket for her parents to hold her before taking her away for autopsy. "Excuse me, replied the nurse. "Would you like to spend some time with your baby before we take her downstairs? We need to get you more stable as well Mrs. Travis."

Talinda lay quiet and motionless. Brandon responded, "Yes that would be fine thank you." He took baby Lydia in his arms. He began to cry as he looked down into her face. "Oh my God Lindy, she is just like you. She's beautiful," He exclaimed through his tears.

Talinda looked over at Brandon and Lydia and realized she had to hold her baby at least once, and so held out her arms. Brandon placed her in Talinda's arms and knelt beside her. They spent a half hour with her before the nurse came to take her away.

"When will we be able to get her for burial services," Brandon asked. The nurse said she would find out for them. Because Talinda would still need to stay in the hospital a day or two for some special tests Dr. Harrell wanted to run on her, Brandon requested and was granted a private room for her off the maternity ward to make things a little easier for her.

She remembered how hard it was for her and Brandon the weeks and months following Lydia's death. All of the tests ran on both Talinda and Lydia had come back normal. There was no medical reason at all for the premature labor and lose of Lydia, except that it was the will and plan of the Father.

It was hard to pack up her room to put everything in storage. Against both their parents counsel, they decided they would try to conceive again as quickly as possible. But weeks turned to months and months turned into years. Talinda appeared to be barren, that was until now......

And now Brandon would not be here to share it with her. The tears began to flow again as she clutched her stomach and cried out, "Why Brandon, why? I need you...I need you."

Her mother, who had arrived just moments before, was on the way up to the room where she was. She stopped outside the room to pray before going in. The Travis' had called Talinda's father when they got in last night to inform them they wouldn't be going to church in the morning after all. So if they wanted to come on to Athens early when Talinda's mother arrived, that would be fine.

As she prayed and listened to the tears of her baby girl, she knew it was time to share with her a pain she had kept hidden for so many years. She had indeed felt God's comfort in her time of need, but had kept her tragedy from Talinda for such a time as this. A time she had hoped and prayed her daughter would never have the pain of knowing.

She now needed to let her daughter know, that she had indeed traveled the road leading to the other side of through. She needed to let Talinda know, that she would make it. It may not seem like it right now, but she would indeed make it. "Too often," she thought as she waited on the Lord to give her permission to enter the room where Talinda was. "We mothers are not transparent enough for our young daughters. They see us as a flawless superwoman, above pain and temptation. But they need to know our struggles. They need to know our pain and disappointments. They need to know God that you will answer prayer and comfort in the time of need...they need to know."

"Mother!" her thoughts were interrupted by Talinda who looked up through her tears and saw her mother standing in the doorway.

"When did I move into the doorway," Valetta thought.

Talinda rushed into her mother's arms, tears streaming down her face and Valetta began to pray:

Lord...God I pray now for my baby girl,

Father I pray that You will comfort her like only You can. Lord it feels now like it was not so long ago that I needed this same comfort from You. Now I pray that You will be with Lindy, just as you were with me when I lost George and little Daniel. You said You will not leave us comfortless and that Your joy would be our strength. You held true to that in my life Lord, and I know You will be true to Lindy as well. Now have joy Lord, have much joy because my baby needs the strength of Your joy to get through this moment in her life. This is a life changing moment, God. We trust You Lord. We may not quite understand, but we trust You and we love You. You said in Your word as Moses asked You at the burning bush, who he should say has sent him. You replied "I AM THAT I AM", signifying You would be whatever we needed You to be, when we needed it. God, we need You to be a comforter and a bright morning star shining brilliantly in this period of darkness in Talinda's life. Bless her Lord and keep her like only you can. In the matchless name of Jesus Christ our Lord!

Amen

Talinda, not quite understanding or sure what to say, looked up into her mother's eyes with uncertain bewilderment. Valetta, reading her daughters thoughts said, "Why don't we go grab a cup of tea and some toast for you and sit on the Travis' deck. It's a beautiful morning out sweetheart, and there is something I need to share with you." Talinda nodded a silent but puzzled affirmation and followed her mother.

Now, as they sat comfortably out on the deck, Valetta turned to Talinda, who sat patiently waiting for her mother's response to her silent questions. "Exactly who are George and Daniel and what happened to them? Why had she never known about them? And why had her mother kept their existence a secret?"

Valetta grabbed Talinda by the hand, took a deep breath as she looked first down, as if carefully gathering her words, then up into Talinda's eyes. She took another deep breath and began to speak. "Talinda, I know you are full of questions. Right now you are wondering who George and Daniel are? What happened to them and why, oh why, had I never mentioned them before? Remember, when the Prophetess came to church and prophesied to you about your future husband. Remember she looked at me and then said you and I would develop a closer relationship? She gave me a look that exposed the fact that God had revealed my past to her. A past that I swore your father to secrecy about, and made him vow never to reveal it to you. Well, here goes. Sweetheart, your father is not my first husband."

Talinda interrupted, "What! Mom I don't understand? What do you mean...who...?"

"Just listen dear, okay. Let me finish, "Valetta replied as she held and patted Talinda's hand to calm the moment. Then she continued, "I was married before your father, to a man named George McLowry. We were married only for a few months when we found out we were expecting our first child. We had a boy that we named Daniel. He was only a few months old when one day we were on the way, ironically enough, to the hospital for a well-baby appointment. Out of nowhere, a drunk driver ran the light and hit us almost head on. I was unconscious for a week, only to awake and find that I was alone. My husband and baby boy had not survived the crash. I only had minor injuries and the doctors were unsure why it took me so long to come out of my unconscious state. Thank God for George's mother, who had insisted on preserving the bodies, so I could be there at the memorial service. I sat at the funeral in disbelief. In one fail swoop, I had lost my entire family. I was devastated and went into a state of depression."

Talinda was stunned beyond words. She simply could not believe what she was hearing. It seemed so unreal that what her mother was telling her could actually be her reality. She was so happy with her father, so normal. You would have never known she had gone through such a tragedy. There were absolutely no remnants or scars about her past, at least not any visible ones. And even now, she was telling the story with strong clarity. There was no shaking or wavering in her voice what so ever! Talinda sadly realized she had never really noticed much of anything about her mother. She spent much of her teen years trying to avoid her as much as possible. Not attempting in the least, to connect with her.

Talinda was instantly feeling guilty about her relationship, or lack thereof, with her mother. Now, she knew the meaning behind her overprotective and smothering ways.

She now understood why sometimes, she would wake up in the middle of the night to her mother praying over her, or watching her sleep. She now also understood why her mother struggled so much when it came to safety. Often when her father would let her drive at a young age, without license or even a permit, her mother was almost lose it emotionally. She never liked to take unnecessary chances with anything concerning Talinda. She grew up feeling smothered by her mother and resenting her need to know everything, everybody and everywhere she would be. She considered her mother a basket case for most of her teen years and was often embarrassed by her actions concerning her. She remembered words she had spoken to her mother disrespectfully in anger, "You need to know too much information mom," she would always say. "Why can't you be like the other mothers and give me a little space sometimes?! I'm not going to disappear!" Talinda felt shame about the way she had treated her mom in the past. She realized now the fear her mother must have operated in, of losing yet another family to unforeseen tragedy. Talinda could feel the tears begin to flow again.

"Talinda," her mom grabbed her hands again and looked deep into her eyes. "People will often say that the things you go through are not for your need, but for someone else's. Sweetheart, no matter how hard or terrible you may think of your current situation. There is someone who has and is surviving worst. And their testimony will help you to survive. In time, yours will help someone else to survive tragedy as well. The one thing you think will totally destroy you. Will ultimately create a powerful ministry in you and through you."

Talinda asked through her tears and confusion, "What...I mean how...I mean mom, how did you get through the feeling of devastation, the depression? Over the last forty-eight hours there have been moments when I felt strong and...and felt the presence of the Lord. Other times, I've felt hopeless."

Valetta pulled Talinda into her arms for comfort. She sighed, "He sends the comforter sweetheart. You have to open up to the Holy Spirit. Just as God manifested himself in an audible voice to you yesterday, he will manifest himself to you, and visit you again. He will dear, and you will be made whole by him, if you allow it. But know this sweetheart, in your pain, God will still require ministry from you. You will rise to the occasion at the appointed time. The Spirit of the Lord will lift up a standard baby girl. He will come in and dissipate your flood. Just stand still and see his salvation dearest. I will be here with you every step of the way. I have taken an extended leave from work. Most of my patients have agreed to online and phone sessions. The others have been reassigned to other physicians."

Talinda felt a strange calm and peace at her mother's words. She remembered the visitation they had at pastor's office the day before. She knew with surety that she would indeed make it to the other side of through. She also knew she would need the experience of her mother in the days and weeks to come. She looked forward to getting to known her mother on a different level.

"Mom," Talinda said and then paused. She was unsure about how her mother would handle the request she was about to present to her. After pondering the thought for a brief moment, she decided to just ask. "Mom, do you have any pictures of my big brother and your first husband? When this is all over, do you think we can sit down and view them together? I would love to see them."

Valetta, with tears in her eyes replied, "Sure sweetheart. Somehow I knew you would ask that question. So I brought the photo album with me. I think it will be good for me as well. I haven't viewed the pictures since I sealed the book, over twenty four years ago."

Talinda leaned into her mother's arms and rested in the peace of God she felt through her mother's touch. She knew her relationship with her mother would never be the same and that they just advanced, to a new level.

~Chapter Six~

A few moments later, Helen poked her head out the door of the kitchen and said, "Sorry to interrupt you two, but we need to be getting over to the funeral home, and start making the arrangements."

"Okay thanks," Talinda replied wiping her tears. She turned back toward her mother and said, "Yes...mom we have a lot to cover today, so we better get started. I still have a few youth I need to contact as well."

"Alright," Valetta replied. "Give me a minute to get my pad and color portfolio out of my suitcase and I'll be right with you." Valetta was a psychiatrist by occupation, but has always loved wedding, formals, and banquet planning. She often playfully threatened to leave her practice and go full time as a wedding planner. She had a wonderful natural gift for color and floral arrangements. And since Pastor Tills didn't want the look of a funeral but a celebration, she didn't have to worry about the design looking too festive for the occasion, because festive is exactly what they had in mind.

"Okay mom, I need to freshen up a bit as well," Talinda responded to Helen.

"Have you eaten yet dear," Helen asked Talinda. Talinda responded with a childlike tone, "Yes I had a piece of toast and a cup of hot tea my mom brewed for me, so I'm okay for the moment..."

Cutting her off, Helen exclaimed in an "I know what's best for you" motherly tone, "Don't you think you need a little more than toast? Breakfast is an important meal and you shouldn't be drinking caffeine dear...I mean in your condition."

74

A somewhat sarcastic and defensive Valetta replied, "Oh no worries, it was decaf. I carry a few packs in my purse where ever I go. I've learned over the years of ministry, that sometimes only God knows what kind of food we need. What he had for me to share with my daughter was sustaining for her soul and spirit man. But to save time and get some natural nourishment into little momma here..." she said as she pulled Talinda in kissing her on the side of her forehead. Talinda smiled in response, "...we can grab something more nutritious on the way over to the funeral home."

Talinda was feeling a little uneasy and surprisingly defensive about the "I know what's best for you" accusation of her mother-in-law. She looked up at her mother and responded, "Okay mom, we better get ready to go. I'll go freshen up and you get your portfolio." She then turned to Brandon's mother and said, "Don't worry Mrs. Helen, I feel fine. Ever since I thought I was pregnant, I haven't been able to eat much more than toast when I first rise in the morning. Breakfast is usually a distant follow-up after settling my stomach." She turned back toward her mother in a "we're the only two people in the room tone" and said, "Mom, I guess little Brandon is going to do me the same way you said I did you. First toast to ease the way and then breakfast." They share in a private laugh as she turned back toward Helen again and said, "Mrs. Helen, give me about twenty minutes to get dressed and I'll be ready to go. I'll try to hurry, because I know we have a lot to do in a short time." Talinda's tone is somewhat harsh towards Helen as she turned and headed into the house to change. She didn't bother waiting for a response from Helen or her mother.

Valetta, a little unsure what to say to Helen because of the awkwardness of the moment, left to go and grab her portfolio and any other materials she may need for the day. But she couldn't help but to feel a little vindicated. Talinda had verbally and openly sided with her and taken up for her with Helen for the first time since she entered the Travis' lives. She gloated inside at the joy of the moment. But it would be short lived.

≈

She closed her eyes and let her mind race back to the moment they met. It was her junior year in college at the University of Georgia. She was in the intern phase of her degree, as a physical therapist there at the local hospital in Athens. She was due to receive a new patient the next day. A football player who had been injured on the field several weeks earlier and had undergone surgery. She had been in attendance at that game and remembered cringing as he went down, knowing his leg had to be broken. Sure enough it was and six weeks later, after he recovered from the surgery and the cast was removed and replaced with a removable brace, she would meet her future husband-to-be, Derrick Justice Goodfellow II.

"Those guys always looked so different out of their uniform," she remembered thinking. There he was. He looked helpless, adorable and in obvious pain. "Here, let me help you," she said as she assisted him into the chair for processing.

"Thank you," he said in a very sexy, sweet, but vulnerable baby boy voice.

"Wow," she thought. "There is just something about him." She cleared her throat and said, "Okay, let's start by checking all your information and get your computerized chart started. That way, we can track your progress. Please look this over carefully and make any corrections needed."

"Thank you," he said again. He took a moment to look at the chart and handed it back to her. "Everything looks correct ma'am."

"Oh please, don't call me ma'am. I'm a student just like you, I'm on my intern this year," Nevette replied. She was unsure why she was slightly embarrassed by his comment.

"I know who you are, Miss Nevette Naythia Graham, I was just respecting your position," he said with a sexy smile.

"Oh, okay...uhmm...ahh...," Nevette had not quite expected that answer and wasn't sure how to respond. She just continued on in a professional manner. "...Let's proceed, so we can get you in the whirlpool tub to loosen up those muscles before we begin. Okay let's see, Derrick Justice Goodfellow Jr."

"Ah, excuse me," Derrick interrupted. "That's the second, not junior."

"Oh, pardon me, Derrick Justice Goodfellow II," she said with a sarcastic smile. "I see your middle name is Justice, wow, how unique that is."

Derrick responded, "I don't really care for my middle name. I mean, who gives their child a name like Justice? You can imagine the jokes growing up, "Justice of the Peace" and "Justice for all" were the most popular. I inherited it from my dad. You would think after he went through a childhood of teasing he would have spared his son from it. But nooo," he replied. He shook his head as though thoroughly amused by his

76

own statement. "He said, if he endured, I would too. So, I guess my son will be called Tre for short," he ended his statement with a chuckle.

"Uhmm...Tre...cute. Well somebody in your family sure liked it," Nevette replied.

"Yeah, I guess you could say that," Derrick exclaimed.

"Well I think it's sexy, and I rather like it," Nevette replied.

"Since you put it that way," he said with a school boy smile as he raised one eyebrow. "I will allow you to call me Justice."

"Why thank you kind sir," Nevette replied with a smile.

"I rather like your middle name as well," Justice interjected.

"What mine?" Nevette said as she pointed to herself surprised. "Actually, most of my family calls me Nay Nay. That's short for Naythia. Nobody really calls me Naythia. It's my aunt's first name. She was named after her two grandmothers and my great-grandmothers, Cynthia and Naytalia. Naythia is a cross between their two names."

"Well it sounds very regal, like it belongs behind a royal title...like Queen Naythia," Justice replied with a very serious chuckle.

"Okay...well, I guess I'll return the favor and allow you to call me Naythia," Nevette responded in a very girly "oh he looked at me" tone.

After he was all checked in, she helped him over to the heated whirlpool tubs. As they were in route she said, "You should have been told to wear some swim trunks or shorts so you wouldn't have to change."

"Yeah, I have them on under my breakaway gyms pants," Justice responded.

"Great," she replied. "I can give you some privacy to get ready if you like."

"No need for that," he replied. At that moment, he pulled off his shirt and ripped off his gym pants. Nevette wasn't quite ready for what she saw and was taken aback by how proportioned he was. He was milk chocolate smooth and ripped in all the right places. She could feel her body temperature rising. His beautiful caramel brown eyes were mesmerizing. His six pack was tight and he had a brilliant smile to boot. Although she didn't know him personally before that day, something told her his personality was brilliant as well.

She smiled and shook head as she thought, "Mmmmm...I bet those massive arms can hold you oh...so...tight, yet tender at the same time. What are you doing girl, you're supposed to be professional, get your head in the game...no pun intended."

Still caught up in her thoughts, she was interrupted by Justice as he said, "Excuse me Miss Graham, exactly what is it you want me to do?"

"Oh, my, God I'm sorry. Ahhh....let me help you into the tub," Nevette responded. She was embarrassed that she had been caught daydreaming. She hoped that it hadn't shown on her face, what was going through her mind. Justice had given her a knowing smile that both melted her and made an already embarrassing situation worse.

"Are you sure you're strong enough to lift me?" He asked with a chuckle. "I mean, I'm pretty heavy for such a petite little pretty thing to have to support."

Nevette could feel that she was losing composure as she thought, "I know I'm way too young for menopause so where is this hot flash coming from? Whew, this is overwhelming, but baby you can lift me if you want to!" Instead she responded, "Don't worry we're trained on how to assist you, without allowing you to put too much pressure on your injury or on us."

After she assisted him into the whirl pool tub she gave him some additional instructions before she left him to soak. "Okay, Derr...I mean Justice," he smiled, "It will take about ten minutes for your muscles to warm enough for us to begin to maneuver them, I'll be right back."

With Justice safely down in the pool she went off to gather all the materials she would need for her session with him. She wanted to look back to see if he watched her walk away. But didn't know how she would respond if he was, so she looked straight ahead and proceeded to the supply room. "Why I am so nervous?" She thought.

Upon her return she went through the therapy session with him. "Let me know if this is too painful as we go along. The idea is to loosen you up so the re-strengthening process can begin. It takes time, so don't rush the therapy. Besides, you could re-injure yourself and we don't want that."

Justice responded, "I don't know, if I would keep the same physical therapist, re-injury might not be such a bad thing." All Nevette could do was smile, she didn't know how to respond. So she just continued to move him through the therapy.

As the session came to a close Nevette exclaimed, "There, your first session is complete. Now was it as unpleasant as you imagined it would be?"

78

"A little more intense than I thought. But overall, you're very gentle," Justice responded.

"Thank you. Could you please fill out a comment sheet on your way out? Do you need help getting your sweat pants snapped back up?" she asked.

"Yes please," he responded, "That would be great. It's still kind of hard to bend over." She hadn't expected him to say yes. No one had ever said yes before and she wasn't even sure it was proper protocol.

As she helped him with his snaps she couldn't help but to ask, "Earlier when you said you knew me, exactly what did you mean by that? Where is it that you know me from?"

"Tell you what," Justice replied, "May I share that with you later after a few sessions."

"Sure why," Nevette answered. She was puzzled and quite curious with his request.

"Let's just say," he started to answer but then paused. He showcased that gorgeous school boy smile and really began to toy with her. He touched her cheek and continued, "I want to give you something to look forward to over our next sessions."

She stepped back out of his reach as she thought, "Oh, so you think that hunk of a body isn't enough, mmm...if he only knew." She responded with a modest but curious, "Okay." She hoped she didn't have a silly schoolgirl crush look on her face. She was relieved the session was ending, because she had all but lost it.

Over the next few weeks the sessions got easier and easier for Justice. His therapy was ahead of schedule. They enjoyed each other's company more and more in each session and Nevette looked forward to his appointment time. She had even created a few extra sessions that he hadn't needed, just so she could be with him. She soon realized that she was falling for him. He was charming and very easy to talk too. She was very excited to find out that Justice had given his life to the Lord earlier that year. Nevette was amazed at how comfortable she was with him. She was usually very uncomfortable when she had male patients. Something, she would have to get over, considering her choice of profession.

Although Justice seemed to both relax and excite her simultaneously, things were about to heat up dramatically, and take a commanding turn.

As the day's session was coming to an end, Justice turned toward Nevette after he was dressed and said, "You asked me where I knew you from six weeks ago at our first session."

Wow, had it been that long? Nevette had completely forgotten about that and responded in a surprised tone, "Oh yeah, I had forgotten about that. You mean I finally get my answer?" He smiled, but turned very serious all of a sudden.

Nevette somewhat alarmed asked, "Do I really want to know the answer? You're seriousness is making me nervous."

"Don't be," Justice responded. "It's not anything like that." He paused and then replied, "Okay, where do I begin? Okay...uhmm...okay...ahhmmm...," he shook and smiled to himself. He sighed as though a heavy burden had just been lifted off his shoulders. "...Okay, just jump right in there Derrick," he said aloud as though having a private conversation with himself. He looked deep into Nevette's eyes with an intensity that penetrated to her soul and said, "Naythia, I am so in lo...I am so attracted to you."

Those words not only startled and relieved Nevette considering she knew she was falling for him, but captivated her. She took a few steps backwards creating a comfortable space between them. She could sense that she had stopped breathing and hoped she wouldn't pass out for lack of oxygen. "Oh my God, what's going to happen? Is he going to kiss me? Breathe, Nevette breathe," she silently coached herself.

Justice continued without pause moving toward her, making up the ground Nevette had put between them. He said in a low, sexy nut sincere tone, "I have been for a long time. You'll be surprised to know that before we broke off into our majors, we shared a lot of the same classes our freshman and sophomore years together."

"Really," Nevette managed to reply in a normal tone. "I don't remember you." She was trying desperately to change the atmosphere in the room, because at the moment the momentum wasn't in her favor. She could feel was yet again losing the battle to control her emotions.

"That's because football players, even though they are on campus still do a lot of online sessions. Whenever football and training schedules coincide with classes, you know football wins. Most of the time, I was in and out of class before the lectures would begin and end," he replied.

80

Nevette silently tried to calm down. His straight forwardness had caught her off guard. He had very much invaded her space and his smile was undoing her.

Justice again continued on not waiting for her to reply. He stroked her cheek and said, "I was so infatuated with you. You loved God and I was very new to Christianity. I was almost always at the campus bible study where you taught. I just knew you had to be a preacher's kid...or something." He paused for an instant shaking his head with that take you over the top smile and slightly chuckled. "I didn't think I was anywhere near your league. I was so intimidated by you and crazy about you at the same time. I sat in the back of the chapel, so I could stare at you unnoticed. It was a very wild time for me. But, I learned to control my emotions and began to respect you as a fellow Christian, even though you had no idea I existed. When I got hurt, I prayed so hard that you would be my therapist. I praised God and was so excited when I saw your name on my records for my physical therapy sessions."

Nevette was in complete shock. She desperately tried to process everything she had just heard and respond in a timely manner, in a coherent tone. But she knew inside, her speech was all but normal. All she could think to say, as she again moved out of the reach of his touch was, "Of course I knew who you were. Who doesn't know the football players? But I didn't know you personally before you walked, I mean hobbled into physical therapy. Whew, I'm just trying to process all of this...it's a bit much."

"I know," Justice replied. "And I'm beginning to think, that I may have messed up our remaining therapy sessions. I hope it won't be too awkward for you now. I mean, can you still be comfortable with me?"

"Derrick, I know we can still be friends. At least, I would like to think that's what we have become," Nevette responded.

Justice moved a little closer to her and said, "Friends is not exactly what I'm aiming for here. But, if that's what gets you through this moment, I'll accept it for now." He smiled with a sexy chuckle then continued, "Because, believe me, I'm fine with it all. I'm already looking way past friends, princess. Are you sure you'll be okay, that won't be awkward for you?"

Nevette backed up again and said, "Derrick, I think I'll be okay. I mean I'm a little taken back by all this, but surely I'm mature enough to handle it."

"You see," Justice responded. He again moved close to her, erasing the space she put between them. "You've already changed. You called me Derrick for the first time since our first session. I like to hear you call me Justice. No one else does and before you started, I didn't even like the name." He paused momentarily and reached out, lightly slid his finger across her lips as he said, "And besides, it rolls sooo sexy off your lips."

"Whew...oh...my my my, God please help," she thought. She felt like she would just hyperventilate and pass out at any moment. She pulled it together and responded, "Wow...I'm sorry. I guess I'm a little more affected than I thought. But honestly Derr...I mean Justice, I'll be fine if you're fine. I do love the friendship we have formed. I wouldn't wish for it to change either." Once again, she backed up a little more to a safer distance from him.

Justice took full advantage of the situation. He moved forward yet again. But this time he totally invaded her space. He smiled and said as he lightly played with her hair, "Change is exactly what I want. But for now...well...I guess I'll see you next session."

"Ye-yes," she responded in a shaky voice. "Your pool sessions start then. I think your leg is strong enough now." She tried desperately to sound normal, whatever that was, because she was too arrested to move away from him. Her back was almost against the wall and she had nowhere left to go.

Smiling, he let her off the hook and said as he headed for the door, "See you in three days." Justice nodded in her direction as he left the therapy room not waiting for her response. Nevette just stood there in silence and waited for him to leave the therapy area, before she fell back against the wall and let out a sigh of relief.

"Oh my God, what just happened," she exclaimed. "Is this him Lord, did you send this man to me? Oh my God, I don't know what to think, I just...don't know. We are so compatible, we get along so well. He is so easy to talk to, and oh my God, he is soooooo sexy!" She shook her head as if trying to get her thoughts together, "You shouldn't be thinking this way girl. If the mothers in the church back home knew your thoughts right now, they would wash your brain out with soap! Well, guess there is only one way to find out what he really wants," she thought. "Tell him I'm a virgin and waiting on that special man God is preparing just for me and see how he responds. That will probably end the infatuation." It would be three days before the

82

next session. "How am I supposed to sleep the next seventy-two hours!" she said out loud.

≈

Helen stood on the deck for a few moments after Talinda and her mother left. She was feeling quite wounded by Talinda's words. She couldn't remember the last time Talinda called her Mrs. Helen. She had been mom to her for seven years and sensed she had offended them both with her accusing tone. She knew Talinda and her mother were not extremely close. She had often taken somewhat of an advantage of that situation, always being the "understanding mother she never had".

Now she felt like instead of being Talinda's mother in this time of bereavement, she had been reduced in rank to mother-in-law status for the first time since Brandon first brought her home to introduce her to them. She realized for the first time that she had somewhat taken on an arrogant pride against Talinda's mother over the years. Because she felt she was closer to Talinda than Valetta had been. And at times, gloated on several occasions when they were all together and Talinda would address her as mom, in Valetta's presence. She often sensed Valetta's jealousy concerning their close relationship. She often times added fuel to the fire by contradicting and challenging advice that Valetta had given Talinda, winning the battle of the mom's. But now all of a sudden, she felt like an uninvited outsider in the relationship. She failed at forcing back tears as she reentered the house. She knew she could easily lay the blame of the emotions, to Brandon's death, should anyone inquire of her.

There was an awkward silence as Helen drove them to the funeral home in Athens, GA. They were all feeling the tension of the morning. As they pulled up to the funeral home and stopped, Talinda's mother Valetta broke the silence.

"Okay, ladies listen. I've been saved a long time and gone through too much, to start giving the devil any kind of victory in my life now. I know the enemy was at work between us this morning. He wants to divide and conquer and I for one am not going to let him get away with it. You all had an awesome experience with God on yesterday and the devil wants to undo it, by putting us at odds with one another today. True to the word, he comes immediately to *"steal, kill and destroy."* I can admit I was a little offended by your words Helen. I'm sure my tone conveyed my offense. But, I want to take the time to apologize. Not just for today, but for all the times over the years, where I was ever sarcastic or offensive in my tone toward you. I was always a little upset when Talinda would address you as mom and was somewhat jealous of the relationship that you two had developed over the years. Because of my past, I wouldn't allow myself to enjoy my family. I operated in so much fear of losing them as I had George and Daniel to a drunk driver. And when she called you Mrs. Helen this morning, I gloated in the moment. But I was almost instantaneously convicted by the Holy Spirit, because of it. We have to remember what we are gathered together for here. It's not about us ladies. It's about Brandon and it's most definitely, always about God. I am happy that Talinda has two women in whom she feels a mother connection to and can turn to in time of need. I am no longer insecure in my relationship with her. I would like for both of you to accept my apology. The enemy would love for us continue on in offense, but I am right now choosing love, forgiveness and joy for my life."

Talinda, with tears in her eyes, turned toward Helen and said, "Oh mom please forgive me, both of my mom's. Today, I really connected with my mother and allowed her into my space for the first time." She touched Valetta's hand, who responded with a smile through tear stained eyes. "And I found myself surprisingly defensive when I felt you were attacking her ability to care for me. I am so sorry. And mom," she said as she turned back toward Valetta, "All these years I never gave you a chance to be a close part of my life. I kept you on the edge, because I thought you were too strict and withdrawn from me and daddy. Now, I know it was protective love and fear. I am so blessed to have two loving and caring mothers to see me through this pregnancy. Too the both of you, I am so sorry."

"Well," a completely broken Helen exclaimed through her tears. "It appears the Holy Spirit has all of our numbers this morning, as has indeed called our houses. Valetta, I owe you a huge apology dear. I never had a daughter, we only had Brandon. When I sensed that you and Talinda weren't close. I took advantage of it. I often gloated in the fact that I was closer to your daughter than you were and that she would call me mom in front of you. I know now, that was flesh on parade. I could not and would not ever, be able to take your place. This morning, when you were having your private moment on the deck, I felt left out of Talinda's life for the first time. I didn't know how to handle it. For the last seven years, I had been the one whose shoulder she would cry on and come to for advice. I found myself very jealous of your time together this morning. I was trying desperately to let Lindy know, that I was still the one she could lean on and knew what was best for her.

Boy was I ever wrong. You two have a natural bond and shared an experience that I will never fully be able to relate too. I mean, I have lost a son. But the both of you have lost a husband, and have the maternal connection that I will never be able to sever. I also think that Talinda needed a testimony. She needed to know by experience that God...through God, she would recover and be stronger than ever. Both of you please accept my deepest and most sincere apologies. You're right Valetta, the enemy does want to come in and steal our experience from yesterday. We must really have a work to do for the Lord, for the enemy to spend so much time planning attacks against our families. I'm so sorry and ashamed at my behavior."

Valetta rising to the occasion yelled out with her fist in the air, "Now there devil, you hear that! We're still standing! We love and forgive one another and we are still standing! All you've accomplished is to make us stronger and closer than ever before, you lose again!"

At her words their tears turned to joy and laughter and they began to praise and magnify the Lord. Talinda remembered what God had spoken to her the day before and exclaimed with a loud voice, "FORGIVE THAT HIS WORK MAY BE COMPLETE!" Helen repeated what Talinda said as though confirming the declaration.

Valetta asked, "What's that all about?"

Talinda responded, "Yesterday, when we were in the pastors office. The presence of the Lord was thick and he spoke to us in a loud voice. One of the things he said was to forgive, that his work may be complete. I am beginning to fully understand what he meant. I thought the Lord was just talking of his son's work on the cross, but he is also talking about Brandon. We are going have to forgive the gang leader that killed Brandon, that his work here may be complete. I believe that God is going to use this tragedy to save the life of the gang leader that stabbed Brandon. I also now believe that He is going to use me, to lead him to the Lord!"

"Oh my Lindy, what an awesome responsibility and anointing God has placed on you. We serve such a loving God," Helen replied with tearful eyes as they walked into the funeral home, still in awe and praising God.

~Chapter Seven~

Serenity's Touch funeral home director was exceptionally nice and professional at the same time. He had known the Travis family almost all of his life and was counted among many who were an influential part of Brandon's life growing up. Talinda was yet again overwhelmed at how God was aligning the right people in her life in all the right places. "Only a sovereign God could orchestrate such a master piece like this," she thought. She had to stop and praise God and give him the glory. She wasn't concerned with where she was, or who was there, it was just her and God and she magnified him. Helen, Valetta and Mr. Thurman the funeral home director, praised Him in concert with her, letting her have her moment with God.

≈

"What an awesome and incredible God we serve. We just made all the arrangements in two hours," Valetta exclaimed.

"My soul does magnify the Lord for his goodness," Helen interjected.

"Now we just have to get back to Decatur to prepare the church and the youth for the home going service," Talinda added.

"Well, what are we waiting for," Helen replied. She then turned to the funeral director and said, "Mr. Thurman, this is the paper you will need when you go to pick up Brandon."

"Thanks Mrs. Travis," He said as he took the paper from Helen's hand. "It's still hard to believe little Brandon is gone, but I trust God, and I know you do to Helen."

"That I do, Isaac...that I do," Helen answered.

≈

They drove back towards Decatur after returning home to retrieve clothes for Helen and Valetta. They decided it made more sense for the ladies to all stay in Decatur that night, to finish everything needed for Brandon's service. They shared about the goodness of the Lord as they drove along. Talinda still had not begun to settle in totally to the fact that Brandon would not be returning to her. But, as they pulled into the driveway and she looked up at the house, she had a sinking feeling.

Talinda stopped and had to brace herself just inside the doorway for just a moment as she started to walk into her and Brandon's home back in Decatur, GA., a suburb of Atlanta.

"What's wrong dear?" Her mother asked in unison with Helen. Helen stood right behind her, and supported her by the arm.

She was overwhelmed with grief. She was finding out that emotions surrounding it can be brought on by certain things or places. Talinda replied and tears fell from her eyes, "I...I can feel...Brandon." She paused briefly and continued, "As soon as I entered the threshold, I could feel his presence. He's all over this house. He's a part of everything and I just suddenly felt so alone. For the first time, I felt...alone. I have been so concentrated on everything else that I never thought about coming home without him. Or the fact of knowing that he is never going to be here again. It's such an overwhelming feeling. I think I need to step out on the deck and get some air."

"Sure sweetheart," Helen assisted her outside. "Do you want me to remove some his pictures or anything in particular until you feel more comfortable?"

"No!" Talinda cried out in alarm of not having Brandon's things close by her. "I mean, I'll be fine with them. I just need a minute. I just wasn't quite ready for the emotion of the moment."

"Do you need anything Talinda?" Her mother asked.

"No mom thanks, but I'll be fine. If you don't mind, may I just have a little time out here alone please?"

"Sure dear," her mother replied and walked back into the house with Helen.

Helen turned toward Valetta after they had stepped back inside the house. In an almost surprised voice she said, "Oh my Valetta, I hadn't thought about what impact coming home would have on her. I mean, I've lost my son and being in his house makes me feel closer to him. Almost like a part I don't have to let go, if that makes any sense at all. But Brandon was her husband...I can't imagine how I would feel knowing I'm never going to be with the love of my life again. That I won't lie beside him. Everything in this house is about the both of them. The memories here must be overwhelming. I just never thought..."

Talinda's mother interrupted as she replied, "Helen...I did, I remember how I felt the first time I returned home without my family. But, Talinda was doing so well, I didn't mention to her that it may be a difficult moment." Almost in tears again she continued, "I can't believe I didn't pray with her about it before we returned. It was in my thoughts, but I just didn't do it...she seemed okay. Much stronger than I was after I lost George and Daniel...I just...I didn't..."

Helen, cut her off as she grabbed her by the hands for comfort and said, "Now Valetta don't. Don't start second guessing yourself now. You're right, Talinda seemed like she was going through like a trouper. She comforted me when I was at the point of total breakdown when we first got to the hospital. You had no way of knowing which event would be hard for her. I think we have all been operating on auto pilot here and now the reality of it all is starting settle in. We will all have to just take one day at a time. We'll give her space as she needs it, and being there when she needs it. The feeling you had after losing George is something you can share with her later tonight. Now I'm really glad we planned to stay here with her. Besides, the men spent a lot of time around town today taking care of minor details and might want a men's night to reflect as well. Roger is probably being the host of Athens' favorites right about now," she managed to chuckle at the thought before she continued. "Talinda will need a mothers touch tonight."

"Both her mothers," Valetta replied as he touched Helen on the shoulder for reassurance that she was just as important to Talinda as she was. "And thank you, for not allowing me to beat myself up too much. I just want to be all she needs me to be right now. She is more delicate than she seems and I am a little worried about her and the baby."

Helen breathed in deeply and responded, "Yes Valetta, I'm a little worried too. But that's why God has us here. Thank you for including me. Together, we will all make it to the other side of through."

They both sat there at the kitchen table conducting idle talk. Mostly their eyes and minds were on Talinda who seemed to sit motionless on the deck, almost like she was frozen in time. After about thirty minutes, they decided they needed to intervene on her self-imposed solitude.

"Okay Valetta," Helen said nervously. "I think she has been out there an unhealthy amount of time. I don't mind allowing God minister to her, but I'm beginning to feel despair for her. I think we better bring her in now."

Valetta nodded her head in agreement and said, "Yes you're right, I'll go get her." She stood and took a deep breath. She brushed her clothes, pulling slightly at the bottom of her shirt tail as she proceeded toward the sliding doors leading to the deck, as if straightening her clothes will give her some added strength for the task at hand. But as they looked up, to their surprise, Talinda stood and came into the house where they both were. Now, all of a sudden, she was unsure what to say. Talinda broke the silence.

"Mom...and mom," she smiled slightly which gave them encouragement and relief. "I know you were both in here worried about me. For a moment, I was worried about me as well. As I sat out there, the peace of God started to engulf me. I sat in silence, letting the Holy Spirit do his work. But then he told me to get up and go inside. That he would fight off the spirit of despair and I would be okay. He told me to allow myself to rely on him and at the right times in the right moments, he would be there for me." She paused and continued, "I'm thankful, you will both be here with me tonight although originally the reason was to finish the arrangements. We only have a few more days before Brandon's memorial service on Wednesday. With the viewing set for Tuesday evening in Athens, I could really draw strength from both my mom's being with me. I don't want to be alone."

"Oh, sweetheart, we all need one another right now," Helen responded.

"Yes, we most certainly do," Valetta interjected.

"Thanks," Talinda replied barely above a whisper because the tears were flowing again.

"Oh Lindy," they responded in unison. They gathered in a group hug as Helen began to pray:

Father,

89

We solicit Your Holy Spirit right now to comfort Lindy. For that much Lord, we all need Your comfort. Father, we don't understand why life suddenly seems to unload on us. Even though we have our weak moments God, we do trust You. God I pray that You will continue to be with Lindy and Father, give us the words to say. Father, we surrender our feelings and emotions to You. And pray for Your strength Lord, in our time of trial. Father we pray now for little Brandon Jr. who is nestled securely in his mothers' womb. Let her receive comfort and peace even from him Lord. Let their special bond begin now Lord while he is yet in her womb. Let his movements of life bring her comfort in knowing that she will soon be able to hold in her arms, the manifestation of her love with Brandon. God, we thank You in advance for all the wonderful blessings You will bestow upon her in the weeks and months to come in the tenure of this pregnancy. Thank You Father, for all that You do and all that You are in our lives.

In the matchless name of Jesus Christ our Lord,

Amen

Talinda responded through tear stained eyes, "Thank you Lord for your continued comfort and thank you mom for knowing the right thing to pray. Thank both of you."

They all exchange hugs, expressing how they both loved and would be there for one another. Talinda smiled as she took in a deep breath and sighed as she let it out. She looked at them both, smiled and said, "Well I still have quite a few phone calls to make. You two need to get your parts of the service together as well. So we had better all get back to work before we run out of time. I have decided because of the time restraint, I will probably dance to a solo and have Jessica ready as a backup in case my emotions won't allow me to minister in dance on Wednesday."

"That sounds like a great idea Lindy,'" Helen replied, "I know Pastor Tills wanted you to dance but it's wise to have a backup.

In the presence of God it's easy to say what you will do. But in the midst of the actual service, you don't know where you'll be spiritually, physically or emotionally."

"I agree," Valetta added.

With that being said, they all begin their assigned tasks for the day. Talinda is busy making phone calls to the youth and explaining to the youth leaders what the pastor had in mind for the service, when Nurse Gregory stopped in on the first scheduled visit to check her and the baby's vitals.

Talinda had talked to several of the youth members who had informed her of Brandon's courageous acts the night of his death. She sat in amazement and awe of God's power in the life of a Christian, when Veronica's knock at the door brought her back to reality.

"I'll get it, Helen yelled over her shoulder as she answered the door." Both Helen and Valetta where settled in the living room. Valetta worked on color palettes and flower displays. While Helen was writing out the information about Brandon's family tree and looking through photos on her laptop to be included in the program. Talinda was at the kitchen counter making phone calls.

"Hello, may I help you?" Helen asked after opening the door.

Veronica extended her hand as she said, "Yes, my name is Veronica Gregory. I'm a nurse at the OB/GYN clinic assigned by Dr. Johnson to check in on Mrs. Travis and the baby to..."

"Oh yes, yes. I remember him saying someone would come to check on Lindy over the next few weeks. Come on in, she is in the kitchen right around the corner to the left."

"Thank you," Veronica replied as she stepped inside the Travis' home.

As much as they wanted to crash the appointment because of sheer excitement, Helen and Valetta decided not to intrude on the visit from Nurse Gregory.

"Excuse me, Mrs. Travis. I'm here to check on you and little Brandon." That statement struck Talinda by surprise and she gave Veronica a deer in the head lights look. "Oh," replied Nurse Gregory, "I shouldn't have said that, I mean...called the baby little Brandon. I'm so sorr..."

"No that's okay," Talinda responded, "I guess I am so in awe of all God is doing, I almost forgot about the vision from yesterday at the hospital morgue. You are correct; his name is Brandon Travis Jr." Talinda smiled and welcomed Veronica with a hug.

She found the heartbeat through the stethoscope and paused momentarily, not quite sure if she heard what she thought she heard and smiled at Talinda. But, unable to be sure she decided to keep her theory to herself until further tests could be run at a later appointment at the hospital. She assured her that little Brandon is doing fine and allowed her hear the heart beat through her stethoscope.

"Wow," Talinda exclaimed through tears of joy. "It's his father's heartbeat! Even though it sounds like there's an echo or something, it's definitely Brandon's heartbeat." Veronica didn't reply, not wanting to give any indication about the heartbeat, other than it indicated a strong and stable fetus. But she did decide to ask Talinda something else.

"May I ask you something Talinda?" Veronica said cautiously.

"Sure," Talinda replied in a knowing tone.

"Have you found out anything else about what happened Friday night? I understand if you don't want to talk about it, I won't be offended," Veronica said in an uneasy reserved tone.

Talinda took a deep breath and smiled at Veronica to reassure her that it was okay subject to pursue. She looked up momentarily and began, "I'm fine talking about it. I mean, I still have my moments, but I now know God had and has a plan. I was told that Brandon was attempting to minister to Quavis the 23 year old gang leader about Christ's sacrifice of His life and blood for us. Quavis, catching them off guard pulled out a knife and said, "Well Jesus follower, be like this Christ you're talking about. Give me Raymond or give your life in exchange for his lifetime commitment to the Knights. Because, just like you just said about your God, only shed blood can get you out of this gang. So put your money where your mouth is, preacher boy!" I was told Brandon sacrificed his life to get Raymond out. I should be angry, but all I feel is compassion for the Knight's leader for some reason. I want to be mad. I'm trying to be mad, but it's not working. I don't know what God is doing right now. But whatever it is, it's going to be big. I mean, I know he's going to use me to minister to Quavis. But there is more, there is much more."

Veronica replied, "You never cease to amaze me. You have God in your life for real. Because girl, I'm mad and angry for you. God answered your prayer for another baby and this little punk gang thug, stole your husband from you..."

Talinda put a finger over her mouth to stop her from talking and said, "Weren't you listening? Brandon gave his life for

Raymond. Quavis didn't take it. For whatever reason, God allowed it all to happen. Raymond is a very special young man to me and Brandon. And this gang leader is to God, he just doesn't know it yet."

Veronica cried, "I wish I had your faith and your love for others, I'm still so angry."

Talinda replied with a puzzled but comforting tone, "Why Veronica? Before forty-eight hours ago, you didn't even know me. You never had the opportunity to meet Brandon, so what are you really angry about?"

"That's not true," Veronica exclaimed. "I do know your husband. I mean not a on a personal level. He ministered to my niece Sarah, after my sister shot her father in the court room for molesting her about ten years ago, because that creep of a husband she had married was going to get away with it. Brandon helped little Sarah as much as he could after she ended up in foster care. We were in school at University of Georgia at the same time. I always felt so guilty, because I could have gotten Sarah. But, I was in school and not willing to give up my career to care for her. Mom and dad were not stable enough health wise for the courts to grant them custody. I was young and selfish. Brandon has been a giving person all his life and this little creep just ended it!"

Talinda took Veronica by the hand, for both comfort and reassurance and replied, "Brandon's life, though short in relative terms, was long and full. He fulfilled his purpose. His job was to lead Raymond to the Lord. Be a father figure in his life and show God to a godless nation of young gang members. He succeeded, but I have to finish that work that his labor will not be in vain. I have to forgive that Brandon's work may be complete. For the gang member and I now see for you as well, Veronica. I have to forgive for you, Quavis and others to see the true nature of God. So, I ask again Veronica, what are you really angry about? Because, I don't think this is all about Brandon. There's something else going on here, isn't there?"

Veronica was now in tears and at a loss for words. All she could do was shake her head in agreement to Talinda's words.

Talinda still held her hands and said, "Veronica let's pray." She shook her head in agreement, still unable to speak because of the sheer power of the moment. Talinda began to pray. Helen and Valetta, who had been ease-dropping in the other room, both bowed their heads in support of Talinda.

Father,

We come now before You in the name of Jesus Christ and ask again, for Your love and comfort. Lord, we are beginning to see that although we don't understand everything. We must trust You with everything. God I pray that You will give Veronica peace. The sweet of peace Your Spirit that Your word declares, passes all understanding. Father I pray that You will send the Holy Spirit to Veronica to comfort her and remove any guilt she may be feeling about Sarah. And Lord God, dissipate the anger she feels. Give her resolution to her hurt through the comfort and power of the Holy Spirit. Father, I pray that You will lead and guide her concerning Sarah and reunite them Lord God. Father, we know that if we delight ourselves in You, You will give us the desires of our heart. Father, teach us how to delight ourselves in You. We will honor You God with everything that is within us.

In Jesus name we pray,

Amen

Veronica was overcome with the presence and power of the Holy Spirit. The weight of His presence in the room sent them all to their knees and ministered to them individually.

After what seemed like an eternity, Veronica was finally able to stand. The weight of the Holy Spirit had lifted, and she managed to say softly, through swollen tear stained eyes, "Thank you, Mrs. Travis. It has been so long, since I felt God's presence. I have been running hurt for so long that I forgot what wholeness in God felt like. I was so angry with God for allowing those ladies to say such mean things about me...to crucify my character and falsely accuse me. God ministered to me through the power of the Holy Spirit. He said that because I didn't understand who I was in Him, or my gift, I succumbed to their pressure and their ridicule. It was because I didn't realize that the things I saw when I looked at people. Or, the things that I knew about them that I shouldn't, was a prophetic gift from God. I allowed them convince me that there was something

94

wrong with me. I listened and received the erroneous report, that I must be a devil in disguise, to know so much about them. That I must be consorting with the enemy for material gain. The truth is I didn't know why I knew what I did. No one taught me about gifts in operation. And I don't know why I understand now. Other than the fact, that I've been in the pure presence of the all mighty God and His divine knowledge has empowered me. I feel so...so..."

"Free...powerful...liberated just to name a few," Talinda finished Veronica's sentence with tears of joy streaming down her face.

"I'm so glad I know Jesus for myself," Helen interjected in a shout of joy.

"And He's sweet I know," Valetta chimed in with joy waving her hand in glorious fashion. They all began to praise and magnify the Lord.

"Now I understand," Talinda said in the midst of the praise.

"Understand what?" Veronica asked.

"When David said, "Oh magnify the Lord with me, and let us...," she waved her hands in an inviting circular motion around the room at each of them as she is continued. "...Exalt His name together! There is something about praising God with other saints that brings on a different anointing, a different presence. One that you can't get all by yourself, we need one another in good times and the bad. Because where two or three are gathered together...,"

Valetta interjected, "Preach preacher."

Talinda finished, "...I AM is in the midst of thee. Oh Hallelujah to the lamb who sits on the throne! Who was...," she said again as she looked around the room pointing at each of them as she added a new attribute about God. "...And is, and is to come! Veronica, let God finish in you what He started. You're not here by accident. Out of the midst of every tragedy and circumstance, is a powerful testimony and an elevation in the spirit realm. Surrender to the Holy Spirit and let God use you, amen."

"Amen...Mrs. Travis...amen," Veronica replied.

"None of this Mrs. Travis stuff, its Talinda or Lindy. We are sisters in Christ." She looked up toward heaven and said, "Oh God, I'm so in awe of You and what You are doing in our lives. Tell Brandon," she said as she placed her hand on her stomach and started to cry. "Tell Brandon that I love him. That I miss him...and I promise I will stand strong...I will keep the faith."

They all stood there silently in support as Talinda continued through her tears, "Tell him I will do what thus saith the Lord...I will...I will!"

Saying those words, she fell to her knees and they all joined her. They allowed God to be God. She wept and was comforted by the Holy Spirit and his divine touch.

After they got up off the floor a second time, Helen turned to Veronica while giving Valetta a knowing smile and said, "Veronica, with all this excitement it may not be a bad idea for you to check the baby's heartbeat again."

"Sure, if you would like..." Veronica started to reply.

Talinda interrupted her, "That won't be necessary I'm sure I'm fine. I mean, what can go wrong in the presence of God..."

But before she could finish she is interrupted by Helen who turned to Veronica with a knowing wink so Talinda couldn't see it, "Veronica, I think maybe you should still check her. All this excitement may have raised his heart rate quite a bit...you know what I mean?"

Veronica, finally catching on said while trying to keep from smiling, "Oh yes...maybe I should...you never know. We want to make sure little Brandon's vital are good and strong still after all today's events."

"Oh, honestly," Talinda replied with a protesting response as she walked across the room back to the kitchen table. She sat back down on the stool. It allowed her to sit at a good height off the ground so Veronica wouldn't have to bend over so much. They left Helen and Valetta in the living room about to burst open with excitement. They were trying very hard not to let it to show, as they sat there with a "we just want to make sure you're okay mother's look", on their faces.

As she retrieved the stethoscope from her bag and started to check again for a heartbeat, she thinks about Sarah and said, "I don't even know where to find Sarah. No one has heard from her since she moved here to Atlanta with the last foster family. I keep hoping I'll run into her. But, I'm not even sure I'll recognize her. For her safety and emotional wellbeing, they didn't want family members to have contact with her until she was a certain age. She should be about sixteen or seventeen by now."

"Well, if its God will, and we know it is. You'll find her, just believe," Talinda responded.

After a few minutes Veronica said, "Ahhh...there it is...a nice strong heartbeat." She looked up at Helen and Valetta who were

96

just on pins and needles and said, "Okay you two grandmas, do you want to hear the heartbeat?"

They both scream in unison with excitement, "YES!" Then Valetta said more calmly, "I mean...," clearing her throat. "...Sure...I mean since the opportunity is available."

Talinda smiled and said as they both jump up together and practically race across the room, "Oh now I get it...check the heartbeat huh...too much excitement huh...you never know...huh! Mom, you guys should have just said you wanted to hear the heartbeat."

Valetta, not really listening to any of them is holding back tears of joy while she is listened to baby Travis' heartbeat. She beckoned for Helen to kneel and gave her the stethoscope. "Well...we didn't want to intrude." Helen slyly said after she had kneeled down, as she squealed in delight now and she listened to the heartbeat.

"Now Helen Travis, repent for that lie," Valetta laughed out at Helen's response. "You know that was our plan all along. We were going to find a way to hear that heartbeat before Veronica left today." At that being said, they all burst into laughter.

"Hold still Lindy, you're moving around has made me lose the heartbeat...oh, there it is. Wow...awesome!" Helen is so ecstatic that she can hardly contain her actions.

"Okay, Helen give it up. Let me hear one more time before Veronica has to go. She is on the clock you know," Valetta said in a sarcastic but jokingly way.

Helen declared as she stood up, "That little heartbeat is just going a mile a minute and nice and strong. Almost like an echo is in there, it's so fast. It's always been an age old myth, at least the elders would always say, that boy's heartbeats were generally slower than girls. But that has to be a myth, because God said we're definitely having a boy!"

Helen's declaration about the echo clarified what Veronica thought she had heard as well. She only smiled at that response and said, "God knows and He's in control."

"Yes, He is Veronica," Talinda interjected trying to keep still while her mother listened and smiled at the sound of the heartbeat.

"Oh, the guys are going to be so jealous when we tell them we got to hear the heartbeat," Valetta said as she is handed the stethoscope back to Veronica.

Helen eyed Veronica, not quite sure that she had revealed everything there was to know about little Brandon's heartbeat. But she decided not to say anything at that particular moment.

"Okay, well like your mom said Talinda, I am on the clock so I had better be getting back. I am going to schedule and ultrasound for you after Brandon's home going service. I'll call to let you know the date and time, once I get back to the hospital."

"Ultra sound?" Talinda asked nervously. "Do you think something is wrong with little Brandon?"

"Not at all," Veronica replied. "Just want to check his position and get a projected date of delivery."

"Oh...okay," Talinda replied with a sigh of relief.

"You will be at Brandon's service won't you?" Helen asked Veronica.

"Why, sure of course. I get the feeling it won't be like any other funeral I've been to," Veronica replied. "Well, let me get back to work. I'll call with your appointment Talinda."

"Okay that'll be great, let me walk you out," Talinda said as she followed Veronica to and out the door.

After they left, Valetta turned to Helen and said, "So you heard the echo too, huh?"

"Yes, Valetta. What does that mean? I mean, it was so strong but it had a beat within a beat. At least, that was how it sounded," Helen replied in bewilderment.

Valetta declared, "Well, psych is my area. I'm not an obstetrician, but in medical school we often went to the other fields and sneaked in on what they were doing. We would discuss among ourselves as students what we learned that day. And, if I'm not mistaken, an echoed heartbeat means there is the possibility of twins, or the positioning could be off."

"Oh my God...oh my God...twins," Helen squealed in delight, "I knew it... I knew it...I could tell by the look on her face when I said "echo" that something was up. I was just hoping that there wasn't anything wrong with the baby."

"Now now, Helen calm down," Valetta cautioned. "Let's not mention this to Talinda. Obviously, Veronica isn't sure or she would have said something. So, let's just keep this between us until after Brandon's service and see what the ultra sound says. We don't want to get our hopes up and we don't want to over excite Talinda. She may be acting strong but she is still very fragile."

Helen was so excited she had to grab Valetta's hand to calm down. She replied, "Okay...you're right...oh this is so exciting. Oh God, thank you...thank you for giving us these babies. I miss Brandon so much and knowing that a part of him is here helps me to handle the emptiness I feel inside. It eases the sharp pain of his death. Oh God... I thank you...Oh God, I just thank you...You are Lord...and I trust you."

Valetta replied, "Amen," as she continued to hold Helen's hand.

"Well, we better get ready to head out to the church," Talinda said as she reentered the house. "Everyone agreed to a rehearsal tonight and finish in the morning. Considering we only have one full day left before Brandon's Memorial service." She paused for a moment then continued, "Those children really love Brandon."

Helen and Valetta suggested they stop to grab a bite to eat before heading over to the church. They didn't have much of an appetite. For the sake of Talinda and the baby, they kept promoting food to make for the fact, that she only ate a few mouthfuls at each sitting.

While they were practicing Valetta and Helen were bringing in the finished decorations. They would take the time to set to start setting up the sanctuary, so there wouldn't be much to do the next morning at the final practices. Beatrice Tills walked up and assisted them as they were carrying everything in.

"Hello, Mrs. Travis and Mrs. Thompson," Beatrice said she walked up. They almost in unison returned a hearty, "Hello."

"Please don't be so formal dear, Helen and Valetta will do," exclaimed Valetta.

Helen responded in agreement with Valetta, "Yes Beatrice, we are all equal women of God here."

Beatrice replied in a relaxed but reserved tone, "Oh, I didn't want to assume anything, or try to force friendship..."

Helen cut her off, "Friendship!" She replied in a stern but nurturing tone. "Beatrice, we are all sisters in the Lord and we all love Brandon and Talinda. Therefore, we are all in this together. You and your husband were like second parents to Brandon. I know you're hurting as much as Roger and I are. Therefore, there is no absolutely need for you to feel insecure. After yesterday and today with all the revelation, comfort and rebuke we have received from the Lord," she paused to look at Valetta after that comment with a smile. "We hold no ill will toward anyone. We are all just trying to hold one another up and make it through this so the healing process can begin. Brandon is gone. Nothing we can say or do is going to change that fact. But we rejoice that he is with the Lord. Our main focus has to be Talinda and the baby she is carrying. Beatrice, we understand how you and Pastor felt on Saturday. Rest assure we hold no blame to the leadership here."

Beatrice was unable to hold her tears. It was as though Helen was inside of her head. She responded, "Yes, Brandon was like a son to us. Denson and I don't have any children of our own, so our young ministers and members have always been our babies and we are so protective of them. Denson and I have been so broken. We have decided that we will not continue with the program. It's too dangerous and we could not bear the thought of losing another minister..."

Valetta, now cutting her off exclaimed, "Oh no, Beatrice! You and Denson cannot do that, or everything is in vain here. All Brandon's work and the sacrifice..."

Beatrice interjected, "But..."

But before she could say another word, Helen interrupted her, "Valetta is right, we cannot allow the enemy to win one single thing here. He didn't take Brandon's life. He sacrificed it to get that young man out of the gang life for good. He bought him out with his life. To close the program now is to say to Brandon, that Raymond's life wasn't worth it...that none of these young peoples' lives are. Listen to me Beatrice. We know just like us, you are hurting. But don't let your emotions speak louder than your mandate from God about these young people. Because emotions have a loud voice and will override the spirit in situations like these. Brandon would be devastated if he were here and remotely even heard of the program being considered for termination. We just won't hear of it. God is doing a great work here. We must *"Forgive that His work may be complete"*. I will never forget what God has mandated for us, forgiveness is a must. Just as receiving the forgiveness is a must. Beatrice, we have to love and forgive and continue in what God has started here through this ministry."

Beatrice held her head in her hands as she cried. She declared, "But it hurts so bad, we feel so guilty...oh God, please take away this overwhelming pain, despair...and confusion...oh God!"

Helen and Valetta knelt right there in the foyer with Beatrice and Helen began to pray,

Father,

We come before You now, in the name of Your dear Son Jesus Christ. God, we are yet again standing in the need of comfort. Lord we know confusion is not of You, so we come against it by the authority of Your Son and command that it to leave right now. Father, as we lay our hands on Beatrice we pray for Your comfort and Your peace on her life God. Father, we rebuke a guilty conscience because we know that is not from You. Satan, you will not stop this program from going forward because we are committed and we stand against you enforced by the power of the Holy Spirit. We serve you notice today that you will not win. We choose to walk in love, forgiveness and peace. We will stand Satan...and we will stand united in faith. Father, comfort Your daughter this day. Speak to her heart Lord. Your servant needs Your touch.

In Jesus name we pray,

Amen

They looked up and saw that Talinda and all the youth had joined them in prayer and support. The youth began to lay their hands on their first lady and pray for her one by one. They had words of comfort, support and gratitude for her and Pastor Tills for believing in them and not deserting them as so many others had done in the past. For such a young group, they offered many words of wisdom and peace.

Talinda being filled with joy unspeakable and a bit overwhelmed at the moment, looked up to heaven and said, "See sweetheart...they were listening to everything you taught them. They got it baby...they got it...and now they not only believe it, they are operating in it!"

She then made her way to First Lady Tills. Knelt beside her and said, "Brandon would be so proud of this moment. This was his mission mandated from God. To take troubled youth, and through the work of the Holy Spirit, teach them about compassion, and give them hope. To let them see that there is integrity in the church and there is love in the pews; to give them a sense of pride and instill in them the drive to succeed;

to teach them that they don't have to be a product of the streets, because they were reared there; to let them know that God can and will break generational curses in their lives. This was his mission, first lady...and it must continue."

Beatrice could only nod in affirmation. She was too overwhelmed in the presence of God to form any words. God had ministered directly to her heart through these youth today. He had used them in a mighty way to confirm the call of the church. She just sat there as they all did, basting in the glory of God's presence.

Suddenly, Raymond stood up and yelled through tears, "It's all about you God...who am I to feel guilty...who am I to walk in despair...who am I to feel worthless...who I am Lord...who am I...I tell you who I am...I'm a child of the most high God and much has been sacrificed for me...no greater love God...no greater love. You said in your word in John 15:13–17...You said, *"Greater love hath no man than this, that a man lay down his life for his friends. Ye are my friends, if ye do whatsoever I command you. Henceforth I call you not servants; for the servant knoweth not what his lord doeth: but I have called you friends; for all things that I have heard of my Father I have made known unto you. Ye have not chosen me, but I have chosen you, and ordained you, that ye should go and bring forth fruit, and that your fruit should remain: that whatsoever ye shall ask of the Father in my name, he may give it you. These things I command you, that ye love one another."* He then dropped to his knees and repeated over and over, "Yes Lord, yes Lord."

Talinda listened in awe and thanked God for his goodness. She got up and went over to Raymond. She knelt beside him and grabbed him by the hand. She looked him straight in his eyes and said, "Now I know why Raymond...now I know why. You have the same passion for God's word as Brandon did. You two are cut from the same mold, that's why there was such closeness between you two. That's why we called you our son. You have his passion...you have his love. Brandon always said you were special...that you had a pure heart. He could see through the past. Through the violence, the gang tattoos and the lingo and he saw your heart. So you continue to stand strong. You continue to listen to God, don't let the enemy come in and convince you that anything that has happened is your fault. Look at me son...it's not your fault. Your dad freely gave his life for you."

At those words Raymond began to cry loudly and shake under the power of the Holy Ghost. He had struggled with so much guilt since that night and had even contemplated suicide. The last three days had been torture for him. But he was able to release everything at that moment to God. He normally spent every day at Talinda and Brandon's house. He even had his own room there. But the last three days he had disappeared. He was in solitude and Talinda had worried about him. But since he wasn't legally her son, she couldn't force him to come home.

Talinda continued speaking to him, "Brandon chose to give his life because you were worth it to him...and if it had to be done all over again and he knew the outcome beforehand, he would still choose to do the same thing. Take advantage of the life that has been given to you and given for you...give God all you have Raymond. God, I pray now that You would fill him with your Spirit......."

No sooner than the words left her mouth Raymond began to speak in unknown tongues. They all praised God with him and you could hear other youth began to pray for the power of the Holy Spirit to fall on them. Not allowing the moment pass, Valetta and Helen laid hands on half the group and Talinda and Beatrice on the other. By the time God was through those teens were strung out all over the foyer and the hallway. Absolutely no one was speaking English. The Holy Spirit swept through and filled the entire group. The power of God was so thick, that you could see the glory cloud and you could feel the midst of rain.

What seemed like hours later, but was probably more like twenty minutes or so they were released by the Holy Spirit. Talinda decided that she would give the parts to everyone to memorize because it was now getting late in the day. They decided they would run through the program one more time to give Helen, Valetta and Beatrice time to set up the sanctuary. They would come back in the morning for a final rehearsal. After the youth helped the ladies unload the rest of the decorations they proceeded back into the gym to rehearse while the sanctuary was being decorated.

Helen gasped as Valetta opened and unfolded the materials and flowers, "Oh Helen this color scheme is just gorgeous, and everything looks so regal."

"Thanks Helen, a "Heavenly Origin and Heavenly Return" is the idea that I attempted to portray," Valetta said as she looked at each piece paying careful attention to reshape everything just perfect. But before they could start to set up the sanctuary, Talinda joined them saying that the youth wanted to know if they could have the memorial service in the gym instead. They wanted to say goodbye in their sanctuary, where they were ministered to by their pastor.

"Oh, I think that would be an excellent idea," Beatrice replied. Together, they set up gym while the youth were rehearsing. They shared the space well and it gave them opportunity to see how much room was needed so they would know where to place each decoration. Everyone seemed to just flow so perfectly together. The aroma and presence of the Holy Spirit lingered and everyone just enjoyed the ambiance. Helen, Valetta and Beatrice had the initial work done and decided to finish in the morning because Talinda and the youth didn't want to give away everything they had planned for Brandon's service. So they waited in the sanctuary for them to finish rehearsing, each telling their Brandon stories to the others.

Jessica danced so beautiful and majestic that Talinda decided to allow the youth do the whole program. She walked in the sanctuary and addressed them with another request. "We adults just need to get out of the way and let God work through these young people. We don't need to get in there and mess things up. Brandon and I were the youth pastors. This should be about them not us, so we will let them decide who will do what and pay tribute to their pastor and mentor the way they would like to. We are gonna get together tomorrow morning at eight o'clock for a final run through and they will let me know what they come up with for the special presentation. They will decide the order of the program. First Lady, would you talk to pastor about possibly allowing Raymond give the eulogy and assist with the altar call?"

Beatrice responded with excitement, "Wow, sitting here thinking of all God has done in these young people today. Realizing that this is the result of a lot of labor on yours and Brandon's parts, as well as theirs, I was just thinking the same thing. I'll talk to him. I'm sure he'll be fine with it. You're right, he was their pastor and you are their co-pastor. This is and should be about him and them, not us."

"Thanks," Talinda responded.

Before going back to the house they finished the entire decor for the service. They also finished and faxed the program detailing Brandon's history and family to the printers. The youth were in the sanctuary deciding the order of the program and

104

stayed after all the adults left to discuss who would do what. Talinda smiled as she saw the look of excitement on their faces. They were going to be able to express themselves and show their appreciation the way that they wanted to. There was a sense of pride and determination on everyone's face. Talinda was happy that she both heard and obeyed the Holy Spirit. They said their goodbye's to the youth and headed off the get take out for a relaxing evening at home. Beatrice left as well for the evening, leaving the key with Raymond to lock up after the youth were finished.

~Chapter Eight~

"Okay," Helen said to Talinda and Valetta as they exit the church toward the car. "Where should we stop to pick up dinner before we head home?"

"Well...," Talinda, being very surprised that she even has an appetite, replied in a childlike forbidden fruit tone. "I was going to say a Fatboy's greasy burger and fries...but...I know you guys wouldn't approve. So I'm game with whatever you both decide."

They all laugh as Valetta replied in that "I know you didn't" motherly tone. "Yes ma'am little mamma, you're correct in your assessment. A greasy burger and fries is so not happening."

"Hey," Helen interjected. "Why don't we just stop by the supermarket and pick up a few things for soup, salad and sandwiches. That's light, but filling and easy on the stomach. We don't need anything laying heavy on us."

"Good idea mom," Talinda replied with a faraway look in her eyes. There it was once again, from nowhere. She was overrun with emotion and was fighting back tears.

"Oh dear, what is it Lindy, did I say something wrong," Helen responded as she touched Talinda on the shoulder.

"I don't know what happened. I was just overcome by emotion. I don't know where it came from...it was...just...there," Talinda said as she wiped away tears.

Valetta pulled her in for a hug as she said, "Sweetheart, your emotions are going to be all over the place for a while. You're pregnant and you just lost your husband. At any given time, you don't know what will do it, a smell...a sight...a sound. You never know what's gonna trigger a memory. Just take one day at a time dear. It's going to be difficult some days. The realization that Brandon is not going to be here, will hit you hard some days. Other days, you'll think of him and smile thinking of fun memories. Sometimes, it will seem like he is right there with you and you'll feel comfort in that. Other days your feel despair as the realization of permanent separation sets in. But in time you will feel normal again and the hole in your heart will heal."

"Thanks mom," Talinda responded as she continued to wipe away tears.

"Oh my precious, precious baby," Valetta said as she just held Talinda in her arms. "Go ahead and cry. You don't have to try to be so strong, it's okay."

Helen came in the other side for a group hug and said, "That's right Lindy, don't think you have to always try be so strong. We're right here for you. It's okay to let go and just cry sometimes. It doesn't mean you're not trusting God. You're human and you just lost your husband. Not to mention you're expecting. That's a guaranteed combination for a sudden release of emotion." Talinda burst into tears of laughter at Helen's comment.

After getting soup and sandwich supplies they exit the market heading back to the car. They actually looked forward to retire at Talinda's house for a ladies only evening.

As they approached the car Helen turned to Valetta and Talinda and said, "Hey, I just thought or something. Well, I think God thought of it for me. Why don't we invite Beatrice to join us for dinner tonight? I think it's important that we include her in our life right now."

"I think that's a great idea," Talinda replied. "I'll call her and see if she wants to join us." She got off the phone with Beatrice and said, "Good, she says she'll be right over. I could tell she was excited about being a part of ladies night. Thanks for thinking of her mom."

"Hey," Helen replied. "We're all in this together and we have to show God's love. Lip service goes nowhere. Christians need to be people of action."

"Amen to that Helen," Valetta replied.

Shortly after they arrived home the doorbell rang. Helen got the door and welcomed Beatrice, who expressed her appreciation to them again for including her for dinner.

As they all work together in the kitchen they are engaged in small talk about Valetta's work. They were talked about anything but Brandon.

"So Valetta," Helen asked. "What is the worst case, I mean client personality you have ever had to deal with in your career.

I mean, do you analyze serial killers, pedophiles or anything crazy like that? Or is it more like family therapy?"

Valetta chuckled slightly as she answered Helen, "Mostly family or individual therapy, including a lot of pedophiles unfortunately. But every now and then you're called to help the FBI on some pretty big cases. You know...to be an expert professional witness on the psyche of a murderer or determine the defenders competency to stand trial. You'll be surprised just how many people try to use the insanity plea. It's really amusing sometimes, because in their attempt to show their insanity they will often end up showing you how they committed the murder. They try to talk in circles and the third person, like they watched themselves do the crime. Like some sort of out of body experience or something.

There was this one lady recently who was a real piece of work though. It took me quite a few sessions to decipher through what was reality and what was her attempt at proving her incompetence. I can't go into the specifics of the case but she was playing out a real horrifying past to explain her psychopathic behavior. The more I listened to her, the more I realized it was actually from a movie. She was telling or retelling the story line of a movie. The only reason I caught on to what she was doing was because it just happened to be from a very old movie that we had to analyze back in college.

We had to take movies from all different centuries and era's and determine, before knowing the ending, the nature of the person's psyche. It was a game the professors played with us. The one she was coming from was a movie that the average American person wouldn't have watched or even remembered. It was one of those foreign films set back the 50's. So you know it was kind of cheesy and the special effects were generic. But it was a real interest holder, I mean if you're into that sort of twisted story line. But those were the best kind for us to analyze.

Anyway, she was surprised when I started to finish her sentences and thoughts. She soon realized that I knew exactly what she was doing. She smiled and said, "Can't blame a girl for trying." I mean...are you kidding me? You just killed three people on a vengeful rampage. And you say, you can't blame a girl for trying...!" She sighed a moment before she finished her sentence. "...I learned that you really have to master the art of detachment early in my career."

They all share in laughter at Valetta's closing statement. Talinda chimed in still laughing, "I bet some of them really are coo-coo for cocoa puffs though huh?" More laughter filled the room as they took their soup, salads and sandwiches and retired to the living room floor to eat and continue in conversation.

After they settled in and were almost finished eating Talinda reluctantly asks her mother, "Mom...I mean if you're comfortable...I would love to see the pictures of George and Daniel."

Valetta smiled as she responded, "Sure princess. I'll get them." She went into one of the guest bedrooms to get the album out of her suitcase. While she was gone Helen turned to Beatrice and briefly explained the situation to her to bring her up to date. Valetta returned with a very elegant scrapbook and sat back down on the floor beside Talinda. They all gather around as Valetta began her journey into her past. A place she has not visited for over twenty four years. She took a deep breath as she opened the book to expose her past hurts. Now, she would know if she really was on the other side of through concerning Daniel and George.

≈

Over the next few days, Nevette found herself thinking more and more about Justice. She just couldn't shake him. Most guys would have never admitted to a girl what he had to her. He was vulnerable and he had put himself in a position to be rejected or worse to be laughed at. He was so genuine, she just couldn't shake him. This next session was going to be very tense. She wondered how she was going to get through it without acting like a silly high school girl being asked out by a football star for the first time. "There's that pun again." She laughed as she shook her head.

Finally, the day of the session came and she was a ball of knots. When he walked through the door she was busy getting the equipment ready for his session and didn't hear him come enter.

"Hi Naythia, I see you're getting ready for me," he said in that low but boyish send you over the top sexy voice of his.

"Oh Justice," she responded as she jumped slightly because he had startled her. "I didn't hear you come in."

"Sorry," replied Justice, "I didn't mean to startle you."

"I'm okay, was just caught up in what I was doing that's all." She paused to take a deep breath and said, "Listen Justice, can we talk for a minute before starting your session? I rescheduled the session after yours so we would have more time."

109

"Sure," he replied slowly. Because of the serious nature of her countenance he wasn't sure if he wanted to hear what she was about to say. "Naythia, I offended you didn't I?" Justice asked with sincerity. "I knew I would mess everything up by telling you how I felt, and coming on so strong."

"No Justice," Nevette interrupted. "It's not like that. I am very flattered by what you said a few days ago. But I was just a bit taken back by your straight forwardness. I have been thinking of how I would respond for the last three days, and well here goes. I was bought up in church and yes I am a preacher's kid. My life has been full of scripture, prophecy and prayer. I wanted to make a difference in peoples' lives, you know. I wanted my life to say, Christian. I also wanted my life to say, purity and holiness." She paused for a second or two because she could feel her internal thermometer rising. She had his full attention and his gaze was undoing her emotionally and sensually. She shrugged past the moment and continued. "Justice I'm a virgin. I made a vow to God and my family that I would keep myself for my husband. So whenever any man shows any interest in me I'm very honest and straight forward about my convictions. I don't want to lead you on. I do enjoy our friendship and pray it can continue after this, because......"

"Wait a minute," Justice interrupted her. "Nevette Naythia Graham, do you think what I shared with you the other day was an elaborate come on, a rouse to get you into bed? I know I came on pretty aggressive but it was only because I wanted you to understand how strongly I was attracted to you. But I would never defile or devalue you in any way."

"No," Nevette now interrupted him and thought at the same time in a soprano toned, "roll your neck black woman", attitude. "Did he just call me by my whole name?" She couldn't help but chuckle at her reaction. She responded, "I didn't think that at all Justice, I just didn't...," she paused briefly and took a deep breath. She gathered her thoughts to ensure she was relayed the correct message to him. "...How can I say this? Being very flattered by your feelings, I didn't want to send you the wrong message. I wasn't sure what message my body language implied. Because to tell you're the truth, my emotions and hormones were all over the place and I wanted to respect your feelings."

"And I yours," he replied. "I probably came on a little too strong, please accept my apology."

110

Nevette reassured him, "Apology accepted, and yes it was a little strong. Flattering...but strong. I didn't know what to do, like I said, my hormones were all over the place."

"Yeah tell me about it," Justice replied.

At that moment all his emotions told him to just grab her and kiss her. But instead, he resisted the temptation. They stared at each other for what had seemed like an eternity until Nevette broke the silence. "We better get going before we still end up in the next therapists' pool session."

Justice replied with an, "I really want to tell you how I feel" sexy voice, "Okay...friends?" He said as he extended his hand as if calling a truce.

"Friends," Nevette responded as she extended her hand in a professional manner to accept his handshake. Justice smiled at her uneasiness. He marveled at her purity and innocence.

She was in her wetsuit already so she asked Justice if he needed time to get ready for the pool. As she removed her robe Justice exclaimed, "Oh...Jesus please help me!"

"Are you okay Justice?" Nevette asked in a concerned voice.

He answered in a boyish "cat that ate the canary" tone, "Ahhh...yes. You took that robe off girl and almost sent me into cardiac arrest."

Now fully embarrassed and flattered at the same time. She replied, "Justice, are you going to be a good boy today?"

He replied with a boyish smile, "I'm going to be good...what?!" He looked at her with that sexy send-you-over-the-edge smile. Nevette gave him an "I don't believe you" look. "What?!...I'm going to be good," he replied with his hands half lifted in a "who m" type of posture.

"Just go get into your trunks," Nevette said with school girl smile. But as usual, he had swim trunks on underneath his gyms pants and just ripped them off, came out of his shirt and was ready. She tried desperately not show a reaction to him in brief style swim trunks. He had always worn gym shorts type trunks on all his previous therapy sessions.

"Oh God, this man is so fine...please Lord help my emotions today," she thought as she began to explain the routine for the day's session. The session was going well and they were in good conversation as usual. Justice had regained most of the muscle mass his leg lost during the six weeks in which he had had to wear a cast. His therapy was almost complete.

Nevette was so nervous. She hoped that it wasn't showing. Every time she had to touch him to guide him through the therapy, she could feel her internal thermometer rising. She felt somehow today their relationship would change, and she was right.

As they neared the end of the session, she slipped as she reached across his body to grab the therapy floaters that were getting out of her grasp. He caught and held her up by her waist and grabbed the floaters for her.

"Thanks," she replied. She was barely able to muster a sound above a whisper. She could feel her body tremble at his touch. She was so nervous because he wasn't just holding her. He was...*holding* her.

"No problem, can't allow my favorite therapist hurt herself now can I?" Justice replied but did not release his hold on her waist. Their eyes met and they were face to face. They just stared in each other's eyes. Justice gave in to his emotions and kissed her with such passion, he had to release the floaters to hold her up and close to him with both hands. She literally melted in his arms. He grabbed her arms and placed them around his neck as he continued to kiss her.

The other intern therapist, Lindsay Armstrong had walked in at that moment. She never looked up as she said, "Okay Nevette girl my session starts in ten min...oh I am so sorry." Nevette pushed off and broke the connection with Justice. He released her from their embrace and was standing behind her scratching his head and looked up and away in an "it wasn't me gesture."

Nevette couldn't believe what just happened. She turned toward Lindsay and said very awkwardly, "Okay, ahhmmnn, thanks Lindsay...uhmm...I'm sorry I went over my time, uh..,"

"There is no need to explain," Lindsay responded with an "uh huh" smile. "I'll give you to a minute to end your session, be back in five girl."

"Thanks." Nevette sighed and turned her attention back to Justice. He was ready to pick up where they left off.

As soon as Nevette turned back toward him she said, "Ahhh...you said you were going to be good...what was that?"

"What was what?" Justice replied as he pulled her back into his arms. He kissed her again said, "Baby, I am being good. I am so in love with you and I will wait forever...I will wait. I will not devalue you with the pressure of cheap sex, as God is my witness. I will love and cherish you. I will treat you like a queen. Our intimacy will begin and end with a simple kiss. I promise I will not pressure you to go any further than that." He took full advantage of the moment and kissed her again and again. He placed his hands on both sides of her face leading slightly behind her head so he could control the intensity and length of the each kiss. In between kisses, he continued to express his true feelings to her.

She was absolutely lost it. There was nothing simple about his kiss. Not only did they send her into the stratosphere, but feeling the full length of his body through their embrace took her to a place she was both unfamiliar with and terrified of. If she didn't break the connection soon, she feared she would enter into a place of no return and lose everything she worked so hard all her life to protect.

Desperate to regain control, she finally pulled away and said, "Derrick, we have to stop. Our session is over and oh my goodness I need some air...or...or something. Not to mention I'm going to put Lindsay behind, and we'll all three be in the dean's office. I thank God it was her that walked in and not the chief therapist."

"I'm sorry Naythia," Justice replied. "I would never dream of dishonoring you. I just...I just lost it. I am usually more in control of myself than that. But girl, you just do something to me. I've waited, hoped and prayed for this moment since the day I walked through those doors for the first session. Please accept my apology...I mean...I don't want to do anything to jeopardize any future relationship between us. Oh God, I don't know what I mean...I'm sorry." He paused and thought to himself, "Oh God, I'm out there too far to turn back now." He continued," Nevette I......"

Nevette cut him off. She interjected, not really knowing how to react, and absolutely mortified of what he would to say or do next. "I think we had better just get dressed," she managed to reply.

After they were both dressed they met at the door way of the physical therapy ward.

"Derrick, you were my last session today. I think we need to talk. Why don't I meet you downstairs in twenty minutes and we can go sit in the lounge area of the lobby?"

"Okay," he turned to walk away but turned back. He came right up to her and said, "Naythia?"

"Yeah Derrick, what is it?" She nervously replied.

"To be honest. I'm not sorry about this at all. I mean...I'm not sorry that I kissed you. I'm definitely not sorry that I told you I'm in love with you...because I am. It's been shut up in me like fire for a long time...burning out of control. Oh...and please, baby,"

113

he paused and smiled at her with a knowing smile. He chuckled lightly as he softly caressed her face and said, "Call me Justice."

She could only smile and shake her head side to side as she turned to walk back into the ward. He watched her until she was out of sight and then proceeded downstairs.

≈

"Wow mom," Talinda gasped as she viewed the picture of her big brother Daniel. "I looked just like him as a baby. I mean, that's amazing considering we have different fathers. I must look more like your side of the family than I thought I did...wow."

Valetta responded as they all continued to look through the scrapbook, "Yes, you two could have easily been mistaken for twins at birth. I remember how hard and comforting that was for me when you were born. I both cried and rejoiced, partly because God had blessed me with another awesome gift of life. But also, that gift was so much of a reminder of the past hurt. My family didn't want me to marry your father. They said that I was rebounding and I couldn't possibly love him. It had only been about two or three months since their death when I met Victor. They just didn't understand, I was lonely and all I knew how to be was a wife. That was what I lived for, to love and be loved. To me it made perfect sense. Love doesn't have a time limit, it is what it is."

Her mother's words struck Talinda center mass of her heart. They had hit their target dead on. She was indeed her mother's daughter because already she was lonely. It was as though her mother was inside of her thoughts and heart. She knew exactly how her mother felt and hoped that the presence of the baby would ease that loneliness she felt and now knew, would only get worse as time went by. She pondered in her heart if any man would ever measure up enough to take Brandon's place in her heart. But quickly dismissed that thought because the mere fact that she existed, answered that question. Her father had indeed measured up in her mother's heart. She knew at that moment, that she would indeed marry again. She was just like her mother. All she ever wanted was to be a wife. That desire, she knew would never leave her.

As she continued to ponder her thoughts Valetta stated, "I remember that it took a few years before I was ready to have another baby. But finally you came. I remember suffering very severely of postpartum depression. But I soon turned the

114

depression into obsession and protection..." she sighed as she looked at Talinda, "...over protection I see now. I struggled enjoying my new family for fear of losing them. Which was just as bad if not more dangerous. Over the years, I managed to successfully push my baby girl away from me. It was a very trying time. One I could have not gotten through, except the power of the Holy Spirit that came into my room one day and began to plug up the holes of the past."

She could feel that she was speaking directly to Talinda's heart. She followed the inspiration on the Holy Spirit. She took a deep breath and said to her daughter. "Sweetheart, it seemed so many times like break-through would never come. But God was faithful even when I wasn't. He was faithful, even when I blamed him and was angry with him. Oh, I never said it out loud. But my actions screamed it at him. But then the sweet power of the Holy Ghost overshadowed me one day. I was in complete arrest and it was at that moment that I knew I would make it to the other side of through. That I would recover and would be able to enjoy the precious new gifts that God had given me. It took your father weeks to even get me to talk to him. I was attracted to him but I was so afraid to allow myself to love. I so afraid that love would be taken away at any moment. Because the reality of life for me was that it could and it had before. But I learned that the power of real love. Is being willing to dive into it with everything you have. All while knowing, that at any moment it could be taken away. It makes you love strong...sometimes too strong. I had to learn to balance it. I remember thinking how desperate I was when you were born. I wouldn't let you out of my sight. I didn't trust anyone to care for you, not even your father. I know I about have drove him crazy and if it had not been for the power of God in his life. I don't know if our marriage would have survived me. But he understood my pain...it was as if God had allowed him to feel it. He always knew all the right words to say and the right times to give me hugs. He endured my obsessive behavior with the both of you. I was just as obsessive with him as I was with you. I had lost my husband and my son in the same night. I was a total maniac when it came to safety. But in time, I learned to trust God with my happiness. I learned that true joy is not determined on your physical circumstance. But on your spiritual circumstance through a proper relationship with God."

They all sat and listened in awe at Valetta's words. They had stopped looking through the pictures. She had their undivided attention and she knew that it was God that was giving her all the words to say. She was merely repeating the words as she heard them being spoken into her spirit by God. She soon realized that she was the only one turning the pages and looking at the pictures. She paused as though pondering a thought and looked up at them smiling.

"What is it mom?" Talinda asked.

She had reached the end of the book. There she had a picture of Talinda and her father. She had placed it in the book with George and Daniel's picture because it was the turning point in her life. It marked the beginning of her healing.

She sported a testimony smile and playfully mushed Talinda's hair as she answered, "Oh it's just this picture of you and your dad. It was on this day that I allowed God show me many things and true healing finally began to take place in me. You were about three years old when I took this picture. We were sitting in the family room and I could hear God say take the picture. But it wasn't until we got them developed later that day in the one hour photo center, that I could see what God was showing me. The look on your fathers' face as he looked at you reassured me that he loved you as much as I did. Although he had not been through the tragic loss of a child or spouse, he had the same fear of losing you and me that I had. But he allowed love to overshadow the fear. Instead of being obsessed he took the energy of the love and just gave it all to us. It was an amazing moment. Oh, I was still obsessive with you, but no longer to a fault. Well, something of a fault because it put a serious strain on our relationship. But you know what," she said as she looked right into Talinda's teary eyes. "I would gladly do it all over again, knowing that the outcome would help my baby get through a trying time in her life. Truly our trials and tribulations are not for us but for someone else."

Talinda just looked into her mothers' eyes as silent tears rolled down her cheeks. She realized just how much a mothers love can sooth every hurt. How amazing God is to give mothers a love that transcends all barriers and eradicates all disappointments and tragedies. There is nothing that a child can do to change a mother's love for it. All she could do was lay her head in her mothers' lap and weep tears of healing. It was as though everyone could read Talinda's thoughts as they all sat with silent tears basking in God's presence that had filled the room. Such a strong yet comforting presence that no mere

116

words could describe. To try would be a futile effort. So they sat and just let God, be God.......

≈

It was well into the evening when they realized the time. And Beatrice taking note of the time said, "Wow ladies, I would like to thank you so much for allowing me to be a part of this special moment. But looking at the time I had better get home. We all have a long day tomorrow. Pastor and I will meet up with all of you tomorrow morning at the church."

"Okay Beatrice, I'll see you out," Helen replied. "Be sure to call or text and let us know you arrived home safely."

"Okay I will," Beatrice replied. She hugged everyone and thanked them again for the invitation to dinner.

Talinda turned to her mother and said, "Thanks mom, for sharing your hurt with me. I know it was probably a challenge for you and I am grateful to God for what he did in me tonight. It was a healing and refreshing moment for all of us."

"More than you'll ever know Talinda," Valetta said as she lightly touched her face and pulled her in for a hug. "More than you'll ever know."

"Well," Valetta said as Helen rejoined them after seeing Beatrice to the door. "We had all better get some sleep. We have a very long and trying day tomorrow. And I for one am just a tad spent."

"Whew, I'm with you there girl," Helen replied.

"Yeah...okay," Talinda responded with a sort of, "I don't want this moment to end", tone. Kind of like when she was young and she had to go to bed early while the adults stayed up longer talking about things they didn't want children to hear. Valetta sensed Talinda's uneasiness about retiring for the night. But decided she wouldn't force anything. She grabbed her hand and gave her a knowing squeeze and a wink as they all hugged and said their goodnights.

"Talinda this is silly," she said out loud about a half hour later as she lie in bed unable to sleep. "You are a grown woman and you are not going to go climb into bed with your mother like a five year old afraid of the dark!" But the more she lay there the more she realized that was exactly what she wanted to do. She had found so much comfort earlier in her mother's words and to be simply put...she wanted her mommy! So she found herself standing outside her mothers' door fighting a silent battle of to knock or not to knock. She heard this knocking noise and was about to wonder where it came from, when she looked up and realized she was actually knocking on her mother's door.

"Come on in Tay Tay," Valetta said in an "I knew it" motherly tone. Talinda opened the door with sheer excitement because she hadn't heard that nickname since her childhood. She stood there silent, and waited for her mother to give the okay. Valetta smiled and threw the covers back and playfully pat the bed. That was it, the signal that it was okay to get in mom and dad's bed!

"I love you mommy," Talinda said as she jumped into bed with Valetta.

"Mommy loves you too princess," Valetta replied. They lay in bed for hours and talked, laughed and cried as well. They tried hard to whisper so they wouldn't wake Helen sleeping in the next room. Talinda asked her mother question after question about George and Daniel. Valetta answered them all. She was surprised at how easy it was for her to talk about George and Daniel and how much she actually wanted to talk about them. She could finally let them have a proper place in her life. There was room for everyone in her heart, she felt balanced. Talinda and her mom both fall asleep shortly after Valetta prayed for God to redeem the time and bless them with the rest of eight hours of sleep, out of an actual three hours.

≈

"The final practice went very well and everything is set for Brandon's service tomorrow," Talinda said to her family as she joined them in the church foyer.

Helen and Valetta were filling the men in on the events from Sunday through today concerning the youth as Talinda walked up. They were convinced that nothing else about God would surprise them. They were awestruck that God filled the entire youth group and that the youth were so receptive to His power.

Talinda nodded her head in agreement and said, "Yeah daddy, it was just awesome. We were glad we decided to come out Sunday night instead of waiting to start Monday morning. The cleanup started after we left pastor's office Saturday, so there were visual reminders of the events from Friday night for them to overcome. They stayed after we left on Sunday and were here before us on Monday. Everyone showed up on time and ready this morning at eight o'clock so they were able to finalize the order of the program in one run through. Everyone did their homework and memorized their parts. They are as ready as to be expected."

118

Pastor Tills and his wife join them as Talinda expressed her gratitude to the youth for their respect and operating once again in the spirit of excellence. But of course Talinda knew it would be much harder for these youth to minister once Brandon's body was in the coffin in front of them. They had so much love and respect for him and vice versa. Brandon had given them his all, and they loved his genuineness to the ministry. They were his babies and it was going to be very hard for them to say goodbye.

Her heart was breaking for them. Brandon was a friend, mentor and father figure to most of them. He had a heartbeat for the youth that could be felt all over the city.

"They were being so strong," Talinda said. "They were trying so hard to be careful what they said. Trying so hard to protect me...they were so concerned about me. They have learned much from Brandon, they are a very unselfish group of young people and we are all so proud of them. They teach you so much about the simple principles of God that we adults often take for granted."

Helen sat down beside Talinda and she began to talk about the wonderful job Valetta has done decorating the gymnasium to lighten the moment. But to no avail because every conversation eventually seemed to end back at Brandon. "Everything is so beautiful Valetta, the colors are awesome and the flowers are exquisite. And Talinda the garment you found for Jessica is so elegant. I was thinking about what happened with them on yesterday, you know...all being filled with the Spirit...Brandon would be so pleased, and proud. This is what he lived for, to see youth flow in the gift of the baptism of the Holy Spirit. You did good Brandon..." she said as she looked up toward heaven. "...You did good son and I'm sure God has now told you, well done." Helen said fighting back tears.

Talinda leaned into her, put her chin on Helen's shoulder and whispered in her ear, "Thank you for always being there for me. Let's just all lean on one another."

"Okay guys, let's go get some food down to that grandson of mine," Roger said to break the solemnest of the moment.

"Yeah that's a good idea Roger," Victor then added in a cautious tone. "Maybe we should drive back to Athens to eat. I mean depending on how hungry we are. Because we have to go to the funeral home for a pre-viewing of Brandon before tonight's service don't we?"

119

That question hit Talinda like a ton of bricks. She had spent so much time getting ready for the service and ministering, that she had been able to block out of her mind the finality of not having her husband with her ever again on this side of creation.

They had previously decided against having a separate viewing and just having the one home going service. They didn't want to put themselves through the emotion of two services. But felt that would be unfair to Brandon's friends and family in Athens who would not be able to attend the actual funeral in Decatur the next day.

But at least at the viewing in Athens that night, they didn't have to do or say anything. They just needed to be there as people paid their respects to the family.

But Talinda knew it would still be hard sitting there in the room with Brandon for hours. How she just wanted this to all be over and she was silently screaming inside at the thought of the events that will take place over the next thirty-six hours.

Talinda responded to her dad's suggestion in a shaky tone, "Yes daddy we do, I'm not really hungry and it's only about a fifty minute drive from here. What does everybody else say?"

"Well, I think we should at least get you a healthy snack Talinda. We could all use something to tide us over, so we're not starving when we get there," Helen replied.

Valetta nodded in agreement. "Yes I agree with Helen. Lindy you do need a little something, we all do."

"Well, if you guys will have us Beatrice and I would like to accompany you to Athens...I mean if it's okay. If it's strictly a family service we'll understand," Pastor Denson Tills said hesitantly.

Helen speaking for the whole group said, "How many times do we have to tell you two, you are family and a very special part of Brandon's life. Don't keep thinking that you are intruding on anything. You're not outsiders. You are welcome. Your ideas are welcome and you input expected." Roger patted Pastor Tills on the back. Beatrice was all teary eyed again and everyone chimed in their agreement with Helen's response.

Roger sensed the solemnest of the atmosphere. He bowed his head and prayed:

Father,

> *We come to You now Lord, praying yet again*
> *for Your comfort Lord. We know that we will have*

to depend on You to get us through the difficult and awkward moments of the circumstances Father. But we trust You God and will give You a yet praise God. We will praise You even in our hurt, pain and loss God. We thank You for the power of the Holy Spirit that is entering in even now as we speak Lord, to give peace oh God of heaven. We love You Lord and we thank You.

In Jesus name we pray,

Amen

Victor gave Roger a knowing gentle squeeze as he rests his hand on his shoulder and said, "Thanks Roger." He then addressed the whole group. "Guys, we're all going to have to be there for one another. We have been in awe of God and His ministering power over the last seventy-two hours. We have had our ups and downs, our good moments and bad, and our strong and weak times. Just remember everybody. Being a Christian doesn't mean that we don't grieve the loss of a love one. It doesn't mean that it hurts any less to lose them, and it certainly not any easier to live without them. But we don't grieve a hopeless lost for we know they are safely tucked away in the arms of the Lord and we will be with them again in eternity. Knowing that gives us a sense of comfort but it doesn't take away the grief. Let God continue to minister to you, because up until today we have only dealt with the manifestation of his death once. But in a few hours we will have to face the reality that Brandon is indeed passed out of this life into his eternal existence, as we view his earthly shell and begin the physical grieving process. God will as he has this whole weekend, give us strength in our times of weakness and comfort us. Let us, as the song says, "Lean on the everlasting arms."

The all chimed in their affirmations and exchanging their "I'm with you and you're not alone hugs", as they went out to their cars to head to Athens, GA. The men drove with Denson in the Till's car and the women were all in the Travis's SUV with Helen driving. The conversation in both cars was idle chit chat. Anything, to keep the subject away from Brandon and the pre-viewing and formal viewing set for that evening.

~Chapter Nine~

As they stood outside the funeral home in Athens, Georgia, Victor Thomas placed his hand on his daughter's shoulder for reassurance. "Okay baby girl, if you like, Roger, Denson and I will go in and do the initial viewing with the Mr. Thurman. You ladies can go freshen up for the actual viewing set to start in a few hours."

They all paused and waited patiently for Talinda's response. Her feet felt like they were buried in cement. She seemed to be frozen in time with a very far off look in her eyes.

Valetta moved to stand directly in front of Talinda to get her attention. Talinda continued to look off into the distance. "Talinda," Valetta paused, to choose her words very carefully, "Talinda sweetheart, right now you're probably thinking that you can't do this...that you can't go in there and view your husband's body. Because doing so means it's true, he's really gone and that you are accepting that this is the end. I know all too well the feeling of despair you must be overwhelmed with right now. Until now, you've been able to disassociate to get through the hard moments. But now, you have to face the full reality of it. Talinda...baby girl your dad and I are here for you, as well as everyone else. You may not think so at this very moment, but you will get through this. I won't lie to you sweetheart...it's going to be hard. You're going to feel like someone is constantly kicking you in the stomach, like there's nothing you can do to stop them and you can't get away from them. Every emotion you can imagine is going to surface. You're going to feel anger, despair, pain, hurt, devastation, just to name a few. Sweetheart you're going to have to fight the feeling of depression and yes...even suicide......"

122

Talinda looked up into her mother eyes, she had read her thoughts. At that very moment she was thinking that she couldn't go on without Brandon and it would have been so much easier if they had been together and both given their life for the cause. She was afraid to speak...afraid to let anyone know that there was even a slight thought of suicide looming around in her brain. But Valetta, knowing her thoughts continued......

"Yes, sweetheart...I know...I know. It's hard to go on alone. But you have something that I didn't when I lost George and Daniel. You have a part of Brandon growing inside of you. His life is preserved through Brandon Jr. Oh my baby...my sweet precious baby girl," Valetta said pulled Talinda securely into her arms. She was now at least crying again showing some normal emotion and life, to every body's relief. Valetta continued, "Just scream baby...just let it out sweetheart. You have been holding this moment back and being so brave for everyone. You don't have to sweetheart. It's okay to let it out. It only gets worse if you try to take to high road on this......"

Before she could say another word Talinda started to scream and shake uncontrollably. She dropped to her knees, and began to lament and wail rocking back and forth screaming out, "WHY GOD WHY? I DON'T UNDERSTAND! I DON'T UNDERSTAND! OH GOD I HURT...I HURT SO MUCH. GOD NO...WHY DID YOU DO THIS TO ME! WHY GOD...HE HAD SUCH A GOOD HEART...HE WAS MY HUSBAND GOD...YOU PREPARED HIM JUST FOR ME. I WAITED GOD...I WAITED! I KEPT MYSELF AND I WAITED! OH GOD PLEASE HELP ME...I FEEL SO EMPTY GOD...I'M JUST SOOO EMPTY...LORD JESUS PLEASE......"

Helen came over to offer Talinda prayer and comfort but was stopped by Valetta, "No Helen...it has to be this way...she has to get it out. If she doesn't let it out it will only be worse later. Trust me...I know. She loves God...she does...she just needs to let these emotions fly so she won't break at the service. The youth are going to need her tomorrow...and she is going to need all of us." She then turned to everyone else and said, "Listen to me everyone, we need to go in together and let our emotions go. We need to allow God to minister to us before the guest begin to arrive. We need to know before they arrive that we are going to be able to handle this. We have three hours before the viewing begins and this is going to be hard. Up until now we have been running on auto pilot. Oh, we have had our emotional moments where we felt despair. But we are about to face the reality of the finality of all of this. It's not going to be as easy as you think. She has to go in now as well as all the rest of you. God will meet us there, and He will comfort us."

Helen held her tears back and replied, "Valetta I know you're right. Even when we pulled up into the parking lot, knowing my baby was in there I was beginning to go south on the inside. I'm desperately trying to hold it together now for Talinda......"

Valetta once again cut her off, "That's just it Helen, don't try to hold it together. Let it out, release the emotion so you and God can deal with it." Valetta turned toward her husband who now stood directly over Talinda as she crying out. "Honey get Talinda up, we need to go inside. It's time to face this."

They entered and immediately they were greeted by the funeral home director who had been waiting patiently inside not wanted to disturb them as they gathered talking just outside the door. He very gingerly said, "Mr. and Mrs. Travis...we have everything set up and Brandon is in the main sanctuary. The programs are on the table and guest book is ready as well. We have placed the items you wanted at his side and the power point presentation is ready. One of my assistants is starting the music you requested now and you may enter when you are ready. We hope that we have presented him well and that you will be satisfied with everything. But we stand ready to make any adjustments needed."

Helen could only shake her head in appreciation unable to speak. Roger responded, "Mr. Thurman, thank you so much for taking care of our son. I'm sure you've done a great job and everything will be fine. You have always been known to take much pride in your ministry and I'm sure there is no exception here. We trust you have lived up to your usual perfection."

"Thank you sir," Isaac responded as tears welled up in his eyes. Both from the compliment and the fact that he had known Brandon all his life and had watched him grow up. He had found it quite difficult to work on him. Although he took much pride in his work, he always thought it was somewhat awkward to be so very good at what he did. He often didn't know how to feel about that, and had many sleepless nights when someone as close as the Travis' were to him had a love one in his care. He shook Roger's hand and couldn't stop the tears that fell from his eyes as he turned to escort Helen into the room. "Okay, Mrs. Helen and Mrs. Travis if you are both ready, it's this way please."

Talinda stood still as the door opened and exposed the finality of her life as she knew it. To her relief, he wasn't placed right in the door and thrust in her face. She gained a little strength. But with each step she took to round the corner to view the casket, she felt her body grow weaker. It was as though she were walking in quick sand. The men assisted the women and Roger caught up to Helen just as she gasped at the first sight of Brandon. She paused frozen in mid-stream of her stride. Then she remembered that Talinda was close behind her, so pressed on, once again in an attempt to be strong. The closer she got to Brandon, the further away she seemed to be from him. It was as though he was slipping away down a hole just out her grasp. She took a deep breath as she took the last step. Now standing at Brandon's side, she looked down into her baby boy's face.

He was clean shaven with a pristine haircut and sharp barber line. His skin was flawless, and even toned. His expression was peaceful and welcoming. She whispered though her tears, "Thank you Isaac...for taking such good care of my baby." Brandon was always very conscious of his personal hygiene and how he both presented and carried himself.

She was surprised at her reaction thus far. She appeared to be holding it together. She didn't feel the desire to cry out that she thought she would be at the sight of her son lying there in state. Roger stood there next to her, patting his son on the hand and telling him how proud he was on the man of God he was and the sacrifice that he had made.

He spoke through his tears, "Brandon...son I am so proud of you. You have fulfilled your ministry. I'm going to...going to miss you so very much. I learned as much from you as you thought you learned from me. Don't worry...we're going to help take good care of Lindy and little...little Brandon." He momentarily lost it crying out, "OH GOD HELP ME! God I'm going to miss my son, he was my only child God. I don't understand God, and I don't really trust the process right now either. You said all things work together for me good. God, how does this fit...I don't understand God...I don't understand. But, I do trust the promise that you're going to wipe every tear from our eye. I will see Brandon again, Lord. We will see him again! I just miss him so much God...it just seems too soon. I've only had him for a short time God...parents aren't supposed to bury their children."

As he wiped his tears, Talinda and Valetta were now standing beside them and they moved over to give them space up by Brandon's head. Talinda leaned over and kissed his forehead and said, "Just as handsome as the day I met you. It's amazing that I have the same warm fuzzy feeling inside, that I did when we shared our first kiss. Brandon, I am going to miss your presence, sweetheart. I'm going to miss your love, your smell, your ministry. I feel so incomplete right now baby...so incomplete. But I have comfort in knowing that you are with the Father and you are with Lydia. By now I know you have been introduced to my big brother Daniel and his father George." At that comment, Valetta smiled through tears as she gave Talinda a slight and loving squeeze. She already had her arm around her for support. Talinda looked into her mothers' eyes for conformation that she was okay with her mentioning Daniel and George. She then continued her conversation to Brandon, "Take care until we all get there sweetheart. And enjoy your Lord baby...enjoy your Lord."

Talinda, like Helen, was very surprised at her reaction seeing Brandon and thanked the Holy Spirit out loud for His strength. The Tills however were not fairing as well. Unlike everyone else, this was their first viewing of Brandon and an overwhelming sense of guilt swept back over them. They had not even rounded the corner to view Brandon's body and they both wept uncontrollably. Victor went over to them and began to pray for strength and comfort from the Holy Spirit. Valetta left Talinda and went over to join her husband in prayer.

Talinda followed her mother. She looked them in the eyes and said, "Pastor...First Lady...you are our spiritual parents and there is nothing that Brandon and I would not have done and will not do for you. Brandon had and I have the utmost respect for you. I do not in any way blame you for anything. This...as hard as it may be and senseless as it may seem, is God's divine appointment for Brandon. God could have intervened, but then where would that have left Raymond. His soul was worth it to Brandon and to God...as well as Quavis'. Please don't do this...don't blame yourselves...let's honor God and Brandon for their sacrifice. Please......"

At her words Pastor Tills stood, still weeping. He began to walk toward Brandon with his wife at his side. When they reached the coffin they stood with their hands on him and began to thank God for the opportunity to be able to be a part of Brandon's life. They thanked God for the ministry that had blossomed in his care, and the many sacrifices that had been made. With each word of prayer, they gained both strength and composure. They turned to Talinda and thanked her for her service and her sacrifice as well.

126

All of Brandon's favorite things lie around the outside of the coffin on display. They all gathered around him, prayed and sang along with his favorite song that was now playing in the background. The presence of God rested upon them and they all knew that they would make it.   There was only an hour and a half before the viewing was scheduled to begin and the ladies decided to go to the Travis' house to freshen up. The men would remain at the funeral home in case there were some early visitor's. They promised that the power point presentation would not begin until they had all returned.

~Chapter Ten~

Even though they knew they were all prepared, the sound of people entering the funeral home sent their minds reeling. It was easy to face it with immediate family, but now the real test was about to come.

Talinda could feel a sickening sensation in her stomach and knew she was about to lose her lunch. Helen who faced her read the situation. She stood up to follow her as she rushed toward the restroom, but was halted by Valetta who stated, "Helen no...you and your husband need to be out here as your family and friends enter, I'll go take care of Talinda."

Helen knew that she was right. She didn't protest and for a moment felt a twinge of guilt. Secretly, she was using the situation to remove herself from the sanctuary before the first guest rounded the corner. This was going to be harder than she thought. Now, along with their own emotions, the emotions of everyone that entered the room would be thrust upon them. Weeping is such a contagious emotion. To no avail she tried to put on her best smile, but resorted to just remaining seated in the front row and waiting for the first guest to view Brandon and then offer their deepest condolences to her and Roger.

In the meantime, Valetta was in the rest room with a cool compress on Talinda's forehead. Her breathing wasn't erratic and so Valetta wasn't worried. She made it into the stall just in time and managed to unleash all her lunch into the toilet and not all over her blouse.

"Okay baby girl, are you ready to go back out now?" she asked in a "knowing" motherly tone. Talinda looked at her with a "do I have to look". But nodded her head knowing full, well

128

her mother wouldn't allow her to hide out in the restroom all evening.

As they entered the sanctuary they could hear people weeping. The Travis' did not have an extremely large family left in Athens. But yet and still, they were all quite close. It was very hard on them to lose such a young member of the family. The majority of the family members would arrive until the next day for the actual funeral service.

Talinda joined Roger and Helen on the front row sitting to the left inside of them. Helen turned to her in between hugs and cards from relatives and friends and asked if she was she doing okay. Talinda could only nod. She felt her emotions taking over her.

Everyone appeared to be holding themselves together pretty well and was able to assist family members who were struggling. Helen was surprisingly very strong throughout the evening. She would weep occasionally, but nothing uncontrollably. They were once again moving in fast forward and the controls were set on automatic. They each now cherished the moment they had with Brandon alone earlier to grieve unhindered and genuinely. Each of them quietly and discreetly thanked Valetta for her wisdom and guidance earlier that evening before the initial viewing with a hug and soft whispers in her ear throughout the evening as the moments presented themselves. Her previous experience and insistence of them to release their emotions proved to be stern but excellent counsel for the task at hand. They were all very grateful to her.

The staff was about to start the power point presentation of Brandon's life, when his cousin entered the sanctuary. It would both conclude the viewing for tonight as well as Brandon's funeral the next day.

He was visibly broken and began to shake with each step of advancement to Brandon. He cried out, "Why twin...why!" As he stood over Brandon's body.

"Oh God Roger its Bernard," Helen said to her husband. They both get up to minister to Bernard. He was Roger's brother's son and he and Brandon had grown up together. They were first cousins and inseparably close. They called each other twin because their resemblance was remarkable.

He managed to speak through tears, "Aunt Helen, I don't understand...why...why God would let this happen...why? Twin has always had favor with God...everything he prayed to

129

God...he answered. Why Uncle Roger...why," he turned back toward the coffin and through red hot tears he screamed, "TWIN...YOU LEFT ME HERE ALONE...HOW COULD YOU LEAVE ME........!"

Roger turned Bernard toward him and began to talk to him. "Listen Bernard, you just said something very profound. You said he has always had favor with God. That whatever he asked for, God gave him. Bernard, son, how do you know that this wasn't an agreement between him and God? How do you know that this still isn't his favor with the father to get what he asked? We just have to trust God and rejoice in the fact that Brandon has run his race and finished his course. That he kept the faith and fought a good fight." For the first time, Roger realized even though he had felt hopeless. He did trust the process. He truly was ministering to himself as he ministered to Bernard.

Bernard looked back down at Brandon, knowing his uncle's words held painful truth. He said as he placed his hand on top of Brandon's, "I love you twin. I'm so remorseful that we hadn't spent hardly any physical time together the last several years."

He cleared his throat as if getting himself together. But he just couldn't get the tears to stop flowing. He mustered a smile as he turned toward Helen and said, "Aunt Helen, how...how are you doing? Whatever I can do for you please let me know?" He once again looked down at Brandon and said, "I promise, I'll take good care of our mother Brandon...I promise."

Those words broke Helen and she shed silent tears as she embraced her nephew. Only the movement of her body showed the intensity of her emotions as she cried in her nephew's arms.

Talinda sat both watching and subdued by his presence. He so remarkably resembled Brandon. He was noticeably bigger than Brandon physically, in height and build. But other than that, it was almost as though she had seen a ghost. She had never physically met Bernard, but had heard that he and Brandon literally could be and always had been mistaken for twins. Their fathers also strongly favored. His presence was very difficult for Talinda. She was stunned to silence giving only a hello nod when she was introduced to Bernard Travis. Brandon had been the only brother he had known. When Bernard went off to the Air Force Academy and then into the United States Air Force as a fighter jet pilot he hadn't seen much of Brandon in the years following. They often wrote each other, and communicated through all the luxuries of modern technology. About a year or so back, Brandon had traveled to Germany to

130

Kaiserslautern to visit him. A trip that Talinda was unable to attend at the time for reasons she now couldn't even remember. In the pictures she could see the strong resemblance but live and in color it was strikingly painful to see him.

"Well," Bernard said as he hugged Talinda, who was still speechless. She slightly trembled at his touch. "It's good to finally meet the woman of Brandon's dreams. You are just how Brandon described you, although your pictures don't do you proper justice," he said as he mustered up a smile. His smile was so incredibly similar to Brandon's that she felt she would dismantle any minute now. Her insides were already affected and she fought to keep it contained. Finally, she managed to get a response to exit out of her mouth.

≈

"Well, I think it's safe to say we've exceeded the friend barrier. We have each other's numbers because of the therapy, so I guess I have a reason to use it other than calling you about my therapy sessions," Justice said starting the conversation off.

"Ah...yeah I think friendship is a thing of the past with us, sooo...where do we go from here?" Nevette shyly asked.

"Look Naythia," he said as he grabbed both her hands in his and lifted them to his mouth to kiss the back of them. "I want to do this respectfully and tastefully, and I want it to be special. Sooo...why don't we go back to our apartments and get changed into nice evening attire? I'll pick you up at your apartment in about an hour and we can go to a nice restaurant to discuss us."

She could only smile because in her mind she had already fast forwarded to the romantic evening she imagined he had in store for her. She collected her thoughts and responded, "Okay, that sounds great."

Justice gave her a kiss on the forehead and said, "See you soon." She watched as he walked away.

"Oh Justice," she called after him.

He turned and responded teasingly as he walked back toward her, "Yeah...what is it? I know...you miss me already don't you?" He said in that sexy voice accompanied by that school boy smile of his.

She smiled and sarcastically said, "Ahhh...no...that's not it, Mr. Wonderful. When you say evening attire do you mean dressy jeans and shirt, dressy skirt and shirt, or....."

Justice stopped her in mid-sentence as he stood practically on top of her and said as he gently stroked her face from temple to jaw and across her lips. "I mean little black dress nice, we're going to Stefano's in Atlanta."

"Oh...okay," responded a very surprised Nevette. "And just what makes you think I'm the kind of woman who owns a little black dress Mr. Goodfellow."

"Oh, you have one," he said. He leaned over into her ear to finish the statement and whispered, "A little black dress doesn't make you're a seductress. It says you are sophisticated, well groomed, gorgeous and very sexy." Not waiting for her to respond he turned and walked away as he said, "One hour...see you then." She watched as he walked out of sight.

Nevette could hardly wait to get to her car and turn the music up so she could just scream! This was her weekend off and she had forgotten her schedule for the next week so she headed back upstairs to get it. Lindsay's session was over and she was closing up the ward for the day.

"Okay, give me the skinny girl, what did I walk in on here today?" exclaimed a very inquisitive Lindsay in a giggly girly tone.

"Oh my, God Lindsay, girl I just want to scream, no man has ever held me like that before. And his kiss, oh, I just melted!" Nevette replied as she placed her hand over her heart letting out a sigh.

"Girl, I've known you for three years and was your roommate for the first two remember. And I can attest to the fact that no man has ever held you at all." Lindsay jokingly replied.

"Ha-ha very funny," Nevette interrupted with a hint of sarcasm.

"Anyway," Lindsay continued. "I knew it was coming, I could tell he was madly in love with you."

"Was it that obvious," asked a surprised Nevette.

Lindsay rolling her head back as she replied, "Girl please, a blind man feeling his way down the street with a cane could see it." They both laughed as they walk toward the door to close up the ward.

"So what now," Lindsay asked.

"Well, we're meeting for dinner in about an hour or so. We're going to Stefano's in Atlanta, so I'll tell you when I come in on Monday," Nevette responded attempted to sound mature and experienced.

132

"Monday!" exclaimed Lindsay as she grabbed her by the shoulder to turn her toward her because she had started to walk away. "No way! You mean I have to wait all weekend to get the details. Girl, stop in tomorrow and tell me something! Hey, and you better be a virgin when you come to sessions on Monday."

"Lindsay, I can't believe you said that to me," responded a surprised Nevette.

"What!" Lindsay exclaimed sarcastically, She sported a sly smile with her hands on her hips and a sister girl roll of the neck, with a pop, pop, pop of her fingers. "Girl you would have lost it in the pool if I hadn't walked in when I did!"

"Lindsay, you are so naughty!" Nevette retaliated back and they share a laugh. Nevette was about to walk away again and remembered, "Oh Lindsay, please tell me you have a little black dress and accessories to go with it!"

"Girl, don't tell me you don't own a black dress," Lindsay replied.

"Would I be asking you if I did," Nevette responded with sarcasm.

"See, that's the problem with you churchy girls, and why I don't go to church anymore. You don't understand sexy. You've been taught all your life that sexy is pornographic or something. Sexy can be sophisticated and elegant, it doesn't have to be slutty. You have the wrong idea about the black dress. You can be virtuous and sexy at the same time. My dress is very tasteful and elegant and it's yours tonight if you like. I'll bring it to your apartment," Lindsay said in an almost offended and more serious tone.

A very surprised Nevette responded, "Thanks Lindsay, and you're right, I have been taught sexy is anything but modest. But, you can't use the excuse of people's misunderstandings to turn your back on God either. I always wondered why you talked about God but wasn't a regular church member. The only person hurting because you're not in church is you. Why, don't you come and help straighten us churchy girls out. There's much we can learn from each other, and with Gods' Holy Spirit as our guide, we can't go wrong."

Now it was Lindsay's turn to be surprised, "You're right Nevette. I used to be so strong in the church. But the women I fellowshipped with weren't human, they were perfect. They didn't make mistakes and they would never discuss life with you. I wanted to understand what it meant to be an anointed woman of God. To be confident in myself and who I was in God.

I never wore clothes that exposed my body or were too tightly fitting. I had too much respect for myself to dress like a street hooker. But whenever I would dress elegantly or wear makeup I turned into a Jezebel in their eyes. I began to think I must not be cut out for God because I liked to look nice, wear clothes that fit properly, and be well groomed. Their clothes always seemed two sizes too big like they were afraid their shape would show. And I wasn't trying to flaunt mine, but I did want my clothes to be flattering on me. It's like they were afraid to be women. If a man has a lust problem, you could be wearing a potato sack and smell like a skunk and it wouldn't matter to him. I think sometimes we spend too much time correcting the women, when sometimes it's the men who need deliverance."

Nevette responded in amazement, "We should have had this conversation a long time ago. I hope you haven't viewed me as judgmental? I like to dress nice and I do, on occasion wear makeup. I just had a problem with what was considered sexy. Over the years, I had several conversations with the elderly woman of my church about life, love and marriage. They inspired me to remain pure until my wedding night. I have to confess, they were a little more than conservative with the single women's attire. But, that was because we weren't married and they didn't want us to unknowingly, open the door for a spirit of seduction to come in. I also have to confess, they may have been a little over the top. But, I also feel that as young single women, that we should be aware of how we are presenting ourselves. Proper teaching is the key to confident but elegant young ladies in the church. I understand how you must feel. Lindsay, I have never seen you wear anything inappropriate. It's too bad you were brought up in a church trapped in bondage. I think maybe, this is something we should address in church with the other single young ladies on Sunday. Will I see you there?"

Lindsay responded with tears in her eyes, "Yes I'll be there." Nevette not willing to allow the opportunity pass by, said "Lindsay let's pray. You need to rededicate your life to the Lord right here, right now." Nevette pulled the door closed to the therapy ward and they knelt down to pray.

Lindsay kneelt but stopped Nevette from reciting the sinner's prayer. "No Nevette, I know all too well what to say. Just agree with me."

"Okay," a surprised Nevette responded.

A very tearful Lindsay prayed:

Lord God,

> *I come before You in Jesus name. The name that is above all names where by men must be saved. Lord, I ask You to forgive me. I allowed people to separate me from You. Father, I rededicate my life to You. I surrender my life to You and I accept the blood atonement Your Son died on the cross to give me. I thank you for placing Nevette in my life God. Truly, she is here on a divine appointment from You. You sent her to rescue me and I thank you, God. Help us to be a blessing to each other and the other young women in our community.*

In the matchless name of Jesus Christ I pray,

Amen.

Nevette responded through tears, "You are a powerful woman of God. Something tells me you never really stopped praying to God. Girl, our lives just got better. And together, we are going to do so much for God!"

They embrace and Lindsay responded, "Thank you and A-men. But right now, we better get you in that black dress before Derrick Goodfellow, *"but you can call me Justice"*..., she said is a low teasing voice, "...gets over to your house."

"Oh gosh! We've been here for half an hour," replied Nevette.

"He'll wait believe me," exclaimed Lindsay. "You get home and shower I'll bring the dress over."

"Okay thanks Lindsay," Nevette said as she hurried off.

Nevette called Justice on her way home. She told him she would need another thirty minutes because she was just now leaving work.

Upper classmen all lived in a singles complex built just for students. It was an up scaled dorm of single efficiency one bedroom apartments.

She was getting out of the shower as the doorbell rang. It was Lindsay, excited and ready to dress her for her date.

Nevette opened the door almost in a panic as she exclaimed, "Oh it's you, thank God. I was beginning to lose it. He'll be here in about twenty minutes."

"Would I let you down? And twenty minutes is plenty of time to get you ready. Are you all showered and shaved?" Lindsay asked.

Nevette all smiles responded, "I'm all ready for the queen of elegance to do her work." Lindsay gets Nevette dressed and throws her hair up in a sweep. She threw on the accessories and highlighted the right features with a little make up enhancement.

Lindsay stepped back and looked at Nevette. "You look stunning," she said.

She turned Nevette around so she could look in the mirror. She gasped as she said, "Wow, is that really me? I look so sophisticated, elegant and tastefully sexy."

"See," exclaimed Lindsay. "I told you sexy doesn't have to be slutty."

"You think he'll like it?" Nevette asked.

"Like it. His eyes are going to pop right out of his head. You may have to drive girl, because he won't be able to see a thing," Lindsay replied jokingly. They both laugh as the doorbell rings.

"Oh my gosh, he's here...he's here!" Nevette practically screamed with excitement.

"Calm down Nevette," Lindsay said as she grabbed Nevette's left hand and gave a deep breathing type of "get it together" gesture with her other hand.

"Okay," Nevette exclaimed. "Let's do this."

"I tell you what," Lindsay said thinking fast on her feet. "You go back in the bedroom and I'll let him in as I walk out to door. Then you come out the back in a minute like you're talking to me and didn't hear the doorbell ring."

"Okay. W-what do I say?" Nevette nervously asked.

Lindsay responded, "Are you for real girl? Say anything...okay, check this out. Walk out like you're fixing your dress. Not really looking up and say, hey Lindsay, how do I look? Then, you'll look up and say, oh Justice you're here. I didn't hear you come in. Are you ready to go?"

"You're a genius Lindsay," a very grateful Nevette responded.

"No, you're just sheltered. Love you...have fun, bye," Lindsay said laughing as she turned Nevette in the direction of her bedroom and gave her a gentle nudge.

Nevette scrambled off to her bedroom rehearsing out loud what she is supposed to say. Lindsay shaking her head in amusement went to answer the door. She opened the door, greeted Derrick and told him that Nevette would be out in a minute.

As she left the out the door, she said in a knowing smile, "She looks stunning. You guys have a good time...ah, but not too good of a time."

He responded with a slight embarrassed tone, "I'm sure we will. Hey Lindsay...thanks...I mean for earlier."

"Uh huh," she responded and smiled a knowing but reassuring smile, as she closed the door behind her.

Justice smiled and turned to see Nevette coming out of the bedroom brushing off her dress. She said, "Hey Lindsay, you think he'll like...," she looked up and saw him, "...my outfit?" She finished the statement with Justice staring at her.

"Wow, you are stunning," stated a very in love Justice.

"Why thank you kind sir," Nevette responded. "Lindsay, you are amazing," she thought.

"Your chariot awaits, Mrs. Goo...uhmm..." He had to catch himself. He cleared his throat and said, "...G-Graham."

"Did he just say...," Nevette thought in a high soprano tone. She pretended she had not caught on to his little slip up and simply responded, "Why, thank you kind sir."

She was so caught up in her thoughts of how she met Justice that she didn't hear him come back into the hotel suite. It appeared that after what seemed like an eternity to Justice and Nevette, whatever Justice ordered was still in the vault downstairs. They apparently thought, they were supposed to deliver it the next day and just bring up fresh fruit and wine the first night. He startled her as he said, "Okay Mrs. Goodfellow, I think I have the room service all corrected now. They'll bring our order in just a few minutes." Justice stopped short of the bed and just stood there, staring at Nevette.

"What is it Justice? Why are you just standing there staring at me?" Nevette nervously asked.

He replied, "Oh just thinking how stupid I am for wasting so much time on room service, when my beautiful bride is here waiting for me to complete her life." He climbed into bed and approached her in a sexy tribal "lord of the jungle" cat like demeanor. He said in a "I'm about to make you climb the walls" tone, "I think I'll cancel room service until in the morning. I have all I need right here."

He kissed her and realized she wasn't as nervous or shaking as before. He said, "Mmmmm.....somebody is very relaxed now."

She placed her hand on the side of his face said just as she was about to returned his kiss, "Somebody....is ready to be your wife." She paused looked into his eyes and said, "Make love to me Justice."

"Ooooo," he said as he maneuvered over the top of her. "Your wish is my command......"

≈

"Yes, it's very nice to finally meet you as well. I have heard so much about you." Talinda replied. She had to momentarily lower her head to break eye contact. She then looked up and continued, "I'm sorry, I was quite disconcerted by your presence. In your pictures I could see the family resemblance. But, I wasn't prepared at just how much you do indeed, favor Brandon. I see why you guys called each other twin. I was caught off guard to say the least."

Bernard smiled again and replied, "No need to apologize. It's I that owes the apology. I shouldn't have allowed this to be the first time that you met me. I should have come to visit you guys before. But, I was so busy building a career, that I forgot to continue to build and preserve family. Guess you could say I was caught up in the cares of this life."

Talinda could feel the room begin to spin. She turned to Helen and held her head as she said, "Mom, I think I need sit down."

With that being said Roger and Bernard assisted Talinda as she took a couple of steps back to her seat. Bernard joined them on the front row and the power point presentation of Brandon's life began.

As they view the presentation, some laugh. Some smile. Some shed muffled tears and while others, sighed. But all enjoyed the little pieces of Brandon that they could all hold on too, memories of his life and ministry from beginning to end.

One by one, those that would not be able to attend the service the next day said their goodbyes to Brandon. They once again expressed their sympathies to the family. Bernard would be at the Travis' house with all them tonight and had shared with Roger that his mom and dad would be flying in to Atlanta the next morning. Talinda had mixed emotions about spending the night with Brandon's double. But all in all, was thanking God for the comfort and assistance of the Holy Spirit that had been

138

with them all thus far. She turned once again to Brandon, stroked his cheek and said, "See you tomorrow sweetheart...for one last time on this side of creation...I love you...I love you."

With that being said, they all turned to leave not wanting to see Isaac close the coffin. They had no desire to endure the experience twice, so asked him to please close the coffin after all the family had left the funeral home sanctuary. Isaac, shaking his head understandably obliged their request. He was close to the Travis' and had grown to love them over the years.

≈

Back at the Travis house, Talinda was feeling a little more comfortable with Bernard. But found was it still difficult to engage in casual conversation with him. It was unnerving to her to say the least, at how similar even their mannerisms were. But at the same time, she couldn't keep her eyes off him. It was almost like having Brandon alive for one more night, in a very weird kind of way. He appeared to be a bit taller than Brandon and had a slightly larger build. But their completions, beautiful eyes and dimples were almost identical.

He sensed her uneasiness and asked her, "Talinda, would it be easier for you if I weren't here. I sort of get the feeling my presence is making this more difficult for you. I could go to a hotel and meet up with you all tomor......"

Talinda cut him off, "Oh Bernard, I'm so sorry...please don't do that. Yes, I was taken off guard when I first met you. The resemblance was overwhelming for me so say the least...but please...stay. It's very important that family is together right now. To be honest, I found myself staring at you and was wondering if I were the one making you uncomfortable. Part of me is very glad you are here. It reminds me of how full of life Brandon was. The other part is struggling, because of the unsettling your presence brings. To be honest, before you walked through the door, I was coming to grips with the finality of Brandon's life on this side of existence...and..."

He finished her sentence, "My presence threw a monkey wrench in the program."

"Well," Talinda replied. "Actually it threw in the whole tool chest!"

At that remark, they both burst into laughter and the awkwardness of the situation just seemed passed, and perfect peace entered the house. Talinda and Bernard sat for hours and filled each other in on their "Brandon memories". Bernard was excited to hear that Talinda was expecting. Everyone seemed to be relieved at the thought that a tangible part of Brandon would be left behind with them.

Talinda was enjoying the priceless memories she shared with Bernard about the love of her life. The more she looked at him and talked with him. The more she found the differences between the two of them and the more comfortable she became.

Around twelve-thirty in the morning, Helen and Valetta who had been engaged in conversation themselves, decided it was time to round everybody up and turn in for the night. Roger and Victor were down in the basement attempting to get involved with the college game playing on the local sports channel. Although no one thought they would get any sleep, the all agreed they at least needed to lie down to rest their bodies.

Before they knew it, it would be time for Bernard get up and leave for the airport to get his parents. They had planned on being at the church by eleven a.m. to check the gymnasium and make any last minute arrangements or changes. They also wanted to be there about a half hour, before the youth began to get into place for the memorial service. Talinda also for some strange reason looked forward to spending some alone time with Brandon. She hoped that Mr. Thurman would be there early with him, to give her one last private moment with her husband.

So, with the agenda set for the next day, they all decided to retire for the night. Talinda rejected her mother's invitation to stay in the room with her that night. She wanted solitude with God to pray and journal her thoughts and feelings of the day's events. And thus they all said they goodnights.

~Chapter Eleven~

Talinda lie in bed after making her journal entry looking up at the ceiling fan, watching it go around and around. It was useless. She knew she was not going to get any sleep whatsoever. She missed Brandon with a passion and had such an empty feeling inside. She looked down at her stomach and smiled at the thought of feeling empty inside. It was such an oxymoron. She was very much pregnant and filled with the love she and Brandon shared growing inside of her. She decided to go sit out on the deck and watch the sun come up, although that wouldn't be for several hours still. She donned her robe and proceeded down the hallway to the kitchen area leading out to the deck. To her surprise, Bernard was already there sitting on the deck drinking a cup of tea.

She made noise as she approached so she wouldn't completely startle him, because he appeared to be deep in thought. Clearing her throat she said very expressionlessly, "You couldn't sleep either huh?"

"Nah, I figured I might as well get up and spend some time out in God's creation and let him minister to me," he replied.

"Oh, I'm sorry. I didn't mean to intrude. I'll leave you to your time with God. I know how important that is right about now," Talinda replied very apologetically.

"No...please Talinda, stay. I welcome the company," Bernard said as he pulled a chair closer for her to sit down. "May I get you something to drink? I'm enjoying a cup of Aunt Helen's famous pomegranate and cherry tea."

"Oh that sounds delicious but no thanks, I'm fine," she said as she sat down. She stared off into the night and she and Bernard picked up in conversation where they left off earlier.

141

"You know Talinda," Bernard said as he stared off into the distance. "The night Brandon died I had actually called my dad and asked him was everything okay. It was almost like the severed twin syndrome you know, when one twin can tell when another one is in trouble." He paused briefly to look at Talinda as if saying "you know what I mean."

Then he continued, "That's just how close Brandon and I were. My dad assured me that everything was fine. Then the very next day he called me back. You know...I remembered looking at the phone seeing it was my dad and somehow I knew that Brandon was gone. As I answered the phone, I tried to prepare myself for what I was about to hear. He said son you were right, something happened to Brandon last night. I'm about to call the red cross so your commander will probably call you into his office soon. We need you to get on the next flight out of Germany. He didn't want to tell me that Brandon was gone but I wouldn't let it go until he said the words. I left work and drove...I just drove. Not in any particular direction with any particular purpose...I just...drove. I needed to just scream, cry and let everything out. Brandon was my brother, my confidant and my mentor."

Talinda just sat and listened. She knew that Bernard was about to say something that she would cherish, a fragment of Brandon that she could keep forever and she wasn't disappointed. Bernard began to reveal some very intimate conversations he had with Brandon.

Bernard stood and then sat right back down and continued, "You know Talinda, I've never seen a man more in love than Brandon was with you. I remember when he first shared with me the vision that God gave him concerning you. He spoke with such a powerful love that I was flabbergasted by it. I said to him, man how can you be so in love with someone that you haven't even met yet and have no real guarantee that you'll meet at all. He looked at me and said, "Because God said so Bernard." Those words penetrated my soul and spirit. When he came to visit me a few years ago the first day he spent more time on the computer with you, than he did with me." He stopped to enjoy a chuckle at that thought, and then continued on, "I teased him that night about being henpecked and whipped. He turned at looked at me in no uncertain terms and said Bernard, when love is as pure as what Talinda and I have you go through withdrawals when you're not in direct vicinity of it. Outside of God, she is like the air I breathe and I feel lost when I can't just reach out and touch her."

Those words both warmed Talinda's heart and tore it up all at the same time. She listened quietly as he continued.

"He said wait until you meet her Bernard, you'll see. She makes a man feel so secure in a relationship. Most of the time, I just want to hold her in my arms and just love on her. When we make love it's so sweet...she's everything a man ever wanted or dreamed of. She makes me want to give her everything, to be everything she needs me to be. He said the thought of another woman being in my life never even enters my mind or loins. I have absolutely no insecurities about our relationship. I know that when I return, she'll be waiting on me and will have something special planned just for me. And just thinking about whatever it is she is going to do, keeps me in such anticipation when I'm not with her." He paused because his voice was starting to quake. He took a deep breath and continued.

"He said to me, Bernard, I have to hear her voice every day. So excuse me for being...whipped, as you call it. But I'm so in love with that woman, and I have to talk to my baby every day." He paused for a second, as if giving what he said some thought for the first time. He started to carefully choose his words as he continued. "You know Talinda the crazy thing is, I remember thinking, wow...now that's pure love in action. I always looked forward to meeting the woman that had my twin turned upside down and inside out." He smiled and shook his head after making that comment.

Talinda just sat there, thinking about the love Bernard described. The love that she and Brandon had shared...the love that she deeply knew she was going to miss. A love that would not be easily, if ever be replaced. For some reason she was very comfortable with him now. She also found that he was the only one so far, she had been able to share fond memories of Brandon with, without feeling angry or depressed. Instead, she felt a longing for Brandon's touch. She was thankful that the lighting on the deck wasn't the best, because silent tears streamed down her face. Bernard continued in conversation without noticing. Maybe he did notice, but didn't know what to say or do, so simply did nothing.

She stood and walked to the end of the deck and looked out across the yard. Her voice trembled as she turned toward Bernard and said, "Oh Bernard, I miss him so much. I know I'm probably more than normally emotional because of the baby, but..." She paused for a moment then continued, "...I just don't know how...I just don't know what to do."

Bernard stood and joined her at the end of the deck. She burst into tears and Bernard instinctively pulled her into his arms, to comfort her. Something she was totally unprepared for. Having the desire to touch him or have him touch her seemed very much off limits. She did not understand the complete comfort she felt in his arms. Her mind was spinning. But then she heard...no it couldn't be...she thought she heard...Brandon's voice..., "Don't worry baby. I got you...I love you so much. You're going to make it through this...you'll see. Sweetheart, just enter into God's rest and Holy comfort. "

Everything inside of her wanted to pull away and just run. Not in any particular direction or destination. Just away from the intensity of the presence she was arrested by. Then all of a sudden, she felt the warmth of the Spirit and just closed her eyes and continued to weep. She knew she was no longer being held by Bernard. A strange nostalgia had come over her. Yes, she knew physically she was being held by Bernard. But it was Brandon's touch that she felt. It was his aroma that she smelled, his caresses that had often comforted her and yes...his heartbeat that she experienced. She instinctively nestled into his chest as she often did when Brandon would hold her.

What she thought she had said silently in her subconscious. She actually whispered in a soft endearing audible tone. A simple yet loving, "I love you sweetheart."

She was startled that she heard the words come out of her mouth. She prayed that she had not audibly said them and that Bernard would not be confused by her declaration. Alarmed, she tried to pull away and out of his arms. "Oh my God, what did I do, why did I say that!" she desperately wanted to be anywhere but there. What would he think of her? What would he think she was trying to do? He was Brandon's cousin for God's sakes!

She just wanted out, but Bernard tightened his grip and continued to hold her. As he struggled to hold her in his arms, he prepared himself to minister the words to her that God had instructed him earlier. His next statement completely calmed her.

It was a divine on cue moment, when he whispered in her ear, "Lindy don't...please baby just listen." Although he knew he was only doing what the Lord was leading, he struggled within because of the overwhelming power of the experience. The love she had for Brandon filled the air.

Her words, although they were directed at Brandon had affected him. He fought off the struggle that originated deep within.

Those words got her complete attention and the struggle ceased. Brandon would say those exact words to her when he wanted her absolute attention so he could minister to her. She knew that it was God speaking through Bernard and she replied just above a whisper, "W-what did you say to me?"

He continued as though she had not said anything. He still held her securely but lovingly in his arms as he replied, "God is so sovereign. I came out here tonight because God told me too. He told me he was going to allow you to feel the comfort of Brandon through me. He told me at the appointed time that I was to hold you in my arms. He told me that I would instinctively know when to do it. That it would be Brandon that you felt and not me.

I struggled with God at first for both personal and obvious reasons. I told him you would probably slap my face if I said and did what he wanted me to. He said he was granting you your desire to feel your husband's heartbeat one more time. To once more hear his voice and allow it to soothe you. It wasn't easy to obey God. And as I struggled to force myself to repeat the words to you, that God placed in my spirit. I knew that this must indeed be God. Because I have the utmost respect for my cousin and his wife and would never dream of the slightest disrespect to either of you. God is saying to you tonight, be comforted my beloved. Receive the gift that I give to you this night. Brandon is safe with me, but tonight, through Bernard I grant you the power of his presence. To ease your troubled heart and bring comfort to your soul."

At those words, Talinda relaxed and melted in Bernard's arms. The Holy Spirit had spoken and reassured her. She rested in the presence of God, being eased by the rhythmic thumping of Brandon's heartbeat. God was healing her from the inside out and she could feel the holes of her soul mending ever so gingerly. Her healing process had begun before the complete end had taken its course. It was so...God to give you what you need, as and sometimes often, before you even realized that you needed it. So there she stayed in Bernard's arms. She whispered her most private, personal and endearing thoughts aloud to her beloved husband. She was being comforted by the miraculous power of the Holy Spirit and said, "With God all things are possible."

Bernard stood silent in obedience and held her in his arms. He was in total awe of the God he served and the lengths he went through to bless his children. He felt the love that Talinda and Brandon had shared through her touch and tears rolled down his face. He now understood the love that Brandon spoke of about and the power of the love they shared. He silently prayed to God thanking him for his many blessings.

The presence of the Holy Spirit began to lift and Talinda looked up at Bernard as they released their embrace. There was something in his eyes that slightly unnerved her. But she smiled nevertheless as she said to him, "Thank you for allowing God to use you to bless me. It's not always easy to be obedient to the Spirit of God. I know that it was both hard and awkward for you, considering any interrupting guest may not have understood the ministry of the moment. I know that had to be in the back of your mind. But you have no idea what this meant to me. You see Bernard, Saturday morning as I sat down next to Brandon's body in the hospital morgue I struggled. I wanted to lay my head in his chest one last time and place his arms around me for comfort and listen to the soothing of his heartbeat. I wanted to hear him I say I love you one more time to me. But knowing there would be no heartbeat or voice of comfort, I couldn't do it. I didn't want to feel the nonresponsive lifeless Brandon. I didn't want that to be my final memory of him. I only vaguely remember saying how I longed for his touch, his voice, his smell and comfort just one more time. God has used you tonight to bless me and let me know that my hurt matters to him. That he hears our cry and will grant our petitions and desires. So thank you...twin."

Bernard smiled as he responded, "I could feel Brandon's presence as strongly as you could. It brought comfort and healing to me as well. It wasn't an easy task, my emotions were all over the place and it was hard to stay in the reality of things. There was just so much happening spiritually. I was so afraid you would think I was trying to come on to you and I even had to convince myself that I wasn't. But I felt that...I knew I had heard God's voice. So, I did something I rarely do when God speaks to me concerning someone so specifically...I obeyed. Too often as Christians, we second guess God's voice and divine instruction. We shrug it off as being our own thinking. We convince ourselves that the person won't understand or won't take it the right way. Or we say that they will think that we think too much of ourselves. But the truth of the matter is, most of the time when it comes to spiritual things, we don't think enough of ourselves."

Talinda sat down as she pondered Bernard's words. She knew they were all too true.

"That's so true, Bernard. Christians are so afraid of being deemed prideful they often don't know what to think of the gifts and mandates God has placed on their life. They are afraid to show confidence in who God has called them to be. Mainly, because other Christians. Who are either jealous or too lazy to establish a "revelational" relationship with God themselves. Will give them a, "who do they think they are", attitude. We can place each other in such bondage," she replied.

They sat and laughed as they shared more Brandon stories and talked about the goodness of God and his word until the sun come up.

~Chapter Twelve~

Bernard looked out over the trees as the sun made its debut bringing fresh mercies from God. Mercies they now both knew they could depend on God supplying daily in their lives, to help them make it to the other side of through. They prayed together for God to refresh their physical bodies. To give them renewed strength, because they had not entered into earthly rest that night. But had however, entered into spiritual rest.

As Bernard walked toward the sliding glass doors that lead to the kitchen he turned and beckoned for Talinda to join him. He read her thoughts and said, "Don't worry. This night was between you, God, Brandon and myself." He smiled and patted her on the shoulder as she walked by him.

"Thanks," she replied and returned his smile. "For everything."

As they entered the kitchen Helen was mindlessly milling around with what appeared to be no apparent direction or purpose. They spoke as they entered as not to startle her.

She returned the greeting, "Oh, hi you two. You're up early...but something tells me that you probably never went to bed in the first place. Roger and I both slept off and on. We tossed, turned and kept waking each other throughout the night. Either of you want anything to eat?"

Talinda was about to say no thank you, but realized to her surprise that she actually was hungry. Besides, Helen wouldn't have allowed her to go without breakfast at any rate. She replied, "Yes mom. May I just have a couple of slices of toast with a bowl of oatmeal?"

"Yeah, Auntie," Bernard echoed. "Toast and oatmeal sounds great...and safe." They all laughed at that response and knew exactly what Bernard was referring too.

Talinda laughed as she gave him a playful punch on the shoulder, "Oh you got pregnant morning sickness jokes this morning, huh? Well, I pray that when you get married and your wife is expecting. She will throw up all over you every morning."

"Oh Lindy that's terrible," Helen replied.

They all laugh at Talinda's response to Bernard. Helen lifted her head toward heaven and thanked God for the gift of laughter that truly is...she quoted, "Good for the soul."

"Amen," Talinda interjected. "And a merry heart is good like medicine."

They continued to laugh, converse and enjoy breakfast together. Helen was all of a sudden feeling quite joyous and decided to fry some bacon, scramble eggs and cut up some fresh fruit. One by one the occupants of the house came down as the fragrance of home cooking and laughter filled the air.

"Well good morning to you all," Helen sang a greeting to her husband and house guests as they entered the kitchen. "Did we wake you? I pray that you all rested at least a little. Please sit down and have some breakfast."

They sat down and all enjoyed breakfast together. The mood was so very peaceful and you could feel the approving and loving presence of the Holy Spirit, hovering over them.

As they finished the refreshing meal his wife had prepared, Roger stood and walked over to the sink with his breakfast plate. As he placed it in the sink he stated, "As much as I am enjoying the peacefulness of the Holy Spirit. We had better get started if we plan on being at the church by eleven. That way Talinda can her private moment with Brandon to......"

Talinda stood and held her hand up to respond to his comment and give time to finish chewing and swallowing her last bite of toast. She very much wanted to avoid the opportunity for anyone to read mixed signals between her and Bernard, so she didn't so much as a glanced in his direction as she said, "Thanks be to God, because He has done great things. He indeed blessed me so abundantly last night. I had my private moment with Brandon. But, we do need to get a move on before time catches up with us."

Bernard was relieved and grateful for Talinda's nonchalance toward him in her reply. He was still so very much in awe with everything that went on earlier that morning. If she would have even so much as glimmered in his direction, he is sure his expression would have spoken very loudly to everyone in the room. He just couldn't seem to shake the warm blissful feeling

149

he felt as he held her in his arms. He silently chastised himself. "Get it together Bernard, you're losing it. It wasn't about you or for you!"

Victor and Valetta eye Talinda for validity of her address. She seemed genuine in her tone and spirit, and they both inwardly thanked God for giving her peace. They had discussed the point among themselves the night before in the privacy of the Travis' guest bedroom. They were a bit unnerved about her scheduled private moment she requested with Brandon before the funeral service today. They had prayed before falling asleep that God would give her peace and closure. They were relieved, to say the least, at her positive and secure demeanor this morning.

"Hey, I just thought of something," Roger exclaimed. "I'm going to call Isaac at Serenity's Touch and see if we can have one of the family limousines to take us to the church this morning. That way after the graveside service we don't have to go back to Atlanta to our car."

"Great idea dad, why don't we take my car? That way, after the service, it will be there and the limousine won't have to make the extra trip back to Atlanta to take mom, dad and I," Talinda added.

"Yeah, those are both excellent ideas," Helen replied.

Helen stood and looked around the room. She asked Victor if he would please lead them in a prayer for God's continued strength throughout the day. That God would both bless and anoint the youth in leading the service. And, also for a special prayer for Raymond, who would be conducting Brandon's eulogy. They all held hands and stood in agreement as Victor petitioned God for the blessings of the day.

Bernard took his Aunt Helen's sedan and left as soon as he got dressed. He needed to have time to retrieve parents at the airport in Atlanta and get to the church in Decatur by eleven to meet back up with everyone before the funeral began. That way they would have a few minutes to unwind and spend a moment with his aunt and uncle and get reacquainted with Talinda's parents. They had not seen them since her and Brandon's wedding.

Roger called Isaac Thurman to make the last minute changes. He pleasantly agreed because it saved him an extra trip to Atlanta.

As Talinda was getting dressed her mother knocked on the door. She wanted to check on her to see if she needed any assistance. She assured her that she was ok, but welcomed the conversation. They talked about how it was for her at George and Daniels' memorial service and the many ways God comforted her through the process. She also warned Talinda about how she suppressed a lot of feelings and kept telling everyone she was ok when she indeed was quite the opposite. Talinda reassured her that she was genuine in her declaration. She had been comforted by the Holy Spirit.

However, she did have some uncertainty about the actual service. But assured her that nevertheless, she indeed felt God had prepared her for the day. She declared that she had complete trust in God that he would keep her. That God had given her closure last night and ministered to her inwardly on a spiritual level. That he had manifested himself and given her complete peace. There was nothing else that she needed to say to Brandon. That she had felt his heartbeat, unfeigned love for her and presence in the room with her last night.

With all that being said, Valetta was satisfied. They all came out of the bedrooms at about the same time. They joined hands once again and prayed for a safe journey before they proceeded to the funeral home.

≈

Shortly after they arrived at the church, Isaac Thurman arrived to place Brandon's casket for the service. He took meticulous care in arranging everything just so. Talinda neither avoided nor intentionally placed herself in immediate proximity of Brandon. She was in full co-youth pastor ministry mode. Making sure that everything the youth needed was in place. That the music was in order and flags, banners and streamers were properly placed around the gym.

About ten-forty-five Bernard arrived with his parents from the airport. Roger felt instant strength and reassurance from God through his brother's presence. Helen and Roger accompanied them to the gym for a private viewing of Brandon.

"Oh Helen," Teresa said. "I don't know what to say or think. Both those boy's belong to each of us. I feel like I've lost my son."

"That's because you have Teresa. Brandon was as much your son as he was mine. Just like Bernard belongs to me as well," Helen answered as they embraced each other for comfort.

Reginald was at a loss for words and all he could do was embrace his brother who all but collapsed in his arms. Roger had been doing so well. He had his moments, but He seemed to just let go when his big brother came into the room. Although he felt comfort and support and gained strength. He also felt like he could just cry in his big brother's arms that had been like a father to him all his life. Their dad had died when the boys were very young. Reginald had always played a father role in Roger's life. Although, he was only a few years older than Roger, he had always been there. It was like the child syndrome of not knowing how hurt emotionally you are, until you see your parent enter the room. Then you just lose it.

Helen and Teresa made their way to Brandon. The men were still in the hallway with Reginald comforting Roger. Teresa stroked Brandon on the cheek as she talked to him about how proud she was of him. How she was going to miss him and couldn't believe this was happening.

"Oh Helen, I keep thinking I'm going to wake up and this all would have been a nightmare," Teresa whispered though her tears.

"I know Teresa," Helen replied. "All the way to the hospital that first day I kept telling myself he is alive. There had been some terrible mistake and he is still alive. When I walked into the morgue, I totally lost it. But now, as I look at him in such a peaceful state, and know the story behind his death. I have come to terms with the fact that he is gone. He died doing what he loved, reaching the youth and sacrificing for them. Oh Teresa, God has done some tremendous things in these youth this weekend. I cannot wait for you to meet them and be a part of the love they share here. He and Talinda have done such an awesome job as youth pastors. God has visited us many times this weekend. It has been a Holy Spirit experience. I have strength I never thought I could have or walk in at a time like this. Brandon was my only child. But God has blessed him and Talinda with a baby. She is expecting and God has shared with her that it will be a boy. So we are all excited about that. She found out the same day that Brandon died. She was able to tell him before he took his last breath."

"Oh, Helen, how awesome," Teresa responded.

They were joined by the men who finally made their way to the coffin. Helen and Teresa moved back to allow the men to the forefront. Reginald just stood there and stared at Brandon. He patted his hand as silent tears stream down his face. They all four stand there comforting one another as Reginald and Teresa say their personal goodbyes to Brandon before the crowd starts to trickle in and the service begins.

Bernard does not accompany his parents into the gym. Instead, he looked for and found Talinda busy in the sanctuary with some of the youth who were just beginning to arrive. She wanted them to view Brandon's body and get over the initial shock before having to minister in the service. She had not allowed any of them to enter into the gym just yet. She was waiting to gather them all together and pray with them beforehand.

He walked up to Talinda in discussion with some of the youth. She saw him out of the corner of her eye and turned toward him which made some of the youth turn to look as well. Jessica just stood there with her mouth open in shock as do some of the other youth. Talinda introduced Bernard to them. "Hi Bernard," she said through a smile. "Okay everyone, I would like for you to meet Pastor Travis' cousin, Bernard. As you can well see, he remarkably resembles Pastor Travis. In fact, they called each other twin."

"I can see why," Jessica replied not taking her eyes off Bernard. The rest of the youth agree and declare the same. Bernard's presence bought comfort for the youth to Talinda's relief. It could easily have had the opposite effect.

"Okay guys," Talinda said to get everybody's attention. "Now, we are going to get ready to go into the sanctuary. The service starts in just under an hour at noon and guests will start arriving soon. So let's pray. Then we will enter the sanctuary together. I want you all to view and have some private time with Pastor Travis before we are bombarded with people. I don't want the start of the service to be the first time you see Brandon. So let's join hands and pray."

Bernard stood in between and held Talinda's and Jessica's hand as they formed the circle. Just before Talinda began to pray, he stopped her and asked, "Talinda, do you think it would be okay if I prayed?"

"Sure Bernard," Talinda responded somewhat surprised. "That would be fine."

"Wow...ahhh," Jessica declared. "He even sounds like Pastor Travis."

Bernard smiled without responding. He looked around the room. All eyes were on him and began to tear up anticipating the prayer about their leader from someone who looked and sounded like him.

Bernard, without giving any commands lowered head and began to pray:

Father,

We come before You, in the matchless name of Jesus Christ. God, we don't always understand Your ways. But we have learned even though our hurt and pain to trust Your ways. Because no matter how hard the hurt or the pain that we suffer, ministry is always required of us. Father, I pray now for these youth, who have been trained up by Brandon. Who have been taught the true meaning of life and sacrifice by a living example in the leader that You chose for them. God, I thank you that You will be with them as they minister on today. As they show their thanks in their way to first and foremost, You God. And secondly, to Brandon. God, You said in Your word that no greater love than this, than a man lay down his life for a friend. Father, they have witnessed a living example of that love in Your servant.

Now God bless them, keep them, and strengthen them. Give them the grace and courage to continue in the ministry that has begun in them through the gift of Your servant. Father, as we enter into the gym, surround them with Your Holy Spirit. Help them to express their grief in a healthy way. I thank you God for Minister Talinda Travis in her wisdom in guiding these youth through a troubled time as she mourns the loss of her husband. As we enter in God, we continue to place our trust in You. We will continue to praise You in all that we do, and we will love one another with a whole heart. Thank you father for Your peace in troubled times.

In Jesus most precious name,

Amen

They youth all stood silent and in tears after Bernard's benediction to the prayer. He was unsure about their reaction and turned toward Talinda. He asked, "Have I done or said something wrong?"

"No," Talinda responded. "You were just the opposite. You and Brandon are almost a carbon copy on your choice of words in prayer. It was like...like listening to Brandon for them and for me. Thank you for allowing God to use you to minister to them, just as he used you to minister to me."

With that being said Talinda turned and walked toward the gym with the youth in tow close behind her. All the Travis's still stood around the coffin talking when the youth entered. When they saw them, they moved to the side to make room for them to come closer. They all began to move closer, together, very slowly. Some started to cry aloud, some stopped in their tracks and dropped to their knees crying. The adults started to assist Talinda in ministering to them. Raymond stayed behind. No one seemed to notice that he had not advanced past the entryway.

It was just as Talinda thought it would be. It was one thing to hear your leader had passed away. But it's quite another to have it manifested into reality. They were getting their personal time in, crying and praying to God about their leader. They were all getting it out and Talinda was relieved that they were coming to grips with it. She was glad she had given them this time with Brandon before the service began. Finally, she looked up and noticed that Raymond stood back in the doorway facing outward. He had not turned toward or made any advancement in the direction of the coffin that held his fallen leader. She walked to the back to talk to him. She tried to no avail to get Raymond to turn around to look at Brandon from a distance. Much less make any advancement toward him. She and Brandon had all but adopted him and he knew Brandon and Talinda as mom and dad. He had not only lost his leader but the only man he knew as father as well. He couldn't get past the thought of the sacrifice Brandon made for him. Talinda was dumbfounded as for what to do when Bernard walked up. He touched Raymond on the shoulder and started to talk to him.

"Hey Raymond," he said ever so softly as he gently gave him a loving squeeze. "I know what you're going through. I know how you're feeling."

Raymond cut him off and leaned forward which pulled Bernard's hand from his shoulder. With somewhat of an angry but low tone, he said, "No...no you don't. There is no way on God's green earth that you could remotely know how I feel right now, so please spare me. I thought I was ready for this...but, I'm not...I'm not. Oh God, please!"

Bernard answered with a graceful tone, "Oh...but I do know how you feel Raymond. This isn't the first time Brandon has put himself in danger to save a youth. He did it for me almost thirteen years ago."

Talinda was stunned, she just stood there and listened unable to move or say a word.

Raymond turned toward Bernard and said, "What do you mean?"

"Well," Bernard continued after clearing his throat. "He took a couple of bullets for me shortly after I graduated from high school. I'm sure Mrs. Travis can attest to the scars he has both on his right side and inner left thigh."

Talinda was in awe. Brandon had never told her how he got the scars on his left thigh or right side just below his rib cage. She shook her head in affirmation as Raymond looked at her for confirmation to what Bernard had just said.

"Brandon was always the good twin," Bernard continued with a slight chuckle. "Although, I always had very good grades in school, I was always trying to prove myself. I got hooked up with the wrong crowd and was trying to be a so called mini dope dealer. Well, one day my mom found some in my room and flushed it down the toilet. Not knowing that on the streets if you cannot produce the money or the dope to your dealer, you paid out of your hide. Brandon went with me to try to talk to them. But they weren't up for conversation and pulled a gun. Brandon...," he paused. He shook his head in an attempt to fight back tears, "...Brandon rushed in front of me. He pushed me and the bullets hit him. They went straight through him and never touched me. Brandon thought quickly on his feet and pulled me down as he fell. He landed on top of me. He whispered for me to close my eyes and be still as we went down. The dealer, thinking he had killed the both of us, ran off. After he left, I said okay twin that was good thinking. I didn't realize until he rolled over off me and blood was everywhere that he had actually been shot. We almost lost him. The paramedics arrived as he was fading out and they were able to revive him and get him to intensive care. After Brandon recovered, I promised him that I

156

would never put myself or him in that situation again. I owed him my life. I went off to the Air Force Academy after that and dedicated my life to serve my country and keep my promise to twin. He later led me to the Lord and I've been going strong for God every since. Raymond, that's what Brandon does, he sacrifices so others may live. If not you, it would have been someone else. Just thank God it was you. And because of it, now you know firsthand what the gift of life is. Now, the best way to thank him is to minister to the people he loved and sacrificed for today, and to carry on in the faith."

Talinda was in total amazement. Her mind raced back to the night Brandon died. If only the paramedics had been five minutes earlier...maybe. "Stop it, Talinda!" She thought. "You said you were going to trust God. Don't start second guessing everything now. You've come to grips with the fact Brandon has run his course...now just stay on yours."

She wasn't the only one amazed. Helen and Teresa had joined them and were just as shocked and amazed as Talinda was. This was the first time they had heard the whole truth about what happened to Brandon that night. He had made Bernard promise to say it was a robbery attempt so his mother wouldn't feel guilty about the incident. Talinda was so in awe her God and the servant he had blessed her to share a life with, for so short a time.

Raymond wiped his tears and began to move forward toward Brandon. With each step, he appeared to gain strength until he stood at Brandon's right side. Bernard stopped Talinda from advancing toward Raymond. He grabbed her by the arm and pulled her back to him and said, "No. He needs this moment alone. Whatever he is going to say needs to be between him, Brandon and God...trust me."

Talinda hesitantly nodded in agreement with teary eyes and leaned into Bernard's chest. They all gave Raymond his time with his mentor...his father. She wanted to be there for him, but agreed that this was the Holy Spirit's mission. Bernard placed one arm around her for comfort and breathed in deeply. Despite all the many times God had used and blessed him with the words and deeds to say, he fought a silent battle that raged on the inside of him.

Raymond was now ready and the youth were recovered and held up remarkably well. It was as though they were in total understanding with God about it. They now just wanted to please their Master and Savior. By representing Him and the mentor He had entrusted their well-being to, to the best of their ability. And, they would entrust the rest to the Holy Spirit.

The youth took their places as the service was about to begin.

~Chapter Thirteen~

One by one, the guests arrived and the gym began to fill at a rapid pace. They were all thankful that they had the mind to move the service from the worship sanctuary. The size of the room, was not the initial motivation behind it their action. They simply wanted to say goodbye to their leader in their sanctuary. But now, they were beginning to understand the magnitude of lives Brandon had touched in his brief life span on this earth. The church worship sanctuary would not have even come close to holding everyone. As it was, the gym was going to be put to the test of maximum occupancy.

The music to Brandon's favorite song began to play as the service began. The first ten rows on the left side that were reserved for close family and friends proved to be nowhere near enough. Talinda had requested for her nurse and new found friend Veronica to accompany the family, in case she should need her for anything during the service. Pastor Tills had asked everyone to please wait until the end of the service to come forward to view the body and give their personal condolences to the family. Everyone politely obliged. They came in and took their seats so the service could begin.

He and Beatrice took their seats on the front row with Talinda, her and Brandon's parents, aunt, uncle and Bernard. As the song repeated itself, that was Jessica's cue to begin her ministry in dance. She danced and worshipped God with all her might. At times throughout the performance, it was hard for her to hear the music through the many Hallelujah shouts. God was divinely showing himself through her ministry of sound and drama. His healing presence manifested in the room.

159

The garment Talinda had chosen for her glistened with the lights bouncing off the many sequins that decked the handkerchief style dress that she ministered in. She was completely lost in the Holy Spirit. It was as though she and God were the only two in the building. The angel wing flags she used in the performance were majestic and flowed ever so freely. Talinda knew all too well the power and the presence of God that often fell in the room through dance, and she sat in awe of Jessica.

She had never seen her minister to this magnitude and knew that her dance would never be the same again. She remembered the moment in her life that God had taken her dance to a new level. Jessica was personally experiencing God. As her dance came to a close, she knelt in front of Talinda and expressed her gratitude to God first and then her leaders. She rose to a cheering crowd that thanked and magnified the Lord. Jessica kissed Talinda on the cheek and whispered a word of thanks to her, for her and Brandon and their sacrifice to the youth. Talinda could only nod, because she was full emotionally and at a total loss for words.

The youth continued with a short drama presentation of Brandon's favorite skit they would minister from time to time titled "The Light in the Window." Brandon himself had written the skit. It was about allowing your light to shine, even when someone has to see it through the window. The theme was that you don't always have to be near a person for your light to shine. A lot of times, he often said, you minister more to someone at a distance. People are watching you wherever you go and across a crowded room, someone will notice your response to a trying situation. Will you past the test? The final line in the play said, "Will you represent God well?" But today the youth added to the closing line of the play. They all stood hand in hand across the front. They faced the crowd and looked up toward heaven. They all said in unison, "PASTOR TRAVIS, WE WILL PASS THE TEST. WE WILL MAKE YOU PROUD. WE WILL HONOR YOUR SACRIFICE, WITH OUR OBEDIENCE AND DEDICATION TO THE MINISTRY. THANK YOU. WE LOVE YOU. AND, WE WILL MISS YOU." They bowed to cheers and a standing ovation. The crowd was in awe of the performance of the youth thus far.

Three youth that were chosen to pray, read one of Brandon's favorite scriptures, and one of his favorite poems. They all spoke clearly and added their personal "Minister Travis" story.

Raymond had been sitting there praying silently to God to be with him, as he ministered before the crowd about his youth pastor and father. It was now time for him to deliver the eulogy. Just as he stood to walk to the podium, a teen walked up the isle and stood in front of Brandon. She was not a member of the church, and none of the youth appeared to know who she was. She motioned for Raymond to please give her a minute. She wept and thanked God for Brandon. As she turned, Veronica gasped...it was her niece, Sarah Carter.

All eyes were on her and you could hear some of the youth as they whispered and asked who she was. She cleared her throat and began to speak. With all of the attention on Sarah, no one noticed a young tattooed gentleman enter the back of the gym and have a seat on the back row. Sarah looked down and then up began to speak. "I know that it is probably safe to say that none of you here know me. I've been sitting here listening to all the wonderful things you all have said about Pastor Travis. Well, when I met him he wasn't Pastor Travis. He wasn't even a minster or anything like that. What he was to me was a savior. I know some of you may think that's blasphemy. But you have to understand what I mean by savior. He was there for me when I was only eight or nine years old and tragedy struck my life. I lost my father and mother in the same day; one to death and the other...to prison." The crowd was perfectly silent and Veronica hung on her every word. As she sat there tears streamed down her face. Partly, because she was happy to see her niece and to know that she was alive and well. The other reason was that right in front of her manifested a reminder of how selfish she had been.

Sarah continued, "I know that I am holding up your program. But when I saw what happened in the newspaper, I knew for some reason I was supposed to be here. I fought the idea of coming because I thought that I wouldn't belong. You guys are all a part of his ministry and know Pastor Travis very well. But if it had not been for his counseling, I wouldn't have made it through the ordeal. He helped me to not blame myself and made sure that I got placed into a foster family that loved God. He would always come by to check on me and never pressured me about anything. He just loved me and showed me God. I'm not surprised to see the youth of this church performing the service today. A few years ago, I was placed in foster care here in Atlanta and I lost touch with him. But by that time, I was secure in my relationship with God. Somehow, I knew he would become a youth pastor. He had a real thing for God and His children. Troubled children like me..." she paused to wipe away tears that fell from her eyes as she talked. "...Children who feel hopeless in their situations. He was the real thing and through him I learned to trust God. Well, thank you for your time," she turned toward Brandon and finished her sentence. "And thank you...Pastor Travis." With that being said, she returned to her seat. You could hear praises to God for the ministry of his servant and she returned to sit down.

Raymond finally made his approach to the podium. He pushed the microphone down and away from him and turned it off. He had the hands free microphone clipped to his collar. He cleared his throat and began to speak. He paused, because his attention was drawn to the back of the gym. Quavis realized that Raymond had spotted him. He stood and prepared to run, but Raymond's first words arrested him and instead he sat back down in his seat.

Raymond took a deep breath and began, "Forgive and it shall be forgiven you. That was one of my fathers...of Youth Pastor Travis' favorite sayings. He had so many that he taught." He paused and looked down at the notes he had prepared. He shook his head and smiled as though having a conversation with someone who was not there. He tore them in half and let them fall to the ground. There was silence. He looked back up at the audience and said, "You know one of the many things that Pastor Travis taught us was to trust the God in us and learn to follow his leading. Ever since mom...," he and Talinda locked eyes and shared a smile on those words. He then continued, "I mean Co-Youth Pastor Talinda Travis, asked me to speak today I had been jotting down little things that I wanted to remember to say. But now that I stand here, they seem insignificant. So, I'm just going to talk about the Brandon Travis that I know and love; the Brandon Travis that laid his life down for a friend; the Brandon Travis that chose to give up everything for my freedom."

Raymond's words were heart felt by everyone in the room. But had the most effect on the lone guest sitting on the back row. He had Quavis' undivided attention. Raymond could hear the words of his leader ringing in his ears. And so, he continued in the direction that God was leading him.

Talinda raised her hand in praise mode, thanking God for the growth in Raymond and all the youth. She was so proud of them and sat there thinking how proud Brandon would be at this very moment. To see them blossom and flow in the spirit. She gave Raymond a smile that let him know he was on the right track and God was well pleased.

Taking cue from his leadership he continued, "I remember the first day that I stumbled, literally, across Pastor's path. I was in small time trouble with small time people. My coaches would always tell me that there was another way. For years I ignored them. I eventually dropped out of school and got into more and more trouble. It didn't take long before my small time people grew into big time people. I woke up one day and realized I didn't want to do this anymore. My intention was to take the gun that I had gotten from the leader of the gang that I had joined called the Knights. Find a quiet place in the park and blow my brains out. I didn't want to do it at home, just in case one of the neighborhood kids would find me before my mother would. I ran through the park looking behind me. Gang life makes you a very paranoid person and I was felt that someone was following me. Well, I ran right smack into Pastor Travis and now, someone really was following me." He paused because his statement drew respectful laughter. He continued, "He saw that I had a gun and took off behind me. He spent almost the whole night with me in the park. There were several times when I threatened to shoot him because he just wouldn't go and leave me to my business. It's like he could read my mind...he knew I didn't want to kill myself. But I knew that death was the only way out of the Knights."

Talinda shook her head in agreement as she remembered the night that Brandon called. He said that he probably wouldn't be home but that he was alright and would tell her all about it in the morning. She remembered how scared Raymond looked when he walked through the door of their home for the first time. Brandon was exhausted, but in such high spirits and he was operating on pure adrenaline.

Raymond looked up from the pulpit at Talinda and smiled. She returned the smile and they shared a silent private moment in a room full of people. Raymond continued, "Needless to say, I didn't kill myself. Pastor spent almost every day with me for the next six months. I was so overcome with emotion the day I gave my life to the Lord. He stood up in church and said..." at this thought Raymond lost it and Talinda began a silent prayer for him through her own tears.

He gathered himself enough to speak. He choked occasionally, but continued, "...He stood up in church and said...Praise be unto God, who sits...who sits on the throne...because this day...this day...this day my son...my son Raymond...has given his life to the Lord...and now we get to share life together in eternity...forever. No one, including my biological father had ever called me son and meant it. I had never been anybody's son. I was always just...just Raymond. But that day, I learned what it meant to be a son and a child of God. I learned what it felt like to have a father. Someone I knew wouldn't judge me and who would always be there for me. I was at their house so much that they threatened to put me on their W-4, and finally just set up a bedroom for me. They bought me all new furniture and everything." That statement brought laughter into the room again.

"You see," he continued. "Pastor was not just a man with a lot of words...he was a man with a lot of love." Raymond walked down off the podium and stood in front of the casket. Looked down at Brandon and said, "I'm going to miss you dad, I felt so lost this weekend." Talinda shifted in her seat as she resisted the urge to go to Raymond's side to comfort him. She shed tears of understanding for her son. She too, had been lost at times throughout the weekend. She continued to pray silently for him.

He continued on, "But then the comforter that you said would come...came...and I..." he struggled through his tears. But was determined that he would finish. He mustered the strength and said, "...I understand dad...I understand. I love you and will continue your mantle. I will pick up my cross and walk in your mantle to......."

Even though they had not rehearsed nor included this in the program. The youth all stood because they the words that Raymond was about to say. It was their motto they recited at the benediction of every youth rally. They spoke in unison with Raymond as he continued, "...Reach the lost at all cost, compelling the youth to breakthrough."

Raymond turned and saw that all the youth had stood with him. He wiped his tears he beckoned for them all to come forward. All together they declared, "PASTOR OUR, JOURNEY WITH YOU ON THIS SIDE OF CREATION HAS COME TO AN END. THE BEST WAY WE CAN SHOW OUR LOVE AND APPRECIATION FOR THE LIFE HAVE SHARED AND SACRIFICED FOR US. IS TO PROMISE YOU, THAT WE WILL MAKE DISCIPLES AND WE WILL SEE YOU AGAIN. WE LOVE YOU PASTOR BRANDON...THANK YOU OFR OUR LIFE!

The church went up in a high praise at the benediction of the service. They began to magnify the Lord as the youth sang Pastor Brandon's favorite praise and worship song.

As they sang the song, Quavis stood in the back and tears rolled down is face. So many things that Raymond said, had seared his heart. He didn't know why, but he felt compelled to be there that day. He was amazed at the scene that unfolded. He even more amazed that no one had even looked for him in connection Brandon's death as of yet.

As Raymond delivered the words about his fallen leader, Quavis shed tears because he himself had traveled that same path. Although he didn't kill himself either, he had not heeded the wisdom of the one who convinced him not to kill himself. Out of fear, he went on to get deeper and deeper involved with gang life. For the first time, he wished that he would have taken the advice eight years ago when he was just fifteen. Advice from a college football player who was home visiting his family on break from the University of Georgia in Athens. He was a star running back, who had recently himself, given his life to the Lord. He ran into Quavis behind the bleachers at the high school football field holding a gun to his head and talked him out of it. He tried to no avail to get young Quavis to give God a chance. Quavis had been running from God and replaced his fear with anger and vengeance; vengeance against a father who never knew him, simply because he didn't want the responsibility of being a father; vengeance against a drug dependent mother who lost him to the court system, never to return to find him. But now his anger and vengeance seemed meaningless. Here he stood, full of regret. For the first time in his thug-filled gang life, he had remorse for someone who had lost their life at his hands. He looked down at his hands. He turned them palm facing up and said loud enough that only he himself would hear, "...so much blood...so much blood." There was no sense of pride for him in this one. Brandon's God had gotten his attention.

He held up his hand to say don't or stop to Raymond, who had begun to head in his direction and left the room. Talinda noticed that something or someone in the back of the room had Raymond's attention. She turned in just enough time to see a teary eyed Quavis has he left building. She turned and mouthed to Raymond, "Another time."

~Chapter Fourteen~

Raymond moved to sit next to Talinda as he announced that the procession would immediately follow the power point presentation. Although they had a large crowd today, time was not a factor. Everyone would get the opportunity to pass through the precession, to pay their final respects to Brandon and the Travis family.

Everyone took their seats as the presentation started. Brandon's life and ministry was put together in a slide presentation to a medley of some of his favorite music. As the last slide played, the screen dulled and the procession of people started to flow through.

Veronica leaned forward and asked Talinda how she was feeling. She replied that she was okay considering.

They had not realized just how many people were actually in the gym until the procession started. They were literally there for two hours to grant everyone the opportunity to say their goodbyes and pay their respects to the family. Talinda was overwhelmed at the love and respect that the city had for Brandon. He had touched more lives than she ever could have imagined. At least more than half of them had given cards to the family.

As the last person took their seat, the family rose to have a final viewing of Brandon before this final chapter of his life would be closed for ever. All but Talinda, she could feel the strength drain from her body. She had been fine until this moment. Although she knew that Brandon had long left this shell and was with the Lord. It was all she had left and now she had to part with it forever. So she sat and watched as Brandon's parents and close relatives bid their final farewell to their beloved Brandon.

It was as though all eyes were on her. She sat glued to her seat. They were originally scheduled to take their cue from her as to when they should close the coffin. But Talinda was frozen in place. Raymond stood alone at the coffin and turned to face Talinda. Then, as though he were on a slow moving escalator, Raymond approached and knelt in front of her. With tears in his eyes he whispered to her, "Mom...it's time. It's time to say goodbye."

Only those sitting on the nearby seats could hear Raymond's words. Bernard stood to help Talinda to her feet but Raymond politely told him, "Thanks...but I think I should be the one to take my mother, to say goodbye to my father."

Bernard nodded in agreement as Raymond held his hand out to assist Talinda to view Brandon one last time. She looked up into his tear-stained eyes and rose to her feet. She knew she had to do this. For Raymond...she needed to. They stood there together and looked down at Brandon with their arms around one another for strength.

Raymond whispered similar words she had heard the night before come out of Bernard's mouth, words of promise. He looked down at Brandon as he touched his chest and said, "I promise dad. I'm going to take care of mom. I'll be there for her and my little brother...I will." He kissed Talinda on the cheek and left her there alone at the coffin.

Talinda stood with no concern that every eye in the building was on her. She felt so utterly alone in a room full of people. Because she knew that from this day forth, the one she beheld would not be there. She leaned over, kissed his cheek, stroked his face and through tears of pain said, "Goodbye my love...until eternity, goodbye." She turned and headed to the isle to exit the room. She had no desire to witness the closing of the coffin on her and Brandon's life. And, she did not want to walk behind it.

She held out her hand to Raymond and said, "Son. Come and take momma to the car." As Raymond escorted Talinda out, they could hear the soft laments of the family members as they closed the coffin. She realized she had chosen wisely. She and Raymond exited the building to the family car that waited just outside the doors of the church.

They sat in the car and waited for the processional to exit the church. As the coffin came by the car they were in, Talinda kissed her hand and put it up to the window of the limousine.

The men's ministry staff was assigned to be the pall bearers. Pastor Tills had not wanted to put the emotional strain of that assignment upon the youth.

The family requested that because there were so many visitors present, that only close friends accompany them to the graveside.

Veronica stopped at Talinda's car as Brandon's parents were getting in and asked her again if she were okay. She assured her once again that she was fine considering. She then asked if it were okay for her to ask Sarah to come to the graveside. Talinda smiled and said, "Sure...do you need me to approach her for you or will you be okay."

"I'm just going to tell her that you would like for her to be at the graveside and she can ride in the car with me, since I'm driving," Veronica nervously replied.

"Don't worry," Talinda reassured her. "God will give you the words to say during the forty-five minute drive to the way the graveside."

"I know he will. Thanks again for everything you and Brandon have done over the years. And all that I know you will continue to do," Veronica replied as she clutched Talinda's hand for silent support. She turned to go find Sarah before the processional left for the graveside. But to her amazement, when she turned to look for her, Sarah was almost standing on top of her. She stood and watched as the scene unfolded with a "longing to be a part" look on her face.

Veronica cautiously tapped her on the shoulder and said, "Sarah, Talinda wanted to know if you would like to be among company attending the graveside service for Pastor Travis. She wanted all the youth whose lives he had affected to be a part of it. You may ride in the car with me if you like."

Sarah seemed to light up at the idea that she would be allowed to be a part of the private ceremony. With tears in her eyes, she nodded her head in affirmation. Veronica pointed her in the direction of her car. Unknowing to Veronica, Sarah knew who she was. She actually contemplated whether she should approach Veronica, when she walked up to her with Talinda's invitation. She had lost her nerve and feared rejection. She was about turn to walk away when Veronica tapped her on the shoulder.

Veronica took an inward moment to ask God for wisdom and guidance about how proceed with revealing to Sarah the real reason she was in her car. They sat and waited for all the cars to get in line for the procession to the graveside. She took a deep breath and began, "Sarah, I'm not really sure exactly what or how to say this. So, I'm just going to come right out with it."

Sarah sat and waited to see what her aunt would reveal to her. Still afraid of rejection, she braced herself for the worst-case scenario. Something she had grown very accustomed to.

"You were probably too young when everything happened with your mom and dad to remember much of anything," she stated. She paused to see what, if there would be, a reaction from Sarah to mind her own business about her mother and father. Sarah continued to sit quietly and so Veronica continued. "You see Sarah, I know the state advised against you having contact with family, so you...," she stumbled over her words. She felt the futile attempt to get them to exit her mouth in fashion that would deem her to appear less selfish, failing to say the least. She finally just blurted it out. "The truth is Sarah, I'm your aunt. Your mother was...is...my sister. I have no excuse to give you for not fighting for you other than my being very selfish at that time. Then when I wanted to try to find you, I was told that it was advised against any of us to try to be a part of your life. So again, I didn't fight. I'm so sorry for that. I know you probably hate everyone that has anything to do with that time of your life. But if you would allow me too, I would like the oppor......"

Sarah put her hand out to stop her aunt as the tears welled up and fell from her eyes. "You don't have to do this Aunt Ronie. I know who you are. I was glad when I looked out and saw you in the seats during the service today. I knew an accidental meeting would be the only way we would probably meet. I don't hold any grudges against you. The main thing Mr. Travis taught me was to forgive. To forgive first myself, that it wasn't my fault. Then my family, so I could have peace. I knew when you asked me to ride with you, that you knew who I was. I knew it wasn't about the graveside service. I hoped and prayed that you wanted to get know me. I want to be a part of my real family's life. I've been from foster care to foster care and while the ones I have been in have been nice people. I was never in any of them long enough to feel like I belonged..." she dropped her head in her hands and began to weep. "...I just wanted to belong. To be with family...real family...my own family."

Veronica wanted to reply but could only cry because no sound would come out her mouth. Aunt Ronie was a name she hadn't been called for eight or nine years. She swallowed hard to get the lump in her throat to ease up enough for her to

169

speak. She reached out and grabbed Sarah's hand and said, "You are with family now. I promise you don't ever have to be without family again. Sarah, I am so sorry that you have grown up most of your life in the same city with family and without your family at the same time. Thank you for not being angry with me...I have felt so guilty."

They leaned across the gear shift and embraced. They held each other and cried until a rap on the window startled them. The funeral director gave them the flag to put in their window and let them know the processional was about to begin. The cars were all in place and the hearse was prepared to exit the church grounds. They gathered themselves, wiped their tears and prepared to move.

Southern people were so respectful of funeral processions. Knowledge of Brandon's death and funeral services had spread throughout the city. Many people paid their respects and held up banners saying "We'll miss you Minister Travis". Others said "Fallen hero". But all showed the love and appreciation that the city had for Youth Pastor Brandon Travis. Talinda was speechless at the support along the route out of town as they made their way to the interstate headed towards Athens to the graveside. She had never known all the lives her husband had touched. And realized she would never just how many there had been on this side of creation.

Bernard watched in awe as well. "Wow twin," he said to himself. "You were a well-respected and powerful man of God who touched many lives and loved to the death." The thoughts he had about Talinda the night before, caused him to ponder how any man could ever have a heart big enough to fill those shoes.

The graveside service was far more intense than the actual memorial service. It was an eternal moment as you watched your loved one lowered to the surface of the ground. It sent chills through you that were hard to shake. Talinda sat, with Raymond on her right side and Bernard on her left. Bernard's parents were on his immediate left and Brandon's parents to Raymond's immediate right. Talinda's parents stood behind them. Talinda held Raymond's head on her shoulder and he cried silent tears as he whispered over and over, "Ministry is always required." It was he father's favorite quote.

Pastor and first Lady Tills performed the graveside ceremony. He spoke words from the heart in lieu of one of the ceremonial prepared speeches in the minister's handbook. Talinda was very much in awe of how everyone just followed the spirit of God. Brandon just kept on bringing out the best in people, even after his departure from this life.

Because of the pressure of the atmosphere and the fact the he knew Talinda was expecting and probably running on empty, he kept the service short. The Travis' had decided they would forego the ceremonial re-pass at the church. They wanted it to end at the graveside. They were exhausted and all secretly worried about Talinda's well-being. They just wanted to go home and do nothing. They had made plans before-hand for the family and the youth department at the Travis' house in Athens for a BBQ the next day.

Just as they planned earlier, Talinda and her parents would remain in Decatur at her house tonight so there would room at the Travis home for Bernard's parents. They would meet at the church at 11a.m. the next day to transport the youth back to Athens. Pastor Tills and another minister volunteered drive the church vans. Talinda and her parents would lead the way to the Travis' house.

Pastor Tills closed out and people still milled around. Some retrieved a memento flower from atop the family assortment on Brandon's coffin. Valetta took meticulous care to take two of every flower in the assortment. She had planned to prepare a scrapbook page in remembrance of Brandon for Talinda who sat and continued to minister to Raymond. His ability to say the final goodbye to his father had proven to be more difficult than that of delivering the eulogy. Bernard assisted her with Raymond.

Helen walked over to Pastor Tills to thank him. "This is exactly how Brandon would have wanted it," she said. The moment was about to overtake her emotionally but she managed to pull it together. Pastor Tills could only nod in agreement. She went on to say, "Thanks again, for taking such good care of my family. Brandon always spoke so highly of you both. I pray that we won't be strangers after this. We look forward to see you all tomorrow at the BBQ. Talinda and her parents are driving back to Atlanta after retrieving her car from the funeral home. You can follow them to the highway. Most of these back roads are unidentified and it can get rather tricky if you are not familiar with the territory."

"Thank you, but it has been our honor to have Brandon a part of our lives," Pastor Tills replied.

"They will also bring our other car back from the church that

Bernard drove to pick up his parents earlier today from the airport," Helen added.

The graveside service concluded and they all prepared to leave. One by one final goodbyes are said until Talinda and Raymond stood alone with Brandon. Raymond, now more in control of his emotions, looked up and beckoned to Talinda as he pointed across the graveyard. Standing at a distance, they see Quavis. He stood and observed the ceremony from across the courtyard. He dropped his head when he realized he is noticed by them. They sense that he also, wanted or needed a private moment with Brandon. They say their final goodbye and return to the family car.

Raymond was amazed that he would not only come to the funeral but would drive to Athens to the graveside to be there for the final service. He had been following the news and daily newspaper to know where the services would be held. Raymond knew this was not normal for him and pondered Quavis' actions in his heart. As they drove away, everyone in every car was silent, meditating in the events of the day. Raymond looked out the window as they drove away and noticed Quavis had walked over to his dads' graveside. He whispered in Talinda's ear so they wouldn't draw the attention of the other occupants. She gave Raymond a knowing smile. Raymond wanted to stop the car to watch Quavis' actions, not being as trusting as Talinda was. But she insisted that they leave him alone. She had felt in her spirit that this would be a turning point in his life and they didn't have to worry about his motive in being there. Raymond rested in his mother's words and once again laid his head on her shoulder for comfort.

Bernard watched them and marveled at the maternal connection they had with each other. Other than the obvious racial difference, it would have been impossible to believe that she and Brandon were not his biological parents. The love was genuine and powerful. The fire inside of him kindled as he watched how she nurtured him. Her touch soothed him and brought peace. Despite that fact that she hurt, she placed his needs in front of her own. They had a connection to spoke volumes to each other, without a single word audibly exchanged between them. He could wonder how powerful to connection between her and Brandon had been. He knew his thoughts concerning her were unhealthy and he forced himself to close his eyes, tilt his head back in an attempt to clear his mind.

172

Quavis stood there, over Brandon's grave and watched everyone drive out of sight. He turned his attention back to the grave workers and watched what the family could not bear to see. As he stood there, his mind raced back over the events of Friday night. Brandon had, without hesitation, given his life for Raymond. Tears fell from his eyes as the last scoop of dirt was placed on top of the coffin and he whispered, "What kind of love is this?" He then turned and walked away.

~Chapter Fifteen~

The youth were all enjoying themselves at the BBQ. The women stood on the deck looked out over the yard. Helen turned to Talinda and said, "This was a really good idea Talinda. Yesterday was very tense for everyone and no one would have enjoyed the food any way. We would have been eating out of sheer necessity. But now, they can do what Brandon has taught them to do. They can celebrate life."

Beatrice chimed in, "Yes, Helen I agree. I think as Christians we get too stuck in tradition instead of following the leading of the Holy Spirit."

Talinda in total agreement replied, "I agree. Yesterday, I was past exhaustion emotionally, physically and spiritually. I just wanted some down time. It was good to go home where no one expected anything from me. I could just do nothing without a ton of people watching me. I felt like a test tube baby most of the day. I was so grateful that I had alone time with Brandon before the funeral to grieve the way I wanted to. I was very surprised at my reaction when I returned home. I thought it would be awkward that first night home after his memorial. But I felt so comforted. I think sheer exhaustion may have had its hand in it also."

She paused briefly as she looked out over the Travis' backyard at all the youth engaged in various activities. She continued, "But look at them all. They are enjoying themselves. Of course, they miss Brandon and his presence is missed. But they are able to talk about him today as they share and enjoy telling the stories of the things he has taught them."

Talinda took a deep breath and again, looked out over the scene. Every game table was occupied. The boys were on the

174

basketball court. Some girls and boys at the volley ball nets and electronic game wars were being played. Veronica was there, as well as Sarah. Talinda was elated when Veronica shared with her how smooth the transition had been for them the day before. Sarah seemed to blend in well with the rest of the youth. It was as though she had been here all along. They made particular notice to include her and make her feel welcome. "They have been taught so well," she thought.

Bernard walked up out of breath and sweaty. Through his deep breaths he declared, "Whew, not as young as I used to be. Those young bucks had me on the run there for a minute. But I got the last shot in to win the game for my team."

"Lucky shot old man!" Raymond yelled in a teasing and sarcastic tone as he threw the ball in his direction. "Double or nothing...or do you need a geritol break?"

The ladies laughed and looked at Bernard for his reaction. Well, he was not going decline a challenge by these young bucks and so, threw the ball back at Raymond. He exclaimed in no uncertain terms, "Geritol...I'll show you geritol my young Palawan."

Everyone burst into to laughter. Raymond replied, "On the court old man...on the court." Before Bernard could reply he ran off toward the driving in between two or three player toward the net.

Bernard followed but not before he turned to the ladies and said, "What have I gotten myself into?"

Helen smiled and said, "It is good to see Bernard interact with them. They are so drawn to him, and it's not just because he looks so much like Brandon anymore. He has showed them that he really cared about them. Not only that he could and would minister to them. He also put himself on their level making a silent statement that he was no better than they were. Youth always appreciate action ministry. We spend enough classroom time with them. Sometimes you have to just let your hair down and cut a rug with them. That's the ministry they will remember and respect, that's why Brandon was so good with them."

"Yes, Helen, I agree. Brandon and Bernard are alike in almost every way. They both love and have a heartbeat for the youth. They both know how to reach and bring out the best in them. The youth are both comfortable with them and have the utmost respect for their authority as well," Teresa interjected.

175

Valetta shook her head in affirmation and added, "As I stand her and watch them play basketball. I marvel at God and eternity. Even though we know Brandon is gone. He will never really be gone. I see him in every face out here today. His love is reflected all over the place." She looked at Talinda smiling and said, "And manifested in others."

They laugh as Valetta pats Talinda's stomach. They were glad that everyone could be at such peace today and thanked God for his peace that passes understanding.

The ball ended up down in the woods and one of the youth went to retrieve it. As Bernard turned his attention to back toward the house and Talinda, he was caught staring by Raymond. "She is beautiful, isn't she," Raymond said.

"What?" Bernard inquired.

Raymond replied, "My mom...Talinda, I see how you look at her. I mean you're trying hard not to but you can't help it. I know you feel guilty because of my dad and you guys being like brothers and all. You know Mr. Travis; I have a confession to make. I knew who you were before mom introduced you to us. Dad told me about you. He said you two were like twins or something and you were very special to him. He said he trusted you with his life and his most prized possessions. He said you would be faithful to us and be here for us."

Bernard didn't know how to respond. He was absolutely speechless. He had tried so hard to hide his feelings and he had been found out by an almost seventeen year old kid. Who he realized, was not so much a kid as he thought. He smiled and said, "Your mother is very beautiful and also very fragile right now. I worry about her. Your dad was right. I will be here for the both of you and you can count on me."

Some of the other guys on the court walked over and Jonathan says, "Is it really true that you fly the fighter jets for the Air Force?"

"Yes," Bernard replied. "I fly F-22's based overseas."

"Wow," Troy interjected. "What a neat job."

Bernard replied smiling. "Yeah, I guess it is pretty neat."

Raymond joins in, "My dad said that it was pretty demanding on your body. I mean, going so fast all the time. He said you guys have special suits you have to wear."

"He's right," Bernard responded. "The suits are fit exactly to your body and regulate your temperature, vital signs and oxygen levels. They can tell when a pilot is in trouble and it automatically releases the precise right amount of oxygen to

176

ensure the pilot remains conscious. The g-force pressure on your body is very taxing. You have to stay in pretty good shape, because I like I said, it's a lot of pressure."

"Wow," Jonathan remarked. "That's just too cool. I guess college isn't such a bad idea after all."

"No," Bernard replied with a chuckle. "Nah. Not a bad idea at all."

Troy asked him, "So like, will you fly for Delta or someone whenever you get out of the Air Force?"

Bernard smiled and he responded, "Probably not. Delta doesn't come close to comparing to the thrill of piloting a fighter jet. I'm afraid that it would probably be too boring."

"I know right," Raymond said as they shared in a laugh. The ball came flying back onto the court.

Bernard went back to join the game and Raymond went over to Talinda and asked could he have a moment with her. She obliged and they went to one of the nearby picnic tables under a tree and sit to talk.

"Why do I feel like I know what you are about to say Raymond," Talinda said as she eyed him with curiosity.

He smiled. She knew him well. He looked down and played with his fingers. He then looked up into her eyes, "Mom, what do we do about Quavis? I mean, I was shocked to say the least yesterday at his presence. He was the last person I expected to be anywhere near dad's funeral. He has never had any remorse about a single person who has died at his hands or anyone else's for that matter. He just never seemed to have any respect for life. Mom, as much as I want to be angry with him I find myself feeling nothing but sorrow for how heavy his heart must be. He has several murders to carry on his shoulders, but something about dad's got to him. It's like it made his load unbearable. I thought the cops would have picked him by now, but I remember that you requested they let it go till after the funeral. In the past, people had been too afraid to identify him so believe it or not he had never been officially charged with murder."

Talinda paused chose her words carefully before she responded to Raymond. She wasn't sure exactly what his question was and so she asked, "Raymond what do you feel God is saying to you about Quavis?"

Raymond looked her square in the eyes and said with no uncertain terms, "We are to forgive him and fight for his life because that is what dad would have done. That's what he did for me. Never gave up on me and he knew all the things I had done, he just showed me love. I think God has Quavis' attention and if we move on it soon, we can be an excellent witness to him."

"Right you are son...right you are. Your dad would be so proud of you," Talinda replied smiling. They continued to talk about how they would attempt to help Quavis before they rejoined the group.

Pastor Tills was led the cleanup committee as they wrapped up the days events. They all pitched in and were soon ready to gather and pray for a safe return home for everyone.

They hugged one another and said their goodbyes. Bernard exchanged telephone numbers and emails with most of the male youth that were present. He told a few of the boy's they should plan to come to Germany for a visit. They were very excited about that idea. Most of them had never even left the state of Georgia, much less the country.

Talinda and Bernard walked to end of the driveway to see them off. Talinda was assured by Pastor Tills that they remembered the way back to the highway.

Bernard inquired again to Pastor Tills, "Are you sure pastor, because I can ride with Talinda as she directs you to the highway?"

"No son, we'll be fine, it wasn't too difficult coming in. You all to need to go relax for the night and enjoy your family," Pastor Tills replied.

Talinda turned to Bernard and said as the vans pulled out of the driveway, "I think you have made some lifetime friends today."

"I think I have. They are an amazing group of young people. You and Brandon have done a magnificent job with them. Their knowledge of the word is astonishing for so young a group. I look forward to returning and visiting them again. I would love to have a few of the boys come to Germany as well," he replied as they turned to walk back toward the house.

She had another out of the blue Brandon moment and a rush of emotion came over her. Her eyes filled with tears as she declared, "Wow, where did that thought come from?"

Bernard noticed she was having a difficult time. He stopped walking and asked her, "Are you okay Talinda, what is it?"

A teary-eyed Talinda responded, "I don't know. As we turned and walked toward the house, nostalgia took me back to the first day I met Brandon. He had just told me of the prophecy he had concerning me. We kissed, had a very passionate and powerful moment with God and then turned to walk back to my house in Virginia. I was just overwhelmed by it. Bernard, my love with Brandon was so powerful. I guess for a while, it will be everywhere. Like my mom said. I need to expect moments like these. But with God, I'll make it through them. I know I will. I have to."

She pondered her next statement and chose her words carefully. She was unsure why she felt she should be cautious about sharing her love with Brandon to Bernard. She couldn't quite put her finger on it, but she felt that Bernard was vulnerable when it came to the love she and Brandon shared. Although she felt completely comfortable sharing it with him, part of her thought that maybe it was painful to him somehow. She shrugged it off and continued, "You see Bernard, when God...when you know beyond a shadow of doubt that God has handpicked the man of your dreams for you, it's so easy to lose yourself in him. And that's what I did, I lost myself in Brandon. We were one and we moved in perfect sync with each other. We were synchronized down to the last millisecond. Now I have to separate and find Talinda again. That's what I'm not so sure I'm ready to do. Oh, this is crazy! I know I'm not making any sense at all......."

"No Talinda," Bernard said as he stopped and turned toward her. "It makes perfect sense to me. Brandon shared some of the same things with me that you have just said. He told me of the powerful love that you two had. He shared with me the vision he had of you, and the preparation that God took him through to prepare him to be your husband. I learned so much about love and how to be a husband from him. I learned the true power of the Word in Ephesians that says, *"Husbands love your wives as Christ loved the church and gave himself for it."* I never even begun to know what true love for a woman was, until I was introduced to the love Brandon had for you. It was overwhelming at times, and I often prayed to God to prepare me for a wife...a real wife who had been taught true agape love. The love Brandon had with you. So I do know how you fell right now and I understand. This whole weekend my mind has been racing back and forth over all the conversations and situations Brandon and I have shared. My emotions as well have been mixed. Sometimes they have been happy. Sometimes they brought tears at the fact that I no will longer have him here for counsel, conversation or mentorship."

As Talinda looked into his eyes and watched as he talk about Brandon. She realized just how awesome the man of God he had chosen for her was. She realized for the first time, how difficult this weekend must have been for Bernard as well. She was speechless and could only nod in affirmation as they continued to walk in silence, back to the house. There were no more words that would fit the conversation. Talinda and Bernard both pondered the obvious awkwardness moment as they reached the house. Everyone had gone back inside and was sitting in the downstairs den.

They discussed the sleeping arrangements for the night in an attempt to see if they could all stay there at the Travis house together.

Victor finally spoke up and said, "Nonsense, we won't hear of anyone sleeping on the couch. Valetta and I will go back to Talinda's tonight. She can stay here and enjoy family time before Bernard's parents fly out in the morning."

Valetta nodded in agreement with her husband Victor. And before Helen could protest, she held up her hand and said, "Helen, I know what you are about to say. We know that we are family and we are not trying to exclude ourselves. But you haven't seen one another in a while and need to cherish the moments you have together. Roger and I are going to stay with Talinda for a while longer and so we'll see you. I plan on staying until I get on Talinda's last nerve and she kicks me out......"

"Oh mom, that's not going to happen anytime soon." Talinda interrupted, "I look forward to having both my mom's support during this trying time. I wouldn't have it any other way."

Those words almost sent Valetta into tears. She managed to muster a smile as she hugged Talinda and expressed her love for her baby girl.

"So it's settled," Victor said firmly. "We'll stay at Talinda's tonight and you will all enjoy family time."

Roger gave in and said, "Okay you win. But you are not leaving this moment I hope? It's still early and we haven't played scrabble yet....."

"Oh God not scrabble," Helen laughed out loud. "Honey, you never win and you can't accept defeat..."

"Now hold on just a minute," Roger exclaimed. "I..."

"Admit it Roger," Helen interrupted. "You're a sore loser. Reginald, Teresa, Bernard am I right?"

Reginald let out a big laugh as he responded, "Sorry little brother, she pegged you right on this one."

180

"That's right Uncle Roger. Aunt Helen's got your number," Bernard confirmed.

Teresa laughed and said, "I plead the fifth."

"Oh come on guys I'm not that bad...," Roger exclaimed as he looks around the room. Then replied with a sarcastic I'm wounded tone. "...Am I?" They all laughed at Roger's expense, and he seemed to take it graciously. And against their better judgment, they sit down to a game of scrabble.

They are down to the last word and letters of the game. There is absolutely no where left for Roger to put his last letter. It just didn't fit anywhere, but true to the word he refused to give up. After five rounds of them telling him his word didn't fit and him arguing and challenging them. Reginald said, "Is somebody recording this. So the next time my little brother swears he's not a sore loser we can replay the day for him?"

They laugh and Roger finally confessed he may have a little problem with losing. But it was because everyone cheated so much. They often wouldn't accept his words, he said in his defense. Once again laughter broke out in the room.

"Well," Victor said as he looked at Valetta then Helen and Roger. "We had better get out of here. We don't want dark to catch us driving." He turned to Reginald and Teresa Travis and said, "It was so nice to see you both again. We need to plan a family trip."

"Yes," Helen said in agreement.

They all exchanged hugs and goodbyes. Victor turned to Talinda and said, "Okay sweetheart. We still have the key you gave us earlier so we'll see you tomorrow."

"Are you sure you don't want me to go with you daddy?" Talinda asked.

"No sweetheart," Valetta replied. "Stay here and be with the family. We'll see you tomorrow."

"Okay," Talinda reluctantly replied. She turned toward Teresa and Reginald and said, "If it's alright with you, I'll ride with Bernard tomorrow to take you to the airport. That way he can drop me off at my house and I'll ride back out here later tomorrow with my parents?"

Teresa smiled as she responded, "Of course Talinda. Sweetheart, you don't even have to ask that. Besides Bernard got us so lost coming out of the airport yesterday, that we thought we were going to miss Brandon's service. I'll rest easy knowing we'll get there on time so we won't miss our flight. And he won't end up in South Carolina somewhere trying to find his way back. The city has changed tremendously since we all lived here."

They laughed and Bernard exclaimed as he looked at his mom with total sarcasm, "Okay Mom, they didn't need to know that. Getting lost yesterday was supposed to be our little secret. In the air everything makes perfect sense and navigation is on point. On the ground things get a little...well, you know what I mean."

They were still laughing as they exchanged hugs and kisses exclaiming how they will miss one another. Talinda walked outside with her parents making sure they remembered how to get home. She reminded them that the garage opener was programed in the car. She texted the code for the alarm as she watched her parents pull out of the driveway. She waved until they were out of sight before she returned to the house.

The Travis house was in no way ready to turn in for the night. They wanted to maximize their time together. Death of a loved always brought to the forefront the need for family unity. They stayed up and shared their Brandon memories as they drank Helen famous pomegranate and cherry tea. They finally decide call it a night and all turn in. Exhausted from the day's events, Talinda's quickly fell fast asleep.

≈

It seemed as though they had just lain down and it was already time to get up. Helen cooked breakfast as everyone got dressed and finished packing. After breakfast, Bernard and his dad loaded the suitcase in the car.

"Okay, everybody," Helen said as they walked out to the cars. "We have to promise one another that we will get together more often. We are family and that's all that's important. We're going to have to start making time out of our busy schedules for at least once a year."

They all agreed as they exchanged their hugs and love. Helen and Roger stood in the driveway as they drove off. Helen leaned into Roger who instinctive put his arm around his wife for support. Helen had not thought saying goodbye to Teresa and Reginald would be so hard. Most of her family had been unable to make the funeral on such short notice. Both her adoptive parents had passed away. She was their only child and didn't have a large family. She treasured the time she had with the Travis', because they were such a close nit family. She was glad they would have Bernard for one more night. His flight back to

Germany wasn't scheduled until the next day. She already looked forward to having the Thompson's and Talinda back over tonight as well. She dreaded when everyone would leave and she would be left alone to remember her loss.

Roger read her thoughts. He said, "I know sweetheart...I know. You'll get through it. Each day will get easier and hey, look on the bright side. In about eight more months, you'll have a grandson to keep you occupied."

She smiled through tears as they returned to the house. They were still a little tired and so they returned to bed.

Bernard and Talinda get his parents to the airport and checked in with time to spare. Teresa looked at Bernard in teasing tone thanked Talinda yet again for getting them there in timely fashion and in a direct route. They all exchanged hugs and kisses as his parents went through security to board their plane.

Bernard could feel the love and anxiety when his mother hugged him. She held on as though it were going to be the last time she would see him alive. He understood and said, "I love you too mom. I'll come home to visit again soon...I promise."

She could only nod. Tears filled her eyes and she released the embrace. Asher and Reginald went through security, they promised their son they would inform him when they arrived home safely.

Bernard turned to Talinda and said, "Well, we better head over to your house, get your parents and head back to Athens."

Talinda replied, "Yeah, because you better bet Helen has this trip timed to the second and knows exactly what time to expect us." They laughed at that comment knowing all too well it was pretty accurate at how Helen was thinking. "I'll call my mom to see if she and dad are ready and we'll swing by there and get them."

Bernard still smiled at the previous comment nodded his head as they turn and began to walk to the train that led to the parking lot.

To Talinda's surprise, her parents were calling her as she was dialing the number to call them. They were up, dressed and already on their way back to Athens. They told them they would meet them there. She had Bernard call Helen and Roger to let them know her parents would probably get there before them and they too were on their way.

≈

The next morning, Talinda and Bernard convinced Roger and Helen there was no need for them to take Bernard to Atlanta, then drive all the way back to Athens. She could just as easily drop him off on her way back home. They all agreed and said their respective goodbyes. But in all actuality, neither Bernard nor Talinda wanted company at the airport. Bernard harbored a secret mission and Talinda was unsure how she felt. She didn't trust her emotions when it would time to say goodbye to Bernard. She didn't want anyone to misunderstand them, because she didn't understand them either. She wanted to have time alone after saying goodbye if she needed it.

The house was now quiet and Helen knew that her true challenge would now begin. There was no one there to occupy her time and she would now be confronted with the emptiness of Brandon's death.

Talinda's parents had decided to forgo the Atlanta traffic to take Bernard to the airport and said she could drop them off at her house unless she needed them to go. She assured them she would be okay because she had to stop by the church on the way home to prepare some of the props and activity sheets for the youths for Sunday morning service anyway. She would continue on because as her husband so eloquently put it, "Ministry is always required."

Bernard expressed his thanks to Talinda's parents for all they had done for his family this weekend and looked forward to seeing them again. He hugged Valetta but when he shook Victor's hand and said, "Sir, even under the circumstances it was nice to see you again. Brandon always spoke very highly of both of you."

Their eyes met and Victor saw something he had not paid attention to the whole weekend. He saw agape love in his eyes, underlined with the pure Eros love that a man has for his wife. He knew this look. Unsure who this love was intended for or directed at, he decided to say nothing.

Talinda promised she would call them when she got to and from her destination's that day. With that being said, she and Bernard were off to the airport. They wanted to get there well in advance for him to check his bags and get through security.

Talinda was anxious about the moment she would have to say goodbye to Bernard. She already felt the emptiness that his presence would leave behind. She also felt that in a strange way, she was saying goodbye to Brandon, all over again. At times, being in Bernard's presence was still just as painful as it was refreshing. She could feel that she was about to lose an emotional battle.

Bernard was not fairing any better than Talinda. He was a ball on knots on the inside. His had stayed up most of the night before and prepared a letter to give her upon his departure. He debated if it were wise at this tender moment in her life to reveal the beast that plagued him.

≈

"Well, this is where I say goodbye...for now," Bernard said as he smiled at her. It would prove harder than he had anticipated saying goodbye to her. But he knew that he could not prolong his departure. He had to go through security and find his gate. He could feel the emotions inside of him raging and prayed silently that he would keep himself together and control his actions. He wanted so badly to give her the letter that was in his pocket but when the time came he chickened out. Everything inside of him wanted to pull her into his arms and kiss her. But once again, feeling very guilty about the war waging on with unquenchable fire inside of him concerning his cousin's wife, he fought off all of his urges and stuck out his hand to say goodbye.

"Oh, don't think you're going to get away with a hand shake mister," Talinda said through a forced smile. Her emotions were catapulting around inside of her and she fought to remain stable. Talinda was having her own private battle with Bernard's departure.

Bernard sensed her struggle, which made it even harder for him to control himself. He knew by the look in her eyes, not the declaration of her tongue that she wanted to be in his arms. He still, however, couldn't find the nerve to give her the letter.

She could no longer deny the fact that she was sad Bernard was leaving. He was so much like Brandon and she cherished the moments they spent together. But on the other of the coin, she was quite relieved he was leaving. She would now be able to begin the healing process without a big reminder of what she has lost standing in her midst and touching her at all the right moments. There were so many things that he did just like Brandon, it was unnerving at times, but comforting all the same.

She said jokingly as she moved in close to him, "We're still family and I think I'm at hug status here buddy."

He forced a smile as she moved to embrace him. As he held her in his arms, he felt so tormented and afraid that she would feel the quickening of his heartbeat. That the love he had for her would just gush out of him uncontrollably. Although he never wanted the moment to end, he knew the longer he held her in his arms the more likely it was his true feelings would be exposed.

As she nestled into his arms she wondered what she was doing? She had a strange sense of security in his arms and found it surprisingly difficult to break the contact.

He was relieved when she pulled away from him and once again said goodbye. He returned the benediction and promised he would notify everyone when he landed in Germany and was safely home. With that being said, he turned, breathed a sigh of relief that his love didn't spill out all over the place and walked through the check point. Talinda watched until he was on the other side and they waved at each other one last time, before Bernard rounded the corner and headed for his gate.

~Chapter Sixteen~

For the last two months, Talinda had attempted to reestablish somewhat of a normal life...a life without Brandon. She focused on the task of learning how not to be a wife, something that she had prided herself in doing very well. She was a nurturer and knew how to care for her husbands every need. She had been taught well by her parents and the elder mothers of her church. Earlier that morning, she had a routine appointment at the OB/GYN clinic to schedule an ultra sound. Everyone on the staff had appreciated the kind words and gifts Talinda had delivered to the OB/GYN clinic. She also sent a wonderful card to the patient care office. She raved about the wonderful service and care she had received from the staff following Brandon's death. She was careful to mention each person by name. She left her appointment in a fairly good mood and drove over to spend the day in Athens with Brandon's parents.

Excited that she was not only going to be able to hear her baby's heartbeat but physically see him, Talinda was overcome with joy as she drove home from visiting Helen and Roger. The ultra sound was going to be a welcome pleasure in the healing process of the loss of her beloved Brandon. Veronica had been such a good personal nurse to her the last few weeks. Talinda was ever so pleased that Sarah and Veronica had been inseparable since the funeral. They moved very quickly and were in conference with her foster parents and the state to make plans for her to be adopted by Veronica.

As she drove home that day, she went over in her mind the message for the youth on the upcoming Sunday. She thought aloud, "Ministry is always required." That was Brandon's favorite saying. She was joyful that she could now have memories of Brandon without them always ending in tears. She, in spite occasional setbacks emotionally, was indeed healing.

She pulled into the driveway and stopped to retrieve mail out of the box on to save the long walk back down the driveway. She didn't have any plans of donning her door again today. While she was joyful, she was also exceptionally tired after her busy day today. She clicked mail icon on her computer to check her emails as she sat down at the kitchen table sifting through the mail she had just got out of the mailbox.

"Oh," she exclaimed after sitting down at the computer. "I have an email from Bernard!" She didn't understand why she was so overly excited about his email. Part of her would always keep him dear in her heart because he was an unofficial link to Brandon, if that made any sense. She knew she was going to have plenty of help with the baby from him and everybody else. She couldn't wait to hear what's been going on in his life. "I hope he's doing okay," she said aloud.

Her mother was due back from Virginia the next day. She had gone home two days ago to take care to some business that she couldn't handle over the phone. Talinda was so grateful to her for staying with her off and on the past few months. She had planned on staying with Talinda for a just while longer to her delight. No one thought Talinda should be alone for the first few months of her pregnancy. Helen, although she wanted to be there, felt that this was good bonding time for Talinda and her mother. And much to Talinda and Valetta's protest, tried not to visit too often.

Raymond had been spending a lot of time at his biological mother's house since the funeral. He wanted to give Talinda some space to be alone, but desperately missed her. Talinda however, would have preferred that he be with her. He always seemed so stressed and out of character after he had spent time with his mom. She finally called him asking when he would come home, in which he excitedly said he would return the next day. He missed her just as much as she missed him. The Travis' had asked about him several times over the past few weeks. They had expected him to stay with them at their house the day they had the barbeque, but he rode back with the youth and went to his biological mother's house. Talinda reassured him that he was welcome because he was family. The look on his face told her he wanted some alone so she had said goodbye to

188

him that day. But she didn't realize it would be a while before seeing him again.

She felt a slight twinge of guilt at being glad her mother, Helen or Raymond weren't there to witness her delightful reaction to receiving Bernard's email. She excitedly sat down and prepared to click on the email when a letter on top of the mail pile caught her attention.

The email would have to wait. It was a letter from Brandon's attorney. She opened it slowly knowing that it probably contained the instructions for Brandon's last will and testament. As she read the letter, she was stunned to say the least at the strange request that Brandon had for her to carry out. There would be a formal reading there in three days with Raymond and both her and Brandon's parent's. But she would also have to travel to Germany to hand deliver a package to Bernard.

The letter said that the tickets for the flight and the arrangements had already been made by the attorney's office. It also said that an official letter had been mailed to Bernard. It was to inform him that she would contact him as soon as the reading of the will was complete. She would know the specifics of when she would be arriving in country. Talinda sat stunned and wondered what could be so important in a package for Bernard, that Brandon wanted her to hand deliver it all the way to Germany. She had an uneasy feeling come over her and a knot formed in the pit of her stomach. She decided to go ahead and read Bernard's email to see if he mentioned anything about it in his letter to her, before she jumped to any conclusions. Maybe he would shed some light on the situation.

Before she opened the email, she called her and Brandon's parents about the reading of the will in three days. Her father had already planned on accompanying her mother back because they all wanted to be present at the ultrasound scheduled for the following week. Valetta shared her, Helen and Veronica's suspicions about the twins with her husband as did Helen with Roger. But no one had informed Talinda of their intuitions. They both managed to hold their tongues but were excited that the ultrasound was scheduled the next week.

After getting off the phone, Talinda turned her attention back to the computer and clicked on Bernard's email:

Dear Talinda,

Just thought would drop a few lines to see how you and my little cousin BJ were getting along. Sorry that it took so long for me to get a letter out to you, but I've been somewhat busy since I returned in country. I pray that you, BJ, Raymond and everyone else are doing well. Please tell them all know that I said hello and I love them. Tell them I promise that I will not be a stranger, even though it's not an easy task to visit from overseas. Maybe, after you have little BJ, if I'm still over here, you can all come for a visit. There's much to see and do here. The neighboring countries are so easy to get to and there's not much travel time involved. I'm sure you and Raymond will all love it over here. Brandon and I had a blast when he visited a few years back.

Talinda, I'm going on and on about nothing in an attempt to avoid the true nature of my writing to you. The truth of the matter is this, and I have to be particularly honest with you. That night on the deck at Aunt Helen's and Uncle Roger's house before Brandon's home going as I held you in my arms obeying the voice of God, my emotions were all over the place. I could feel the love that you had for Brandon and he had for you. It was so strong it was almost overwhelming. I found myself envious of Brandon and I fought off the urge to kiss you.

At reading that statement Talinda paused and got up to walk around the apartment. She wasn't in shock by his declaration. She had sensed something that night and dismissed it. She was however, afraid of the next thing that would be in the email. Had she sent the wrong signal? What did the attorney say to him in the letter he received to spark this conversation from him? He was her husband's cousin. But something inside of her was more intrigued than she wanted to admit. She missed Brandon so and longed for his touch. She guiltily wondered sometimes what it would be like to be in Bernard's arms again. Would she feel Brandon?

She had repented several times at the thought of using him to have an image of her husband in her life, however unreal it

190

would have been. She walked back over to where the computer was. Why was it she was excited at his words? They thrust an onslaught of emotions upon her. She chastised herself. She was now all the more in total anticipation and intrigue at what Brandon has in Bernard's package. What does Bernard know that she doesn't? She finally decided that she wouldn't speculate what the next words would be and just read them. Thus, she continued with Bernard's email:

> *All my adult life, I have wanted to find a woman that loved me half as much as the love I felt you had for Brandon. People have the misconception that men don't love as deeply as women do. But we do. We love just as hard if not harder than women. But because of vulnerability, we don't often put our emotions out there as easily as women do.*
>
> *When you said, "I love you sweetheart", although I knew you were talking to Brandon, I was over whelmed with emotion. Your declaration to him was so pure and genuine...it was just indescribable. As I held you in my arms and you were talking to Brandon and sharing your heart with him. I was so envious of him and the love he shared with you. I not only wanted to kiss you, I wanted to sweep you up in my arms, carry you into the bedroom and make sweet love to you. I wanted the love Brandon had described to me. I found myself longing for the relationship he had with you.*

Talinda paused once again. She shook her head and fought back tears as she softly said, "Oh God please...no...I don't need this confusion right now. Please protect my emotions and give me strength Lord." She wiped her tears, looked back up at the screen and was determined that she would continue reading until the end without another pause. She needed to know what Brandon's attorney had said to him in his letter. But that wasn't going to be the case, because the next group of sentences would prove to be almost too much for her to handle:

> *I found it very difficult to look you in the eyes the next day. I felt so guilty about my*

191

feelings of the night before, because yours had been so genuine, pure and honest. Not that my motive wasn't genuine and a mandate from God because it was. But my own emotions and manhood struggled within me. I had to suppress what I felt for you and only until now could I even get up enough nerve to send you this letter. I wrote most of it the night of Brandon's funeral and was going to give it to you as I boarded the plane on the way back to Germany. But when you walked me to the gate and we said good-bye I couldn't give it to you. All I wanted to do was to pull you into my arms, and kiss you good-bye. Not as Brandon's stand in, but for myself...for Bernard."

She gasped as the tears began to flow. She realized this email had absolutely nothing to do with the letter from the attorney. She declared aloud, "Oh Bernard...please don't do this." This declaration from him was going to make her trip to Germany to deliver the package from Brandon awkward to say the least. Not so much awkward because of him, but because she was emotionally all over the place. She was confused about every event in her life leading up to this moment. Including what she felt about Bernard. She wanted to, scream but instead continued to read:

"I left feeling so guilty and convicted about my feelings toward you. I only now got up enough nerve to finish and email you the complete letter.

I know that what I did that night was God led and I'm not taking away from the experience. I do know for sure that God led me to be there for you. That it would minister to you because I looked so much like Brandon and you would be receptive to my touch. But what I wasn't prepared for was the emotion behind your love for him that would come along with it. You are an exceptional woman of God Talinda and I hope and pray that God will bless you with another love of your life. A woman that understands love the way that you do is mandated I'm sure, to share it with someone.

There are many godly men out there who are looking for a woman who really knows how to love and make them secure in the relationship. Men more often than not, have insecurity in their lives concerning relationships that they never tell anyone about, especially, the women in their lives. Mostly because, they feel their manhood is challenged by appearing weak. But a good woman like you will help them to overcome that weakness. Talinda, you bring out every emotion that a man has and you make him comfortable with sharing them.

Please don't take this letter the wrong way. I am not soliciting your love or a relationship. The memory of my cousin is too fresh and runs too deep. But I had to be honest with my struggles. I just felt like I could pour my feelings out to you. I feel they would be safe with you. So rest easy Talinda, I have since gotten my heart and emotions under control concerning you.

Because I was so certain that you discerned my emotions that night, I felt like I owed you an apology for the way I held you. I almost allowed my own selfish desires get in the way of how God wanted to bless, minister to your hurting heart and comfort your spirit.

Most women don't know how to make a man feel safe in the relationship, but you have mastered it. I now know that I can be comfortable around you and look forward to visiting you and BJ upon his arrival into this side of creation, lol. With the same anticipation that you probably have, I can't wait to hold him in my arms and feel a little bit of Brandon. Take care Talinda. I am so blessed to have met you and hope that, although I have poured my heart out to you, we can remain friends. But something tells me that you are way past mature enough to handle it all. I look forward to an awesome friendship and family tie with you. Until next time, you and the little one take care.

Sincerely,

Bernard

She sat and stared at the words on the screen. As she read his letter she found was back in time to that night on the Travis' deck in Athens. She was going over her feelings, emotions and actions. She knew she had indeed sent mixed signals to him throughout the weekend and again chastised herself for creating a difficult situation. She was unsure how she would respond to his letter. She wanted to choose her words very carefully as not to make an already delicate situation worse. She knew that she would soon be standing right in front of him.

Although he had stated toward the end of the letter that he had gotten his emotions under control, she wondered if that was just a matter of geography. How would their next meeting be? How would he feel? Moreover, how would she feel and react?

She picked up the pen and paper, but then placed them back down on the counter again. She continued to ponder her thoughts, the email and the contents of the attorney's letter concerning Brandon's odd request of her.

She had to be honest about her feelings that night. The truth of the matter was, she was so glad that he hadn't kissed her. She wanted so much to feel Brandon's kiss and physical love just one more time. Had Bernard kissed her or attempted to make love to her, she is not so sure she would have resisted. Everything in her would have known it wasn't right, or that it wasn't Brandon. But the thought of possibly feeling Brandon one more time may have been too much for her to resist, in her emotional state. She hoped that she would have been virtuous enough to say no, but she knows all too well that she is just not sure.

She paused and took time to thank the Holy Spirit that He had controlled the situation that night. Something she hadn't even considered until reading Bernard's letter. His letter, as well as the one from the attorney had her thinking. It ministered to her on a level that Bernard probably did not intend for it too. It propelled her to want to go forth in the women's ministry at her church. She had been an active part, but the information that Bernard had shared with her was something that needed to be addressed. Without sharing any of the details of her and

Bernard's ordeal or her life, she knew she needed to minister to women about love and relationships. She needed to teach woman how to be strong in love, something her parents instilled in her at a young age. She had been taught to love hard and give all. She was grateful that 1 Corinthians 13 had been thrust into her spirit all of her life. And her father often taught about the agape love for mankind and the Eros love between a husband and wife. So she understood love.

But what Bernard said in his letter had struck her deeply. It captivated her thoughts and she struggled at how she would respond.

"Ughhhh...Brandon...Bernard...God. I don't know what to do. Wow, what now?" She said aloud. Knowing full well that a response was in order, she regained her composure, picked up the pin and began to write.

My Dearest Bernard......

To be continued...............

About the Author:

Minister Cynthia Harris is a native of Atlanta, GA. She and her husband of 26 years, Minister Kim Harris are the co-founders of T.O.S.O.T. (The Other Side of Through) Ministries. She spent years in her local church writing the plays for the Christmas and Easter programs. In 2007, her longtime friend and founder of Still Useable Ministries, Evangelist Susan Marshal, solicited her to write a stage play for an upcoming women's conference. And thus, the series "The Other Side of Through" was born. Many of the instances in her works are inspired by challenges, situations and tragedies that have occurred in her own life. She implements the power of how God brought her through when the pieces of began to fall apart and unravel. She is passionate about writing and understands that this is her mandate from God. She aspires to reach and minister to the hurt, confused and lost with her gift of imagination and knowledge of the Word of God, through romance and drama. She was born to write for such a time as this.

Look for exciting new titles from this author.

~ Ministry is always......required! ~

Made in the USA
· Charleston, SC
26 October 2012